HUNTER

EDEN SUMMERS

Cover Image by Stas Vokman Photographer

Cover Model - Konstantin Kamynin

DEDICATION

To gratitude,
Since finding you—truly finding you—my life has changed.

1

HER

THE WEIGHT OF A PSYCHOPATH'S GAZE RESTS HEAVY AT the back of my neck. He's watching me, stalking me, probably already fantasizing about how my bones will break under his fists.

I fight to contain a smile and cross my legs, allowing the hem of my skin-tight skirt to hitch higher along my thighs.

Every move I make is strategic, every slow blink, every bated breath, every swipe of my lace glove-covered fingers along my exposed neck. I've practiced this a million times. I always do, because this needs to be perfect. Second chances are for the unprepared, and I'm anything but.

My auburn wig is for his benefit—the brown contact lenses, bright red lipstick, and fuck-me boots, too. Tonight, I'm an actress, and my role is that of a novice escort—his ultimate temptation.

I stir the toothpick-speared olive around in my martini glass, feigning loneliness.

My mark, Dan Roberts, has to be beside himself with interest, salivating, his palms itching, his cock hardening. He's picturing his hands around my throat, anticipating how hard he'd have to squeeze, and for how long, before I lost consciousness.

I know this because I've watched him for weeks. He's become predictable. All those nights spent in the shadows, stalking him as he stalked other women, has paid off. And it could've been just as easy for the local Portland police to track his crimes, if they'd bothered to take the word of numerous beaten women over the statement from a rich senator's son.

Only they didn't.

Their pockets had been lined with so much green that the evidence didn't matter anymore. Fake alibis were taken as legitimate accounts. Photographs of beaten, bruised, and broken bodies were discarded, just like good ol' Danny boy had done with the women he'd tormented once he'd gained his sadistic fix.

This man is a criminal.

A vile waste of oxygen.

A pathetic piece of garbage.

And apparently, I'm the only one with enough devotion to take out the trash.

From the corner of my eye, I see him approach, stopping directly beside my perch on a cracked leather stool. He jerks his chin at the young female bartender and slides his hand over the scratched wooden bar. "Whiskey." His voice is loud, with an undertone of control.

He loves control.

Lives for it.

I glance at him from the corner of my eye and see no beauty in what people have described as a handsome man. His pale skin is smooth, his raven hair clean-cut and combed. Dark eyelashes frame what I know are deep brown irises, and his lips are lush and inviting. Or they would be, if I didn't know he was a few Froot Loops short of a carton.

I scoot forward on my stool to place my drink on the bar, but deliberately miss my target. The glass topples, the liquid racing toward the man's hand.

I lunge for his wrist, pushing it out of the way to save his immaculate suit, and exaggerate my loss of balance. I topple, my shoulder ramming into him, my stool knocking his. "Oh, my gosh. I'm so sorry."

He turns, those strong, destructive hands clutching my upper arms to stabilize me and my seat. "Are you okay?"

"Yeah." I lick my lower lip, quick, panicked, and nod. "I was trying to stop your jacket from getting wet and made an even bigger fool of myself."

"You're not a fool." He releases his grip and rights my martini glass as the bartender mops up the mess. "Let me replace your drink." Dan turns to the woman behind the bar, not waiting for my response. "When you're done, can you get her another martini?"

"Sure. Just give me a few seconds."

I remain still, the screaming euphoria of celebration contained to the inner walls of my mind. My plan is working. The foundation has been laid.

"Thanks." I grin. "That's kind of you."

"Not entirely. There's a catch to my generosity." He shoots me a glance, his lips kicked at one side. "You have to promise to sit with me until you finish your drink." His gaze slithers down my body, curving over my breasts, my hips, then lower, all the way to my exposed calves.

I will my cheeks to blush. I will them and will them, but alas, I'm not that fucking demure. Instead, I lower my gaze and bat my lashes. "Actually, I don't think that's a good idea. I'm...working." I hitch the strap of my small clutch higher on my shoulder. "It's my first night. I was told to always stay near the bar unless I have an offer."

His thoughts practically crackle in my head. He's thinking how easy this is. How perfect. How serendipitous.

You bet it is, buddy.

"Working?" he muses, palming the two drinks the bartender slides toward him.

"Yeah." I nibble my lower lip, exaggerating my vulnerable, virginal escort role. "I bet everyone can see how nervous I am."

I glance around the dilapidated bar. Nobody pays me attention. It's like my favorite drinking hole on the other side of the city—frequented by depressed drunkards too liquored to notice if it's day or night.

"Maybe a tiny bit." He chuckles, and I try not to cringe at his equally fake facade. "Come on." He swings out an arm, his whiskey pointing the way to one of the free booths in the back corner. "It's only one drink. I won't take up too much of your time." He winks. "Unless you want me to."

I continue to devour my bottom lip. It's my go-to move. And from the way he keeps glancing at my mouth, it must be working a charm.

"I guess one drink can't hurt." I scoot from my stool, grasp the martini glass he offers, and saunter myself to our private destination with the predator close at my back.

My skirt hitches higher with every step, the material creeping teasingly closer to my lace panties, until I slide into the booth.

"Get yourself settled." Dan places his whiskey on the table, his free hand twitching at his side. "I need to excuse myself for a moment."

"Okay." I sip from my glass, watching him over the rim as he strides to the restrooms.

He may be heading for the bathroom, but I know his main objective isn't to use the facilities. He needs to calm himself. To lessen the adrenaline spurring him to make snap decisions.

Day to day, he can fool the average Joe. From my time watching him, I've learned he gets careless when close to obtaining a fix. He turns into a stereotypical addict—jittery, breathless, and unable to control the need to rush to the finish line.

I've triggered his game.

There's no turning back.

He wants me. Needs me. He's hungry for my screams, and that's okay, because I'm just as hungry for his.

This man, although vile and psychotic, is actually quite special. He's not just the focus of another one of my retribution projects. He's more. Much more.

This smug piece of shit could be the key I've spent ten years searching for. He could quite possibly be my Holy Grail.

With a lazy glance around the room, I open the tiny baggie stuck to the inside of my blouse cuff and rest my fingers on the rim of his glass. Fine white powder falls over my palm and into the liquor, the Rohypnol dancing through the liquid with such choreographed perfection I can't hold back a smirk.

The sight is beautiful. Peaceful. Karma in motion.

I dust my gloves gently, brushing off the evidence, then bite the olive from my toothpick and give the concoction a stir. In seconds, the betrayal disappears, dissipating into sweet nothingness.

Every inch of me thrums, pulsing and throbbing from the inside out. The enjoyment only increases when the door to the men's bathroom opens and Dan strides forward with a wicked grin.

He thinks he's good, and I've gotta give it to him, when it comes to being a sadistic son-of-a-bitch, he's a real winner.

What he doesn't realize is that when revenge is the aim, I'm the motherfucking queen.

Years of experience flow through my veins. Retribution is my specialty.

I discreetly flick away the toothpick and paste on a chaste smile as he reaches the booth.

"Everything okay?" I ask as he hovers at the end of my seat, his forehead beading with sweat, his gaze darting around the room.

"Let's get out of here."

"Leave?" A twinge of panic unfurls in my belly, and I shove it down with a sip of gin. I'm the one in control here. Not him. "I can't. I'm working, and you haven't even started your drink."

He grasps his glass and downs the contents in two large gulps.

Big mistake, Danny. Fucking huge.

I release a girlie laugh, the sound obnoxious to my ears. "You're eager."

"I guess I can't help myself. You're a beautiful woman who's nervous about her first gig. My gentlemanly nature means I'm obliged to ease your burden."

I take another sip, a tiny one to ensure I remain level-headed. "And how will you do that?"

"By being your first customer."

Ding, ding, ding. Jackpot.

"Oh." My response is shy, but no matter how hard I try, I still can't get my cheeks to heat. "I wasn't expecting that."

He reaches out a hand. "Come on. Let's go."

"Wait." I can't leave. Not yet. The drugs need time to start their numbing goodness. "We haven't discussed payment."

He reaches for his back pocket and pulls out a wallet. "Name your price."

"That depends on the service."

He retrieves a stack of bills and places them on the table. "Is this enough for a few hours?"

My lips part as I pretend to be gobsmacked by his generosity. In reality, I'm scrambling to stall. "Yeah." I slide my fingers over the money, drag it toward me, then slip it into my clutch. "That's more than enough."

"Come on, then."

He raises his hand again, and I stare. It's still too soon. Too quick. If I leave now, I'll have to think on my feet to slow down this sequence, and although I'm shit-hot and shiny when it comes to this, I'd prefer not to take unnecessary chances on such a special project.

"Can I finish my drink first?"

His mask of charismatic charm falters with the narrowing of his gaze. "I don't have all night, sweetheart."

"Right." *Fuck you.* "Of course not."

I slide from the booth, ignoring his offered hand, and lead the way outside into the chilly night air. "Maybe I should buy a bottle of something to celebrate." I spin back to face the door, only to be stopped by his large frame sliding in front of me.

"I know you're nervous, but we don't need it." His rush for a fix has risen to fever-pitch. His eyes are glazed, his cheeks flushed.

"It'll only take a second." I sidestep, and he shadows me.

"I've got whatever you need back at my place." He walks forward, and I'm forced to retreat. One step. Two.

I raise my hand, placing it on his chest as I plant my feet. "I'm sorry, I'm going about this all wrong. We haven't even discussed logistics." *Stall, stall, stall.* "I have a room within walking distance. It's small and simple and does the job. I'd just prefer if we had something to break the ice when we get there. Maybe a bottle of wine or some whiskey.

7

I know a lot of body parts that taste better when moistened with liquor."

Those plump lips smile down at me, and I see the expression for the threat it is. "With you, sweetheart, I don't want booze."

He grabs my hand in a tight grip, and it takes all my strength not to knee him in the groin like my intuition demands.

"Now, come on." He tugs me along the footpath, toward the parking lot. "My car is down here."

"We don't need to drive. My hotel is literally at the end of the block. It's an easy walk."

"I'm not interested in walking." He tries to charm me with a playboy sparkle in his eyes. "And my place is warm and clean. Not some seedy hotel on the wrong side of town."

If I get in his car, we won't make it to his Lake Oswego home. I'll be driven to an isolated industrial area where he'll try to beat me, rape me, then leave me battered and barely breathing on the side of the road.

No, thank you, Danny boy.

"I appreciate the offer, but I insist on my hotel." I pull my hand away. "Neutral ground, ya know?"

His nostrils flare, and I wonder if he'll drop this bullshit act and drag me, hair first, to his getaway car.

"It's decent accommodation," I exaggerate with a flash of my pearly whites. "You'll like it."

"It's the car or nothing."

My chest tightens. Fear and anxiety collide in a mass of tangled emotions. I can't throw away my one and only shot at this.

At *him*.

But I can't get in that car either. Not now. Not even

8

with the looming promise of his Rohypnol-induced impairment.

Confinement in a small space would mean my fun would end and his would begin. I'd lose my advantage and he'd gain the upper hand. His strength against my strategy.

I have to stick to my plan or let him walk.

God, I don't want to let this fucker walk.

"Then I guess this is where we part ways." My face falls, and I don't need to fake a stricken expression. I'm on the verge of heartbreak, devastated at the thought of this guy getting away, not only with what he's done, but with the information I desperately need. "See ya, handsome."

I give him a timid finger wave and the chance to demand a refund before I turn in the direction of my hotel. I take slow steps, and his pursuing footfalls don't hit my ears. He's not following. I guess he's too frustrated to even ask for his cash.

Shit.

Four weeks of meticulous preparation disintegrate into painful splinters, each one penetrating my skin to exacerbate the failure.

This guy deserved what I had planned. He'd earned it over months, possibly years, of brutality. But losing the connection to my past tears me apart, limb by limb, nerve by nerve.

Anger boils my blood, the potency so rich my throat tightens with the need to scream. I can't turn back.

I *can't*.

Getting in his car is too dangerous. The drugs might not kick in for another twenty minutes. Maybe more. He'd easily overpower me. I'm not stupid enough to believe my years of self-defense, martial arts, and boxing classes could save my ass in a confined space, up against a deranged psychopath.

The knife in my boot is insurance, but I'm not infallible.

I grind my teeth to the point of pain as I trudge the eight-minute walk to the sleazy, pay-by-the-hour hotel, with its flickering red 'Vacancy' sign.

What the hell am I going to do?

I may never get another chance to find Jacob. I've failed. Again. And not only on a personal level, but all those women Dan has abused won't get a vicarious taste of vengeance.

How have I messed this up?

Was the meticulous preparation not enough?

Should I have watched him for longer?

Could I have tried harder?

Risked more?

Fuck.

I pull the hotel key from my clutch and stride to door fifteen—the last room in the single-story complex. I slide my key into the flimsy lock, preparing to lick my wounds in private, when the noisy crunch of asphalt alerts me to a vehicle entering the parking lot. My heart kicks. A sixth sense sends goosebumps erupting along my arms. Or maybe it's optimism.

I want this.

I want it enough that each breath hitches in my throat.

I glance over my shoulder, my limbs throbbing, and come face to face with the impeccable good fortune that stares back at me.

2

HER

I paste a surprised look on my face, placing my mental celebration on hold.

Dan cuts the engine, slides from the car, then slams the door shut.

"You changed your mind?" I ask.

"Yeah." He stalks toward me, his smile stiff. "I did."

I unlock the hotel door and push it wide, allowing him to proceed. "After you."

He doesn't respond as he strides inside, not bothering to scope his surroundings. This smug piece of shit thinks he's invincible, and I can't wait to prove him wrong.

He slumps onto the well-worn bed, the cheap springs squeaking with his heavy weight. A frown spreads across his forehead as he stares blankly at the tiny kitchenette in front of him.

Could my buddy Rohypnol have given him a friendly nudge of disorientation?

"You okay?" I purr, closing the door to the world.

"Yeah." He clears his throat. "You got a glass of water or something?"

"Sure." I saunter to the sink, and the hair on my neck tingles as my back faces him.

Limit vulnerabilities.

Stay alert.

He pushes to his feet while I begin filling a cloudy glass with tap water. Every inch of me is tense, ready to attack, but I continue the monotonous actions, turning the tap off slowly and drying my hands on a dirty dish rag.

I swing around. He paces near the door. Like a caged dog, he wants out, but there is no *out*. Not until I have what I want.

"Here." I hand over the drink and point to the sturdy wooden chair strategically placed between the bed and the stained sofa. "Have a seat and I'll make you feel comfortable."

He takes large gulps of the water, the deep grooves of his frown still intact when he hands back the empty glass. "No." He shakes his head in a mix of confusion and agitation. "Let's go. I'll take you somewhere better than this."

"We have all we need right here." I grab his wrist and lead him forward, guiding him to sit in the hot seat. "I've been practicing something for a while, and I really want to see what you think. Call it an added bonus, if you like."

I place the glass on the unsteady bedside table and slide my hand under the pillow on the bed. He watches as I produce a handful of thick, red ribbon. I sway my hips to imaginary music on my return and let the long lengths of material fall to the floor, dragging behind me.

"This room is a dump," he mutters. "We need to go to my place." He grips the armrests, preparing to stand.

"Don't." I lean over and get in his face. "It will be fun to have sex in here. It adds to the fantasy." I inch closer, his stale breath brushing my lips. "I'm the weak woman in distress, and you're the wealthy, charming man here to save me. But every fantasy has to be earned. Let me earn this. After that, I'll go wherever you want."

His jaw tightens. His features harden. "You've got five minutes."

"I can work with that." It isn't a lie. Once he's tied, his ability to negotiate is over. The game is won. All that's left is the celebration.

I hold his right wrist to the armrest and begin binding it to the wood with my ribbons.

"What the fuck are you doing?" He lashes out, gripping a fistful of my hair—my wig.

I gasp, feigning fear when the reality is anger shooting through my body. "It's a part of the show," I plead. "I just—"

A rustle of noise sounds from the back of the room. In the bathroom. *No*, it must be right outside the window, in the alley. My escape route.

The potential for someone to overhear freezes my blood. It seems to have the same effect on Dan because he releases my hair and scowls at me.

"Hurry up and do your thing." A slur mars his words. "Then we leave."

I nod, quick and sharp, ever the eager escort, and continue binding one wrist to the armrest, then the other. Next, I kneel between his spread legs, sliding my palm over his crotch as I lower. There's no hardened cock behind that zipper, no erection, no arousal. Not surprising. He won't get turned on again until he's in control. Not until he's inflicting pain.

I bat my fake lashes at him and tie his ankles to the chair legs, tightening the last knot against his leg with all my strength.

"*Jesus.*" He tries to kick me and fails under the restriction. "Stupid bitch. That fucking hurt."

I cluck my tongue, stand, and leisurely walk to the bathroom to close the door on anyone in the alley who may plan to snoop on my pleasure. "You're really showing your true colors now, Danny boy."

His face slackens.

I let the situation sink in—my familiarity, his vulnerability.

Warring emotions spread across his face, from confusion to annoyance, then more confusion. "Who are you?"

I shrug and stroll back to stand before him. "Consider me a business partner. We're going to work together tonight."

"Is that right?" His narrowed gaze holds mine as he tugs at his wrist bindings. "Well, I'm more than happy to help a pretty lady. But you might want to untie me. We can't work together if I'm stuck like this."

"You'll do just fine where you are." I move to the bed and drop to a knee to retrieve the folder I stashed under the ensemble. "It's very easy, actually. All I need are a few answers to some really simple questions."

"*Ha.*" He grins. "If you're after information, I'll tell you what I've told everyone else. You're not getting anything until I get paid."

"I'm sorry, but that deal isn't going to work for me. I'll have to convince you to try this my way." It's my turn to smile, the curve of my lips gentle with the slightest hint of cocky menace.

"And what's stopping me from yelling for help?"

"I think the most influential answer is my ability to cut your dick off and dive out the back window before anyone finds the room key."

He snarls.

"There are many more reasons," I continue. "Like, what will Daddy think when another escort makes claims of sexual assault? I don't think the senator will appreciate an additional scandal where you're concerned."

"You fucking cunt."

I chuckle. If only he knew.

"Now, as I was saying. It's very simple." I slide out an image hidden inside the folder and hold it up. "This guy," I point to the man standing beside Dan in the candid photo, "I need to find out where he is."

He doesn't glance at the image, doesn't even acknowledge it. "Sorry. I can't help you."

I inhale slowly and smile. "You sure?"

"Yep."

I nod, shrug, then slam my elbow against his cheek.

His head jolts to the side. His shouted curse fills the room.

"How 'bout now, Dan?"

"You're going to die." He bucks in the chair. "I'll fucking kill you with my bare hands."

I lunge, grasping his throat in a tight grip as I glare. "Let's get one thing straight. You might think you're tough as nails because you hurt defenseless women, but I spend my days fucking up ruthless men. I will cut you. Flay you. I'll slice you open and wear your intestines like a fucking necklace to your own funeral unless I get what I want."

I release my hold and step back.

We're both panting, our chests heaving. Dan glares from under his lashes, his lids heavy. "Something is wrong. I feel like I'm going to pass out."

"That would be the Rohypnol I gave you back at the bar. It's only going to get worse."

His eyes widen.

"It also means we're on a tight schedule. So, tell me." I raise the photo and wait until his attention strays to the

15

image. "The guy standing beside you, where can I find him?"

He squints, his fingers gripping into the chair. "Like I said, I don't know him."

"Danny, Danny, Danny." I cluck my tongue as I return to the bed. I slide my hand under the pillow and pull out a knuckle duster. He watches my return with narrowed eyes as I slide the shiny metal down my glove-covered fingers, then cock my fist.

"Wait," he snarls. "That photo was taken two years ago."

"Where?"

"I don't know. It was a rented property. Some mansion on the outskirts."

"The outskirts of Portland?" My words flow in an excited rush. "Here?"

"Yeah. Here."

"And you spoke to this guy? What were you doing with him? Have you seen him since? And who rented the property?" I fire questions, hoping to maintain the momentum.

He shakes his head, his brows furrowed. "It was a party. A celebration. I only went to pick up a package."

"What sort of package?"

His chin lifts. "Laundry," he grates.

AKA drugs? What a naughty, naughty senator's son.

"And this guy" I tap the man standing next to him in the photo, "is that who you got the package from?"

He jolts his wrists. "Yes. *Christ*. Who the fuck are you? You're getting yourself messed up in some pretty heavy shit, sweetheart."

"Why don't you let me worry about that." I only need the briefest grasp of information. That's all it will take to make another connection. Another lead. "Do you know his name?"

"I can't remember."

Liar.

"Think, Danny." I drop the photo and lean forward to grip his junk. "Think hard."

He winces, but the severity of my hold isn't evident in his features. The drugs must be providing a numbing effect.

I squeeze tighter and twist, achieving a grunt.

"Zander. Zeke. Zack. *Fuck.* I can't remember. Last name was Vaughn."

"Are you sure?" I point to the photo. "You're telling me this guy goes by the name Vaughn?"

"Yeah," he grates. "That's exactly what I'm saying, bitch."

My heart pounds, the inspired reverberations ebbing all the way into my stomach. I can work with a name. That's all I need to inch another step closer to Jacob.

I release his dick. "If you're lying to me..."

His head lolls back. "Too fucking tired to lie."

"Okay. Good." Tingling optimism makes me believe him.

"Are you going to let me go now?" His blinks are slow. Sluggish.

I'm running out of time. "We're just getting started."

He scoffs, opens his mouth, and yells, "*Help.*"

Jesus. I slam the heel of my palm into his nose, cutting off the call, then lunge for the bed. In seconds, I've retrieved the gag from under the pillow and have it pressed to his mouth.

His head thrashes, and he yells through clenched lips as I increase the pressure, banging and smacking the hard ball gag until he relents and opens for me with a growl.

"Good boy." I tighten the strap behind his head, then come back to stand in front of him, admiring my handiwork. "Revenge is such a pretty picture."

He's yelling, mumbling, whimpering behind the gag. Rage glares back at me, but it's a wavering emotion. A sleepy anger that dissipates. He no longer tests his bonds, the mind-numbing drugs making the situation more acceptable.

That won't last long.

"Now that we have the photo out of the way, I want you to know I've been watching you for quite some time." I hope to reignite his fear or maybe a bit of panic. Instead, he looks straight through me. "You enjoy hurting women, don't you?"

He releases a half-hearted chuckle, his eyes twinkling the slightest bit.

"Beating them. Raping them." I grab his hair and yank. "You prey on those weaker than you."

His eyes brighten in bliss. In memory. He's reliving what he's done in that twisted mind of his. Even with his life at my mercy, he's enjoying his accomplishments. But then his eyes close.

Oh, no, he isn't going to take a nap on my watch. It's time to fast-forward the festivities.

"Hey." I slap him. "You've gotta stay awake for this." I'm hell-bent on retribution, but I'm not going to beat the unconscious.

He mumbles, over and over, the same cadence, the same indecipherable syllables. I'm curious enough to lower the gag and give him a chance to confess his sins.

"What's your name, bitch?" he slurs, his eyes still closed. "I want to know what to whisper in your ear when I'm raping you raw."

"Oh, honey." I reposition the knuckle dusters, pressing them lower on my fingers. "Threats don't work well with me."

"You touch me again and I kill everyone you love."

"I wish you the best of luck."

His eyes open, but he's not there. Not really. I doubt he'll remember any of this tomorrow. He'll only have the physical pain to taunt his unclear memory.

I run the cold metal on my hand along his jaw. "Maybe I should cut out your tongue to stop your sweet-talkin' ways?"

He spits at me, the projectile not making the distance. "You're dead."

"Not yet. So, while we're both alive and kicking, I'm going to give you a refresher on the lives you've ruined." I shove the gag back in place and clench my fist. "Cassidy Trelore, twenty-six, broken ribs, broken jaw."

I cock my arm, my limbs heating with approaching euphoria. Then I swing, launching my fist into his ribs. A muffled grunt is my reward.

"Melissa Taylor, twenty-eight, swollen lip, two black eyes, and eight facial fractures." This punch I aim at the middle of his face, cracking cartilage and distorting his nose.

He yells.

Everything inside me tingles in celebration while rivulets of scarlet blood seep from his nostrils toward his mouth.

I continue, naming the women he's assaulted, along with his long list of offences. Each time I land a blow harder than the last, until his face is a masterpiece of reds, maroons, and puffy, swollen skin.

Bree Foster. Carla Kane. Zoey Day. Amanda Scupin.

"Do you like feeling vulnerable, Dan?" I stand in front of him, cupping his clean-shaven cheek in my palm while I run the steel down the other. "Do you like knowing I'm hurting you, the same way you hurt those women?"

His eyes roll, and my stomach swells with disappointment. He's tapping out. Already. Weak fucker.

Then again, I did give him a healthy dose of powdered goodness.

"That's the downside of the drugs." I sigh. "That, and the unlikelihood you'll remember this tomorrow. But I want you to try, Danny boy. I want you to try real hard. Can you do that for me?"

His head slumps forward, a barely conscious affirmation.

I lean in, place my lips near his ear, and close my eyes as I breathe victory deep into my lungs. "Good, because I never want you to forget the night karma finally caught up with you."

3

HER

I leave Dan tied to the chair, drool seeping from around the gag while he slumps forward in unconsciousness. Every inch of me that was numb and emotionless the day before is thrumming with the enthusiasm of a cheerleader at a pep rally.

The buzz spurs me on as I slip through the bathroom window with a pack of my belongings strapped on my back, and strut my cheap fuck-me heels as far as they will take me.

My journey home lasts longer than my magical moments with Dan. I walk a lot of miles, catch two different cabs, and slink down numerous dark alleys to dispose of every item of my costume in a different location.

By the time I reach the bar across the street from my apartment, I'm dressed in my favorite pair of denim jeans, a tight, long-sleeve, plunging top, and my strappy stiletto heels.

The lack of warm clothing isn't appropriate for the January chill, but that's what adrenaline is for. Right? That, and the promise of a stiff drink once I get inside.

I open the door to Atomic Buzz—a drinking hole with nowhere near the edginess or allure of its name—and Brent, the owner, grins at me.

"You're lucky, Steph. I was thinking about closing early."

I glance around, my attention skating over the two elderly guys playing poker near the front window, then around the soulless room to the couple whispering sweet nothings at a table in the far corner.

"And ruin the atomic buzz you've got going?" I ruffle the long blonde strands of my hair, trying to work out the stiffness left from the nasty wig. "It looks like you've doubled your clientele since I was here last."

"Almost." He snickers. "What are you drinking tonight?"

I throw my pack to the floor and slide onto a swiveling seat, resting my hands on the sticky wood of the bar. "Whiskey, neat. Thanks."

Brent raises his brows as he reaches for Johnny Walker, then slides me a filled glass.

Yeah, I know, it's a sick-fuck move picking Dan Roberts' drink of choice, but I'm in a sick-fuck kind of mood.

"I'm celebrating a job well done," I clarify.

"What job was it this time?" He eyes me with interest, as if he's actually invested in my life. Nobody else looks at me like that. No one has in years. I make sure of it.

"The professor had us researching the growing number of assault and rape cases tied to solicitation."

I sometimes wish I could tell him the truth—that I don't work as a research assistant for a college professor who specializes in violent crimes. Having one person in this world to confide in could be a game changer. But trust issues are one of my many colorful traits.

"Which means we're on to a new project by the end of the week." I raise my glass in a silent toast, then take a sip.

"Well, congratulations on having finished studying that fucked up shit." He gives me a grim smile. "You know, my sugar daddy offer still stands whenever you want to quit that horrible job and let me take care of you."

I laugh. "Brent, you've only mastered the daddy part. When you get the sugar, let me know."

The door to the bar opens, and we glance to the guy making his way toward us. His face is turned as he scopes the room, but the black jeans and matching leather jacket tell me he's got enough self-respect not to be seen in a place like this.

"Think he's lost?" Brent asks.

"Without a doubt." I return to my drink, cupping it in both hands. "I'll bet you five bucks he asks for directions out of this hellhole."

"You have such little faith in my fine establishment."

I sip casually, enjoying my salute to Danny boy as the newcomer sits two chairs away, teasing my peripheral vision.

"What can I get you?"

"A Corona." His voice is low and subtle, barely a whisper of response, yet masculine enough for me to appreciate.

"Comin' right up." Brent shoots me a look as he grabs a bottle from the fridge beneath the counter, his eyes wide in exaggerated surprise before he returns his focus to the new guy. "You a local?"

"No."

"What brings you here?"

There's a huff, a pause, then a muttered, "Life."

Brent twists the cap on the bottle, hands it over, and

returns to his leaning post against the back counter. "Steph, look at me."

I frown, because I'm already looking at him.

"This guy is perfect for you. He's quiet and unresponsive, just how you like 'em."

I chuckle, roll my eyes, and raise my empty glass. "You need to spend less time focused on my sex life, and more on pouring drinks."

I chance a glance at my anti-social neighbor and take in his profile. His lips are tight. His jaw, too. There's a wealth of hostility vibrating from him. Even the dark stubble hugging his cheeks has a rough fuck-off vibe as wisps of hair shadow his eyes.

"Where you stayin'?" Brent asks, ignoring the tension.

"Do you always ask this many questions?" the guy drawls, the words smoothly gliding over his tongue to polish his annoyance.

"Yes," I answer. "He does."

Brent laughs. "This pretty little thing," he jerks his head at me, "came in years ago with the same aversion to conversation. Took me eight months to get a name out of her."

A name that isn't even mine.

I ignore the guilt and swivel my chair to face Mr. Reluctant. "You're better off spilling your guts. Just blurt it out. Divulge it all. It'll save the monotony of repeating all those monosyllabic answers."

He glances my way, dissolving my guilt with eyes so clear and hazel I'm caught off guard.

Whoa. Profile view was confronting. Front view? Equally so, with an added hint of panty-melting gorgeous.

Those lips are full and dark. His stare is fierce. The tense features make me want to lick his face, or slap it, just to see how he'd react.

"You know what?" Brent grasps the whiskey bottle and

pours me another drink. "You two are perfect for each other. Silent, secretive, and socially awkward."

I hold in a snort and incline my head. "He's right. He just nailed my Tinder bio." Not that I use Tinder—I can get my kicks on my own, thank you very much—but I know at the very least Brent will get a chuckle from my sass.

What I don't expect is the slight tilt to the stranger's lips. The tiniest lift revealing a dimple in his left cheek. It's devious, devilish, and undeniably delicious on such a rough and intense face.

"He's not going to give up, is he?" he asks.

I shake my head. "Not if you plan on staying here."

His focus doesn't waver. "Then maybe you could lead the way to another bar that doesn't pester clientele."

I'm not usually caught off guard, but this man has claimed that response from me twice in less than a few minutes.

"Hey, now." Brent raises his voice. "I'm just being welcom—"

"I'm fucking with you." Hazel eyes hold mine as this stranger gifts me with the slightest hint of a grin.

I stare for longer than I should, trying to come to terms with all the conflicting aspects of the sight before me. There's something different about him. Something intriguing. Then again, I'm still high on adrenaline, which makes all my responses unreliable.

"So..." Brent clears his throat, breaking my train of thought. "In answer to my question..."

The stranger reverts to his scowl, a blatant sign he's annoyed at being dragged back into the game of Twenty Questions. "My sister got knocked up by a lowlife with a heavy hand. He ended up leaving her as soon as my nephew was born. To help her out, I quit my job, packed my things, and drove here."

"That's…" I want to say unbelievable, because it is. Men like him don't exist. They aren't real. Not in my world. "…admirable."

He shrugs and palms his beer, taking a long pull. "She doesn't know yet. I only got into town tonight."

"Well, I hope you find the lowlife piece-of-shit and give him a dose of his own medicine." I don't realize what I've said until the words are out there, announcing my hunger for vengeance.

He narrows his gaze, looking at me with such intensity I feel his questions sink inside my chest to tinker with my pulse.

"I'm not the violent type," he murmurs.

My heart flutters.

Clearly, I'm not used to men who don't think with their fists. My world revolves around violence. My past, my present, and my future all mesh into nothing but bloodshed and suffering.

This man is a breath of fresh, crisp air against my tarnished lungs. If I had any hopes for my life, any maternal or romantic plans, I might have been tempted to sink my hook and reel him in.

Here fishy, fishy.

I grasp my whiskey and fight not to guzzle it down. "How old is your nephew?"

"Eight weeks."

There's no pause. Not even a slight frown as he recalls the timeline. This guy is fully invested in his family, and I'm a smidge jealous. I used to be surrounded by people like him. Good people. Loving people. But they never looked this severe or harsh. I can feel him scrutinizing me, studying me, just like I was doing with him.

"See what I've done here?" Brent interrupts. "My

pestering has started a conversation. If it wasn't for me, you two would be sitting in silence."

"Silence is good." The stranger swirls his beer with a lazy flick of his wrist. "Silence is comfortable."

"Silence is honest," I add, gaining another fierce stare.

He inclines his head.

Again, my gaze is glued to his. I can't help it. There's something about him that demands attention. Something dark, like I'm used to, and also something promising, which is entirely new to me. I suddenly feel like I want to climb his broad chest and ride his face for hours.

Not a good idea.

I turn back to the bar and ignore my nagging libido as the chatter continues without me. Brent returns to his questioning antics while the stranger resumes his monosyllabic answers.

Their conversation washes over me, sweeping away the brutal parts of the night to replace them with something basic and easy. Something suburban and casual. I concentrate, trying to learn more about him, but my adrenaline-filled brain is darting, looking for a hook to clasp onto.

Unfortunately, it snags onto my attraction. The sexiness.

My heart pounds harder with each muttered word. The minutes tick by with building lust. I glance to the large hands encasing his beer, the thick fingers, the tanned skin.

Hands are my downfall. My Achilles' heel. I can picture his grip around my throat. Clasping my flesh. Burying deep. A shudder slips through me.

Damn it.

I'm due to get laid. That's all. What is the cobweb tally at now? Two months? Three? And my last conquest ended up being more of an unwilling victim. He hadn't realized I was leading him into a sexual research situation and did a runner when I donned my newly purchased dominatrix attire.

But a woman's gotta try these things. I'm inquisitive by nature. Stepping outside the box is what I do. It's how I learn, and grow...and realize my error of spending five hundred dollars on black leather items, including a high-neck bralette and matching web garter.

"How about you, Steph?"

"Hmm?" I blink up at Brent and take another sip of alcoholic goodness. "What did I miss?"

"Laboring work. Do you know of any construction sites in this area?"

Construction? Laboring? Of course this broad temptation has a body built for sin under his jacket.

"Sorry." I shake my head and keep my gaze straight ahead. S*ip, sip, sip*. "Maybe a temp agency could help."

Brent leans into my line of sight, his lips lifting in a knowing smile. "What's wrong?"

I raise my glass. "I'm almost out of liquor."

It's no secret I like to get my sexy on, and my lovely bartender buddy probably thinks I'm too scared to get freaky with this Hulk-like Adonis.

That isn't the case.

Tonight is for celebration, and I don't feel like a sexual rejection to tarnish the memory. The insults from my last escapade are still raw.

That's a whole lot of spandex, sugar.

It wasn't spandex, asshole. It was expensive, supple matte black leather with gunmetal buckles.

Brent fakes a yawn as he refills my glass. "I think I might call last drinks."

I glare, and his eyes beam back at me, taunting—*matchmaker, matchmaker, make me a match*.

Does he think I'm too timid to sleep with this guy?

Really? My sexual appetite is more likely to indicate I'll swallow the sexy stranger whole.

"Yeah," my drinking partner agrees. "I guess I better make a move."

I glance at him, and he's right there staring back at me, strumming my pussy with his caged emotions.

"Do you want to get out of here?" he asks, passive as fuck.

The question not only surprises me, it lassos my womb and squeezes tight. I'm flustered, which is out of character, and I'm also aroused, which isn't all that surprising.

"Yes." I throw back the last of my drink and stand. "But I'm leaving on my own."

Apparently, the mix of adrenaline and whiskey has made me reckless. I'm a panty slip away from taking this guy home. This devilishly sexy man with his shadowy intrigue and penetrating eyes. My heart palpitates. My sternum itches. I want to drag him to my apartment by his dick. I would strip him. Devour him.

Not tonight, Satan. Not tonight.

I need to focus. Regroup. I have a lead to chase tomorrow, and I don't want anything else stealing my attention.

I pull my pack from the floor and scrounge for my purse, only to have the stranger shake his head.

"I've got it." He reaches inside his jacket, pulls out a money clip, and slides a stack of bills across the bar. "This should be enough for both of us."

It is.

More than enough.

I don't know how to respond. I'm uncomfortable with being indebted. I'm also charmed by his generosity. "Thank you."

He grasps his drink, not paying me attention as he raises the bottle. "Don't mention it."

It isn't a gentlemanly request. It's a statement. A demand that I ignore his kindness. It's entirely gruff and anti-social. It's how I usually act—my MO outside of this bar and away from the one man I speak to. It's so familiar I can't help smiling.

This man is me.

"Well..." I beat my desire back with a studded bat. "It was nice meeting you."

He scans me with a quick appreciative stare, from eyes to heels and back again. "I assure you, the pleasure was all mine." There's no inflection in his tone, no excitement, and definitely none of this pleasure he speaks of. But I believe him anyway.

I tingle in places that aren't usually susceptible to flattery. I crave more of his scrutiny. I want all of his attention.

Shit.

I clear my throat to break the trance and sling my pack over one shoulder. "I'll catch you later, Brent."

I don't glance in the bartender's direction. I focus on the door, my head high, and eat up the space between me and necessary fresh air. I fight temptation like a pro, striding my seductive heels toward my escape, until I hear the squeak of a bar seat.

"I'm out of here, too."

That voice slays me. The lethargy. The masculinity.

I pause and glance over my shoulder to see my fantasy approaching, the slightest tweak to his mouth a threat and a taunt, all in one. I should run. Fast. But all the cautionary thoughts are being smothered by the heavy weight of attraction.

There's a hum.

A zing.

It slides down my spine, tightens my nipples, and contracts my pussy in the most delicious squeeze. I'm already convinced this guy could make me come like a runaway freight train, leaving me devastated and deliciously broken.

I want that pleasure. I want the pain, too.

He raises a cocky brow. "You waiting for me, princess?"

Princess? "Seems more like you're following."

"Maybe." He shrugs. "Is that a problem?"

There is much more to his question than the issue of him tailing me. It's about vulnerability. Susceptibility. Deliciously dreamy carnality.

And yes, it's a major problem. Huge. My normally infallible caution is wavering like a leaf in a hurricane. But I can't voice a protest. The words aren't there. Not the right ones. Only those that will be so very, very wrong. "I guess that depends on what you want to achieve."

Thoughts dance behind those lazy eyes, and I want to know them all. I itch to hear his secrets. His darkest desires. I need to know his plans for me, and I want the explanation to come in erotic Technicolor.

"I want everything." His voice is low—pure sex and seduction.

My pussy twists in knots. There's no denying the inevitable. I'm going to succumb. This zing is too vibrant to ignore. I can already taste him on my tongue. The alcohol. The sweat.

I sigh, resigned to my fate. "Then, no, I guess it's no problem at all."

4
___
HER

I LEAD THE WAY ACROSS THE ROOM, THE STRANGER AN inch behind me. When I press my palm against the cold glass of the door, apprehension sinks its teeth deep into my flesh.

I pause, suck in a breath, and attempt to tune out my lust in an effort to listen to my instincts. This is the second time I've led a stranger from a seedy bar with the promise of sex, all in the space of a few hours.

The first didn't work well for Danny boy, and although I crept from that hotel room with a crazy-bitch smile on my face, I need to make sure I don't end up being the victim in this scenario.

"Problem?" The question is murmured with slight humor near my ear. "Don't tell me you've changed your mind already."

I glance over my shoulder and his face is a breath away. He's a mountain of a man up close. Thick and strong in the shoulders, with a heavy hand that lands beside mine on the door.

"Do I look like the type of woman who makes

mistakes?" It's not a flirty tease. He needs to know I own my shit. All day. Every day.

He ponders the question, or maybe just me in general, and rakes his teeth over his lower lip. He gives an almost imperceptible shake of his head. "No. But there's always a first, and I have a feeling I'm going to be a special kind of mistake."

He's a cocky son-of-a-bitch, and damn, his confidence has latched onto my ovaries, and I don't want it to let go until we are both double-digits deep in orgasms.

"Promises, promises." I push the door and walk ahead, not stopping until we reach the edge of the sidewalk. "I live over there." I jerk my chin toward the looming apartment building across the street with the solitary streetlight that illuminates years of neglect. The old, block construction isn't inviting in the slightest. It's cheap and nasty. Just the way I like it.

All the obvious downfalls are the reasons I consider myself lucky to live there. Nobody inside the dark and dirty walls has enough time or money to bother snooping on their neighbors. Most are too busy keeping their own heads above water with day-to-day life. I come and go without notice, not having made any friends in the years I've rented the studio apartment.

"Lead the way."

A firm hand lands on the low of my back, beneath my pack, the touch warm against the thin cotton of my top. I straighten, stiffen, and suck in a deep breath at the tumbles taking over my stomach.

I wait for a passing car, then step onto the asphalt, bringing us closer and closer to approaching bliss. He's glancing around, scoping the area as I enter the pin code into the building's outdated security panel. The one-two-three-four access code is a poor excuse for protection, but in this crime-riddled area it's the thought that counts, right?

I'm only glad the lobby doesn't smell like urine and stale beer today. It means I can pretend this cheap-ass building has a modicum of decency, when clearly, everyone who lives here knows better.

Another few feet of tense silence and we're at the rickety death trap of an elevator. I shove my finger against the call button, and the doors jolt open. He follows, moving to the opposite side of the small space as I lean against the wall, my arms spread against the thin waist-high railing.

He mimics me, arms spread, ankles crossed, and watches while I press the button to floor three. Neither one of us moves, or talks. He barely bats an eye until those doors close. Then he pushes from the wall and eats the space between us in two predatory steps.

I hold my breath, my tingles turning into wildfire as he walks into me. Not up to me. *Into me.*

His hips bump mine. He parts my legs with an aggressive shove of his knee. The silence and staring continue, no words, only actions as he wraps a menacing hand around the back of my neck and grips tight.

Fear jolts through my chest, making me immobile. He's animalistic, not an ounce of warmth in his expression.

I don't know this man. Not his name, not his age, not his hobbies or life goals. He's a complete stranger who has me pinned inside an enclosed space, his strong, calloused hands holding me hostage.

"You look nervous," he growls close to my lips.

I should back out, cut and run from this careless idea. But my heart loses the panicked beat and produces something more adrenaline-based.

I want him. I *need* him. To make the sterile parts of tonight that hover on the edge of my awareness a little less harsh. To make life exciting for all the right reasons instead of those that are wrong.

I lean closer, taunting him with a look I hope is equally as devilish as his own. "You're the one who should be nervous."

His chuckle is barely audible. "It's not my style."

"Mine either."

His fingers clench tighter, as if he's daring me to back out. I won't. Other women might be inclined to run. I still want to ride him and tame the wild beast barely contained in those eyes.

The elevator bounces to a stop and the doors open. He backs away, and I ignore the chill seeping into me as I lead the way onto the threadbare hall carpet.

My door is at the end, the very last room on the left. I sling the pack off my shoulder and pull my keys from the internal Velcro compartment, ignoring any curiosity he might have as I start working on my door.

I have three locks, the last a pin-code-operated deadbolt that is more high-tech than the entire building's security. There's also the small motion-activated camera beaming down at us from above the doorframe.

"Have a problem with break-ins?" he asks.

I cover the keypad, tap in the code—six, five, three, nine—and shove the door wide. "Nope. Not a one."

I'm smart and pre-emptive when it comes to protection. This stranger at my back is a risk, but my blade is hidden in a strap below my breasts, mace is in my pack, and there's a myriad of hidden weapons at my disposal inside this apartment.

I flick on the light, illuminating my studio space that is practically in a different dimension from the rest of the building. The paintings on the walls are huge masterpieces. The kitchen is filled with shiny new appliances. The floor is the finest polished wood.

I've got family money. A whole heap of it. So, I live in comfort. I just choose to do it in a shitty building. I've learned it is easier to blend into the rat race than the wealthy elite.

But I don't get any of those reactions from him. I can't hear his shock, or sense his surprise. Instead, his heavy footfalls approach, his large body pressing into mine, pushing me into the back of the sofa.

A rough hand shoves into my hair, pulling my head to the side, his mouth moving to my neck. "What's a woman like you doing in a building like this, princess?" His voice vibrates along my carotid, killing me slowly.

The endearment is a special gift of misguided appraisal.

He thinks I'm a princess. How cute. Or maybe he's being sarcastic. If so, he gets a gold star.

He sucks on my skin, and I moan. I'm completely unfamiliar with the acute vibrations taking over my insides. So unfamiliar I don't want to speak for fear my voice might make it vanish.

"Who are you?" he murmurs.

I shake my head and nuzzle my ass against his crotch. He's hard and thick, his erection an adamant force behind his zipper.

I swing around, needing those lips on mine.

He sates me immediately, taking my mouth with a harshness I don't anticipate. I'm used to soft kisses. Kind and timid. This is profoundly better. A fierce, punishing collision of lips and teeth and tongues.

His hands find my hips and he grinds into me, teasing me with anticipation. "Who are you, Steph?" He holds my gaze, those eyes as questioning as his words.

"I'm a memory you're going to treasure forever." I grip

his shirt and pull him forward, demanding more of his mouth.

I can't get enough. Maybe it's the way he scares me the slightest bit. The ferocity. The confidence. Or maybe it's narcissistic, because his harshness kind of reminds me of myself. Either way, I'm scrambling for more.

I want. I want. I want.

I glide my hands under his shirt and place my palms on the warmth of his stomach. Another moan escapes me. The ripples of his muscles are like an ocean under my fingers, moving and changing as his hands slide down my back and squeeze my ass.

He's so fucking strong, and I want that strength coiled around me, controlling me. I crave his temporary ownership. Instead of always being the one in command, in charge and under pressure, I want to be owned. To be a puppet instead of a puppeteer.

I claw at those muscles, working my way up his stomach and down his ribs. His masterful lips continue to overwhelm me, his tongue increasing its pace and severity.

My panties are wet, soaked, and my pussy clenches, demanding to be filled. I push my hands farther, learning more of him as I glide them around his back.

I'm about to release another moan at all the overwhelming perfection when my fingertips brush a hard object protruding from the waistband of his jeans.

He stiffens. I do the same.

He tries to recover by continuing the kiss, and I pull away, my fingers still touching the object that is undoubtedly a gun.

I wait for a response to all the questions going through my head, but he gives me nothing. No explanation. No apology. Only the lazy bat of his lashes over steely, lust-glazed eyes.

I inch closer and wrap my hand around the grip. He responds with the raise of his chin and the slightest narrowing of his gaze.

"Why does a non-violent man need a gun?"

"It's a bad neighborhood."

I incline my head, my heart beating rapidly in a mix of fear and arousal. I want to believe him—really, I do—but a lack of ignorance makes it impossible.

I weave my free hand around to sit on his chest, then shove him back while pulling the weapon from his waistband.

He goes with the flow, gifting me with a few retreating steps when we both know he could've tried to hardball his way out of the situation.

"A Walther P22? Nice." It's a serious gun. A seriously scary gun for someone who claims to avoid violence.

I eject the clip, shove it in my pocket, then pull back the slider. "Oh." I release a sardonic chuckle. "And a live one in the chamber. Aren't you a wealth of surprises?"

I guess it could be worse. The clip could be half empty.

He grins, but there's no humor in the expression. "And you sure know your way around a gun."

I shrug and lob the lone bullet his way. "Like you said, it's a bad neighborhood."

He catches the round without breaking my gaze, then again when I throw him the clip.

"Leave."

"You're kicking me out?" He scowls.

"You bet your perfectly sculpted ass I am." He's more like me than I realized—confident around guns, proficient in lies. I can no longer ignore the warning signs that highlight a dangerous man.

His jaw ticks, and those dazzling eyes are back in predator mode.

"Unless you want to play How Many Weapons Does She Have Stashed Within Arm's Reach." I grin. "That really is a fun game."

"Fine." He holds out a hand. "I'll leave."

I stare at his upturned palm and raise a brow. "If you're waiting for a high-five, you've assumed the wrong position."

"I'm waiting for my gun."

"Well, then, it looks like you're gonna luck out twice tonight." I jerk my chin toward the door. "Go. I'll throw it down once you're outside the building."

His hand falls to his side, fisting into a white-knuckled grip. "You're going to throw my gun from a third-story window?"

The upward twist of my mouth isn't friendly. "I hope you're a good catch."

He licks his lower lip, and I'm sure it's supposed to be a threatening gesture with those squinted eyes, but I'm over here still drowning in the gushing wetness of my panties.

I want to hate-fuck him right now. Hate-fuck him so damn hard. Unfortunately, I realize my safety is more important than indulging in my deranged fantasies. And yes, it's a seriously slow reaction I'm not overly proud of.

"Until next time." His mouth has the slightest incline, an almost imperceptible grin, as he turns for the door.

"Oh, sweetie, there's not going to be a next time."

He glances over his shoulder and smirks. "We'll see."

5

HIM

I STALK THROUGH THE LOBBY, PISSED AS ALL HELL THAT I've severely fucked up this situation. Tonight wasn't supposed to be difficult. The plan had been a straight line of simplicity. A fucking breeze.

Then *she* had happened. The distraction. The complication.

"*Shit*." The curse bites through my clenched teeth, bitter and aggressive. "Such a fucking mess."

I have a million different things to do tonight, and one of them shouldn't have been the hot blonde with the sassy mouth. But that's where I've been, in her apartment, ready to fuck her.

I move along the sidewalk, toward the streetlight, my neck craning as I focus on her window—third one up, last along the wall. She isn't there. Not yet. So I stop, arms crossed, and wait.

Then I wait some fucking more, because she sure as shit isn't in a hurry to return my gun.

I'm about to start searching the street for a rock when the glass pane slides upward and her grin comes into view.

She sticks her head out the window, light blonde hair cascading over slim shoulders, those perky tits looking lush and inviting from yet another angle.

Her eyes hold a wicked gleam, and that sexy mouth is a lip-lick away from begging to blow me. There's no denying she still wants my dick. It's written all over her seductive face. Problem is, I can't ditch the stiffness in my pants to pretend I feel any different. My arms throb with my barely contained restraint. I can still feel her hair around my knuckles, can still smell the vanilla scent.

"Ready?" She dangles the gun, holding it lazily by the grip.

"Born ready."

She smiles—she probably gives a sadistic chuckle, and I'm too far away to hear it—then drops my weapon. I watch her watching me until the split millisecond before the gun reaches my hands. Then I'm all business, loading, locking, and placing the P22 back into the ass of my waistband.

"Thanks for the memories," she calls out, then ducks her head inside and slides the window shut.

I focus on the square of glass for longer than I should. Glaring, still seeing her even though she's already gone. Damn that sassy mouth.

Who the fuck is she, anyway? *Steph*, the bartender called her. Stephanie. AKA The Whirlwind Who Became A Bigger Obstacle With Each Passing Second.

She's a loose end, but I can't convince myself to tie that knot tonight. I'll see her again. I'll resolve whatever we need to resolve soon enough. In the meantime, I will pave the way for resolution and return to the regular broadcast of my shit-show life.

I make for the bar, my softening cock leading the way across the deserted street. Behind me, I hear another slide of the window, then her authoritative, "*Hey*."

I pause, my ego taking a few seconds to enjoy her continued interest, then shoot a glance over my shoulder.

"Do you want a tip for future conquests?" she asks.

A tip? This woman wants to give *me* a tip? There's no denying we're both hooked in this impromptu game, but it's clear she has a misconception on what role she's playing.

I shrug. "Sure."

"The only thing a woman wants to find hard in a guy's pants is his dick. Ditch the gun next time."

I grin. I can't fucking help it. That mouth of hers is going to get us both in trouble. Then again, maybe it saved her. "There's going to be a next time?"

She laughs and slams the window closed again, but she's still there, still watching, still holding my gaze with those bewitching eyes.

I shake my head, trying to shake her off, too, and continue across the road to the shitty bar with the catchy name. I don't look back as I shove my way through the front door. I don't need to. I know she's watching. I can feel her stare at the base of my neck.

The same five people are inside. The two men playing cards, the couple in the far corner, and the bartender, who is eying me, probably trying to figure out if I hurt his girl or ended the night in a sexually premature fashion.

"She kicked me out," I admit as I slide onto a bar seat.

His jaw is tight as he throws a bar coaster toward me, the flimsy cardboard skittering along the scuffed wood. "Well, I didn't see that coming."

Funnily enough, neither had I. People rarely catch me off guard. Women never do. Until now.

"Want another drink?" The offer lacks kindness. I'm sure he's annoyed at me for hurting her, and I appreciate his loyalty. It's something I can exploit to get answers to my growing list of questions.

"Yeah. Whiskey." I'd already had a taste for it on her tongue, and fuck me for needing more.

His eyes narrow as he grabs the liquor bottle and begins to pour. He tries to stare me down, and I oblige because it's in my best interest to play the remorseful role.

"I know I messed up." I focus on the coaster, fiddling with the edge like a remorseful motherfucker.

He places my drink in front of me and holds tight until I meet his gaze. "What'd you do?"

"It was nothing."

"Obviously it was something to her."

"Yeah." I concede with a nod and decide to dive straight into the truth. "She found out I was carrying. It scared her off."

He releases my glass and steps back. A clear retreat. "I don't blame her."

"Neither do I. But come on, man." I play it cool. "I'm from the country, and when my sister calls to say this guy of hers is beating her and threatening her with a gun, how am I going to defend her and her kid? I'm not going to apologize for wanting to protect my family. I know how crazy you city people are."

He holds my focus, reading me. "Oh, well." He shrugs. "You can't win 'em all."

I nod. "I know, but she was different. Believe it or not, I actually like her. The woman's a spitfire."

He chuckles, eating up my attraction like a lovesick fool. "She sure is. If I was ten years younger…"

I force a laugh. "Any idea how I can get a second chance?" I raise my glass and take a sip. "She doesn't seem the type to appreciate me waiting out in front of her building in an attempt to see her again."

"Hmm." He leans against the back counter and crosses his arms over his chest. "That's a tough one."

I reach into my jacket, pull out my money clip, and flick over two fifty-dollar bills. "You can't happen to tell me some of her usual hangouts, can you?" I place the money on the sticky bar and slide it over.

His eyes narrow on my hand, then my face. "You bribing me, son?"

"I'm willing to do whatever it takes to get a second chance."

His lips thin. His shoulders straighten. "Your money is no good to me."

Bullshit. The guy might want to believe he's above the incentive, but his darting eyes tell a whole different story.

"You sure?" I hide my growing annoyance behind a relaxed tone. I don't have time for this shit. Not for him. Not for her. If Brent isn't careful, I'll lose my patience, and nobody wants that. "Come on. Just let me know where she hangs out."

He sighs, the first sign of a slight buckle in his resolve. "I don't know much about her. Only a few things I've learned here and there from regulars who talk a lot of shit. So, I'd suggest your money would be better spent getting a decent meal at the Hot Wok at the end of the street." He glances away. "On a Thursday night...at around seven o'clock."

I hide my smirk behind another sip of whiskey.

"And if you're new to the area, you should check out the boxing club six blocks south of here. I think they have classes Monday, Wednesday, and Friday mornings."

Wednesday—*tomorrow.*

I tilt my glass at him in appreciation. "Thanks."

His gaze narrows. "If you fuck with her—"

"I know." I should laugh. If the threat had come from anyone else, I would.

"You do right by her. Even if she isn't interested in what you've got to offer."

"I will." The lies come easily. They always have.

I throw back the remaining liquid, then slide the glass toward him. "Thanks for the drink." I stand, leaving the bills on the counter.

"Take the money with you. You left more than enough earlier."

"Keep it for next time. I have a feeling we'll be seeing more of each other."

He chuckles. "Only if you're lucky."

"Yeah." Or more specifically, if she's unlucky.

I walk outside, unable to help myself as I glance at the building across the street. The third-floor window. I expect to see her there, watching, waiting, and I'm ashamed to admit I'm disappointed she isn't.

She thinks the game is over. That the hook-up failed, and we've gone our separate ways.

In reality, our time together has just begun. The two of us are going to get to know one another, whether she likes it or not. And that's not my fault. It's all on her—her decisions, her actions. Her damn sassy mouth.

I continue along the road, down the side street, to my car. I climb in and snatch my phone from the glove compartment.

Three missed calls, all from Decker, but he's not the person I need to speak to first.

I dial Torian, and I'm not surprised when he doesn't answer. The fucker would be sleeping like a baby while I worked. His voicemail cuts in, and the beep sounds without a welcome message.

"Hey, Torian. There's been a complication." I swallow over the bitter taste of temporary failure. "It means a slight delay in the timeline, but I'll call once I'm done."

I hang up, knowing he won't give a shit about details, and call Decker.

"Where the fuck are you?" he demands in greeting. "You were supposed to check in over an hour ago."

"There was a change of plan."

"What change?"

"A snag with the job. I had to follow a lead."

"You're not a fucking detective. You do your job, get the hell out of there, *then call me.*"

I start the ignition and do a U-turn, going in the opposite direction of where I need to be. "You worried about me, pumpkin?"

"Stressed," he growls. "I was stressed. Big difference."

"That's cute, Deck. Real cute." I creep my car to the intersection and glance up at her building. Her window. She's there, standing to the side of the frame, trying to remain out of view as she peers down at the bar.

My dick pulses, and I'm not sure I even know what I want from her anymore. I should go back up there and finish what I started. I should end this tonight.

But I can't force this. For once, I don't want to.

"Fuck you, *Hunt.*" He snaps my nickname, making it sound like a curse. "So, you've quit working for the night? Is this you calling to punch your card?"

"No. I haven't started." I shouldn't give a shit that she's up there waiting for a glimpse of me, but I do. I shouldn't want to draw her attention, but I itch to do that, too. "I only called because I need you to do a background search on someone."

"You haven't started? You checked out hours ago. What the fuck is going on?"

"Focus." It's a warning to us both. I tear my gaze from her silhouette and turn onto her street, driving away from her building. "The name is Stephanie. She lives at apartment nineteen, level three, six-five-nine Belldore Street." I pause, waiting for confirmation that doesn't come. "Did you get all that?"

"All that? You haven't given me much to go on."

"It's enough. Once you start digging, you'll find more." He always does.

"And what am I digging for, exactly?"

"Anything and everything." I want it all. I *need* it all. "And make sure you get started right away."

"Yeah, I got it."

"I mean tonight, Decker. Now. This is your main priority."

"Why? What happened?"

She happened. Long hair, slim legs, sassy blue eyes, and ruby lips I want stretched around my dick. And they are only the physical attributes. I know once I delve into that mind of hers, the fucked-up shit I find will be even more impressive. "It's nothing you need to worry about."

"Right." He huffs. "I don't need to worry at all."

"It's just stress, remember?"

"You know, it's no coincidence your nickname rhymes with cunt."

I grin. "I'll call you when I'm done."

6

___

HER

I POUND THE PAVEMENT, JOGGING THE SIX BLOCKS TO the mid-morning boxing class due to start in less than five minutes.

I should've been up early to start my research on the names Dan gave me. Instead, I slept in, which is out of the ordinary. Being kept awake until three a.m. with a rabid case of insomnia is also an anomaly. And only one person carries the blame.

Hazel eyes haunted me all night. *No*, they didn't haunt. They taunted. Teased. I hadn't been able to get my pounding heartrate to lessen, which made relaxation impossible. I'd tossed and turned, each movement reminding me of the feel of a dominant man against my skin.

I don't even know his name.

It could be Bob or Jim or something equally lustless. Whereas I currently imagine calling out Ryder or Heath or Drew in the height of passion.

I could scream the fuck out of Heath.

Jim? Not so much.

I push through the door to the boxing class and haul the

pack off my back to scrounge inside, pulling out my black and white sparring gloves and matching defending pads.

"You're late." Adam, my instructor, raises his voice as I walk across the room and dump my backpack on the floor. "We've got even numbers today. So hurry up and pair with the new guy."

"New guy?" I scrunch my face accordingly.

Fuck the new guy. I always work out with Adam. He's the only one with enough respect and guts to challenge me.

"You'll be fine." He juts his chin to the left and I follow the direction, already glaring in the hopes my intimidating squint will earn me a place back beside my rightful partner.

"Oh, hell no." The words whisper from my mouth as my attention fixes on yet another anomaly.

He's here. My insomnia-inducing, weapon-wielding fantasy is throwing air jabs like the rest of the class, his remarkably cut muscles on display through his white sports tank and mid-thigh black shorts.

He meets my glare with soulless, excitement-starved eyes. Yet, every part of me notices every part of him. Not only the taunting lack of familiarity in his expression, but his tauntingly sexy body, too. Every damn inch of my sweaty, heated skin is well aware there isn't an ounce of unsculpted flesh anywhere to be seen on this man. Not on his thighs. Not on his arms. And I'd bet my life, not on his ass, either.

There's definitely no gun hidden on him today, but this time it doesn't matter. The guy is a weapon in himself. A lethal assassin. At least where my pussy is concerned. This visual inspection is slaying my cooch. It's brutal and unwarranted and entirely thrilling.

I stride toward him, masking the need to salivate as if my life depends on it. "You following me again?"

He keeps jabbing at the air as a subtle grin kicks at one

side of his lips. "That's a little paranoid, seeing as though I was here first, and this place isn't even in your suburb."

That's the exact reason I've been coming here for the last three months. It isn't somewhere anyone would expect me to be. I bypass two similar classes on the run here. I even jog additional miles, sometimes doubling back on myself, to ensure nobody follows.

So, yes, I do wave the paranoid flag with pride. But that doesn't mean he isn't tailing me.

"You're serious?" His lips thin, and he stops jabbing the air to stand at his full domineering height.

I drop my gloves to the floor and cross my arms over my chest in response. *Don't loom over me, asshole.*

He scoffs, the sound barely audible as he shakes his head. "No, princess, I'm not following you. But after seeing you in those curve hugging clothes, a guy might just change his plans." His interest stalks my active-wear, flittering over my body like a physical caress. Ankles to chest.

I want to tell him to stop, to back the fuck off, but there's something about the lazy way he appraises me that encourages stupid decisions.

"Thanks, buddy," I reply with a luscious amount of sarcasm. "It's actually funny you mention my outfit, because when I got dressed this morning I thought to myself, 'Hey, if I'm lucky enough to run into that random guy I met in the bar, who just so happened to bring a gun into my apartment, what would be the best outfit I could wear to impress him?' And these were the clothes I pulled out."

"I'm sensing a little hostility."

I raise a brow. "Really?"

He's different today. Tired. I don't like that I want to know why. I don't like much at all about this guy turning up in my life, only his eyes...and his grin...and his confidence, his muscles, the way he kisses...

Shit. I like too damn much about this man.

"You brought a lethal weapon into my apartment. Of course there's hostility." I take my position beside him and fall into routine.

Jab, jab, jab.

Jab, jab, jab.

He does the same, those sculpted arms assailing my peripheral vision.

"I can't believe you're still hung up on me having a gun," he mutters under his breath.

"For starters, it happened less than twenty-four hours ago. And second, no, I'm not hung up on you having a gun. I'm hung up on you bringing it into my apartment. Into *my home*."

"Would it make you feel better if I apologized?"

I freeze, entirely surprised by the question, because, yeah, a sincere apology and explanation would help this situation. But I'm beginning to think a clean-up crew for this mess would be more dangerous than my annoyance.

I don't want to like this guy. Nope. He is already too far under my skin. Continuing dialogue would be a mistake.

"Forget it," I mutter. I train my gaze straight ahead, determined to focus on getting the workout I need, not the workout he could give me.

"Time to pair up," Adam calls. "One throwing punches, one holding pads. I want to see jab, cross, hook. Jab, cross, hook."

I reach for the gloves at my feet, not giving him the option of who will punch first. I need to swing the frustration from my body. To jab, cross, hook this shit out of my system.

"I guess I'll hold the pads to start off," he grumbles.

I glare. At him. At myself. At everything that seems out of place and abnormal. I don't like this. I'm not comfortable with the human interaction or how much I'm beginning to enjoy it.

Every time our eyes meet, that zing hits me.

I loathe it.

"So..." He pulls the worn class pads onto his hands and holds them at chest height. "You don't want an apology, but would it help if I told you I took your advice?"

"My advice?" I throw a hard jab, and he jolts.

He recovers quickly and gives me a game-on smirk. "Yeah. You told me to ditch the gun. Which I did."

I ignore him and throw a cross, packing all my strength into the swing. This time, he doesn't flinch. He barely moves.

"And I can assure you, the only thing hard in these pants is my dick."

A mental image assails me, and I have no idea why my imagination has overcompensated in the package department. Huge man, huge dick. It seems proportionate, but I don't want that visual.

Nope.

It's difficult enough concentrating on throwing a powerful hook without my pussy contracting with his every word.

"Jab, cross," I hiss as I complete the actions. "Hook." I throw everything I have into those punches, driving him backward.

Jab, cross, hook.

Jab, cross, hook.

"Whoa," Adam calls out, coming to my side. "Ease up, Emma. I don't want you scaring away the new guy."

Shit.

I ignore the narrowing hazel eyes staring back at me from my boxing partner and force myself to calm down.

Adam gives a disapproving shake of his head and moves on to the next pair.

Jab, cross, hook.
Jab, cross, hook.
Jab, cross, hook.

"Emma?" The stranger's steely gaze questions me more than the deeply murmured word.

"Concentrate." I cross higher, making him duck to avoid an impact to the face.

"I thought your name was Steph." He crouches, bringing our eyes level.

I hide my apprehension behind a scowl. "Emma Stephens. Some people shorten my surname and use it as a nickname."

Jab, cross, hook.
Jab, cross, hook.

The intensity in his expression increases, and I don't appreciate the scrutiny. I can't blame him for the disbelief. The explanation was poor, especially for my standards. Usually, I'm quick on my feet, mentally speaking.

Today? Not so much.

"Okay, everyone," Adam yells. "Switch places."

I throw my gloves to the floor and pull on a set of pads. Once I'm standing straight and ready, the asshole hits me with a jab worthy of knocking a lesser woman on her ass. I stumble, and he smirks at me.

"Sorry. I'll go easier on you."

"Don't you fucking dare." I hold my hands in place, preparing for the cross. This one is equally hard, but at least I'm ready. The hook, on the other hand, makes me stumble sideways.

He watches me with each swing, staring into me,

holding me captive. The physical exertion and mental games make my heart pound incredibly hard. I start to pant, my breaths short and sharp, almost to the point of hyperventilation.

He doesn't question me anymore, not in words, but those eyes seek answers. They're digging deep, seeing things I don't want him to see.

"Stop it," I growl.

He chuckles, soft and oh-so low. "Stop what? Do you need me to throw softer punches?"

"You know what I'm talking about."

Jab, cross, hook.

Jab, cross, hook.

The more he moves, the more sweat beads his skin, making those muscles glisten.

"Get a drink, guys."

I slump at Adam's instruction, dropping the pads to the floor as I hunch, all my muscles squealing in agony.

"You did well." My tormentor pats me on the back, his actions and words equally derisive.

Fuck him. Fuck him for starving my libido. Fuck him for the insomnia. And fuck him for playing mind games.

He's messing with me, and he already knows enough to entice him to snoop. I straighten, my nostrils whistling like a damn bull with my labored breathing as Muscle Man stands at my side.

"What's wrong?" His grated whisper brushes my ear. "You look livid…and let me tell you, it's sexy as fuck."

A shudder jolts through me, the vibration culminating in my nipples.

Something isn't right. I don't know what it is. I can't see through his brain-numbing fog to understand it.

It's intuition that tells me to get out of here. I lean over, scoop my gloves and pads off the floor, and walk for my backpack. I rip the bag open, the zipper grinding under the pressure. I shove my stuff inside and haul it over my shoulder before stalking to the door.

Nobody tries to stop me. I have no friends here. No one knows me.

I push outside, and cold air hits my cheeks, bringing clarity. As cute as it was to think I had a similar personality to this guy, we are nothing alike. We never will be.

I'm not normal. Not my past and not my future. I don't fit in, and I don't want to. I need to remain under the radar, and it feels like this guy has nailed a neon sign on my ass.

I start down the sidewalk and hear the door push open behind me.

"Wait."

His demand has no effect on me.

Liar.

Of course it does. I want to plant my feet and confront the hell out of him. I want to ask him why he's hassling me, why he's paying attention when I've skated by unnoticed for so long. I want to know why the hell I'm torn with every action and every word where he's concerned.

And I seriously want to know why I can't stop picturing the size of his dick and how good it would feel down the back of my throat.

I keep walking, getting as far away from stupidity and craziness as I can. Even now, I'm hoping he follows, and I don't know why.

Why? *Fuck.* Why?

I don't understand. Nothing makes sense, and still, the feeling is a nagging force trying to break free from my chest.

I want him to continue, and I need him to stop.

"*Wait.*" This time the request is growled in the deepest command.

I start to jog, making my way along the street, past the

fruit vendor and up to the second-hand store when strong fingers grab my elbow, pulling me to a stop.

"Why did you run out?" His frown bears down on me. "I thought we were having fun."

"*You* were having fun. This isn't enjoyable for me." It's messy and chaotic.

"We had chemistry last night." He releases my arm. "It'd be a shame to let it go to waste."

"We also had a lot of alcohol."

He scowls. "You weren't drunk, and neither was I."

He's right, and I can't bring myself to admit it. I've gone years without an emotional link to anyone apart from my friendly bartender. I've been alone and strong. Now I feel weak with my need for...*something*. I can't even pinpoint my attraction to this man. It's just there, hovering like a gas cloud.

"Let me buy you a drink tonight." There's still no enthusiasm ebbing from him. Not even the slightest glimpse.

Why is that entirely endearing?

I scoff. Maybe because he's the polar opposite to the last guy I dated. My stomach hollows at the reminder, and I push out a heavy breath to wash it away.

"I'm not much of a drinker." I tear my gaze from his and focus on the second-hand televisions playing in the window, my lack of interest raking over sitcom reruns and numerous news feeds. "Last night was a one-off."

"Then dinner. We can go to that wok place at the end of your block."

I'm about to decline the offer when a news flash crosses one of the television screens.

Senator's Son Found Dead.

I blink through the hallucination, trying to make the words disappear.

My heart stutters, and my world narrows to those four words. *Senator's. Son. Found. Dead.* Then Dan Roberts' face takes center stage.

Numbness seeps into my limbs, and the sound of the busy sidewalk disappears—the street traffic, too. My pulse echoes in my ears. There's only my thundering heartbeats and that news headline.

Pounding arrhythmia and panic.

Fear and hysteria.

I've killed a man?

I shake my head. *No.* I've never killed anyone, even though there have been numerous people who've tempted my restraint. I am the self-appointed person who gives criminals a dose of their own medicine when the legal system fails to provide punishment. I give victims revenge, and assholes a chance to change their ways.

I don't do death.

That is for a higher power to decide.

"What's wrong?" That voice sounds near my ear, and I squeeze my eyes shut to find focus. "Are you okay?"

I breathe through the delirium and finally blink to find him staring down at me, his forehead wrinkled, his lips tight.

"I'm good," I whisper. Then louder, "Just light-headed from the exercise."

"You need food." He scrutinizes me, reading me, and my cheeks heat under his surveillance. Under my guilt.

I step back. "I need to get home."

"No." He follows, matching me step for step. "Tell me what's going on."

I glance back at the television, finding the breaking news replaced with some sort of telenovela. Maybe it was a figment of my imagination. Maybe I'm losing my ever-loving mind.

"*Just leave me alone.*" I run, sprint, ditching him somewhere along the way.

I don't stop. I reach the end of the block, then the next, and the next. I don't glance at the cars that blare their horns as I cross numerous streets. I don't pause. Yet, I can't outrun the nightmare clipping at my heels.

I don't kill people. I couldn't bring myself to do so. No matter how vile or disgusting a criminal's actions are, I always make the punishment singular. I contain the pain to the guilty party. Because once that life is snuffed, an intricate web of people become affected.

The parents who live for their only son are devastated. Those nieces and nephews who dote on their uncle are heartbroken. The innocent sisters and brothers are filled with anger and confusion.

I can't be the person who inflicts that pain.

Maybe it's already too late.

Maybe I already am a murderer.

Fuck. I should've dug deeper into my research on Dan. There could've been a heart condition. An allergy to Rohypnol. *Hell.* He could've choked or had trouble breathing after I fled.

Oh, God, I'm going to throw up.

I push my legs even harder, reaching the corner of my building with shaky thighs, my chest heaving, and there he is, leaning against a black Chevrolet parked in the loading zone.

A sexy car for a sexy son-of-a-bitch.

"What the hell is going on?" He strides toward me, a thick black sweater now hugging his upper body.

"Stop following me." I sniff, my nose leaking from the vigorous exercise. "Get out of here."

"You took off after saying you were light-headed. I wanted to make sure you were all right. Clearly, you're not."

"Clearly?" I swipe at my stupid nose with my wrist.

He moves in front of me, his gaze softer, on the verge of kindness. "You look like you're about to cry."

I straighten and blink through his ignorance. "You're an idiot." I won't cry over Dan. I refuse. My nose tingles due to exertion. My eyes burn because...damned if I know, but it isn't from building tears.

I sidestep and hustle for the front doors, entering the pin code through blurry vision. He's at my back before I'm inside, and I no longer have the strength to tell him to leave.

"At least let me call someone. A friend. Or family."

A harsh laugh escapes my lips. There is nobody here for me. No friends. No family. Nobody and no one at all. Not a single soul.

I make it to the elevator and press the button. The doors open, and he follows me inside, always following, always there.

I slump into the corner, my arms hugging my chest.

"Give me your phone." The stranger holds out a hand while he presses the button for my floor with the other. "I'll call someone to come look after you."

I ignore him, too focused on Dan's face as it takes over my mind. The snide smile, the laugh, the voice. The feel of his ribs breaking beneath my fist. The crack of his jaw. The sound of his muffled shouts.

I press a hand to my mouth and the other to the elevator wall to hold myself upright. The floor jolts to a stop, and bile rushes up my throat, demanding to be free.

Please let me make it to the bathroom.

I lunge for the doors, pull them apart, and sprint for my apartment. I'm blinded by horrible images as I release dead-bolts and enter the pin code. Dan's hair, his eyes, his mouth. I can see it all.

What's your name, bitch?

I shove inside my apartment, dump my backpack, and rush to the toilet. There's barely enough time to collapse to my knees before the contents of my stomach leave me in a heaving purge.

Through the rise of bile and partly digested toast, the face of a murdered man stares back at me. Haunting me.

I want to know what to whisper in your ear when I'm raping you raw.

I grip the toilet, my stomach convulsing over and over and over again until there's nothing left to give.

"Are you still going to tell me nothing's wrong?"

That voice pulls me from the panic, stripping away the memories of one man and replacing them with another. I wipe a hand across my mouth and glance over my shoulder, finding him leaning against the doorway.

"Get out." I push to shaky feet, flush my breakfast, and reach for the cabinet to pull out my toothbrush and paste.

"Did you know the guy?"

I rinse my mouth with water, load up my brush, and begin scrubbing. "*Leave.*" I scour the vomit from my mouth, cleaning my tongue and teeth and everywhere in between.

"The guy on the television," he clarifies. "The senator's son."

No, I didn't know him. He was a stranger, even after I killed him. I grasp the counter and focus on my reflection in the mirror. I'm pale, my eyes wild, with strands of hair stuck to the sweat on my cheeks.

"Was he a friend of yours?"

"*Shut up.*" My head throbs with each beat of my pulse. I can't think. It hurts to breathe. I start for the door, needing space, needing room. I try to push by him, and he doesn't budge. "Get out of my way."

He doesn't. Instead, he shoves from the frame, stands tall, and stares me down.

"I said, *move.*"

He squares his jaw, preparing for a fight I'm more than willing to give. I have to get this toxic sludge out of my system, and thrusting it out is the only way I know how.

I cock my fist and swing, already anticipating the painful contact that never comes. He ducks, weaves, and steps back in a flash of movement that makes my head spin. I swing again and again, each attack thwarted by his quick reflexes.

I keep advancing, keep punching, keep trying to distract myself from reality.

I pounce forward. *Jab. Cross. Hook.* My knuckles graze his chin. Almost impact.

His eyes narrow and that harsh face hardens. "Enough."

I can't stop. My arms have a mind of their own. I can't control my thoughts. Not the blinding flashbacks of what I did to Dan, or the snapshots of what he'd done to other women.

I swing again, and this time the ferocious intruder grabs my wrist, wrenching it down and twisting. I'm spun in a circle until my back is plastered against his front, his other arm smothering my chest. He holds me in place, trapping me while I hyperventilate.

"I said, enough," he growls in my ear.

I whimper and sag against him, my heavy breathing lessening in the long, silent moments he holds me.

"Was he your lover?"

"What?" I struggle to break free and fail. "*No.* He was a disgusting excuse for a man who deserved to die long ago."

The truth shocks me. But it *is* the truth.

"Then why the breakdown?"

"It isn't a breakdown." Now I'm lying, because the reality is, I'm scared. I'm terrified of being sent to prison. Not because of what could happen to me once trapped inside. I'm petrified I'll die behind bars while the person who destroyed my family runs free.

I can't fail them.

I refuse.

"So, storming out of boxing class, running away from a conversation, and then violently vomiting is a common thing for you?" He scoffs against my neck, making me shiver. "I guess my first impression was wrong. Here I was thinking you had a massive set of balls."

"I don't need balls." I buck against him, and the faintest hint of his erection has me sucking in a sharp breath. "But it's nice to know you were thinking I had a set to match your own. Is that what turns you on? My massive balls?"

"No." His laughter is low and sinister, barely audible as it flitters over my neck. "I'll be honest and say everything about you turned me on last night."

Those mind-numbing tingles sink deeper inside me. My arms, my legs, even my toes buzz from the potential distraction.

"Everything about you *still* turns me on," he whispers.

I close my eyes, sinking under his confounding spell. He's not begging me for sex. There's no passion. No heat or urgency. His words are cold and emotionless, yet still coated with a devilishly seductive edge I can't ignore.

I need to learn to ignore it.

He knows where I live, which wouldn't be an issue due to my security measures if he'd become the one-night-stand I intended him to be. But now he also knows I've lied about my name. I've told him I have weapons stashed in my apartment. And he's aware of two of my regular haunts—Atomic Buzz and the boxing class I now have to quit taking.

He's chipping away at my privacy, and I need those pieces back.

I wiggle in an attempt to break free and ignore the

heavy weight of disappointment when he lets me go. I face him, and the simplicity of what stares back at me turns my insides to mush.

He's not smiling. No, those lips are a flat line. His arms fall limp at his sides. There's no warmth or seduction. No cocky smirk. Just him. Just eyes that sink into me, whispering promises beyond my wildest fantasies.

Everything about you still turns me on.

His confession washes away the panic, and in its place, arousal blooms.

He stalks toward me, and I hold my ground, tilting my head to maintain contact with those predatory eyes. He brings us foot to foot, almost hip to hip. The looming wall of a man stands before me, expressionless, emotionless, apart from all the devastatingly calm superiority.

My mouth salivates.

His hand snaps up, aiming for my chin, but I smack it away. He grins, tries again, and fails after another one of my slaps.

My turn, big guy.

I launch my hand at his throat. He doesn't defend himself. He stands there, letting me wrap my fingers around his neck as his eyes flash. I'm taunting a bear. Poking the giant. I wonder if he'll crush me, mentally or physically.

"We can spar all you like." His offer brings chills. "But I'm sure you'd prefer it without any clothes on."

The temptation of his statement wraps around my chest. *Squeeze, squeeze, squeeze.* He's right. So painfully, unbelievably right.

"No." My grasp on this situation is slipping, sliding. My fingers grip the cliff's edge, but the ground crumbles beneath my grasp. "Get out, before I make you leave." The demand clogs my throat, coming out in a garbled mess.

"You don't want that."

"Don't I?" Fuck him and his incredibly clear insight. "Will my knee in your junk prove otherwise? Or maybe you need my fist in your face."

"Have at it, princess. I'm no stranger to pain."

7

HER

I BELIEVE HIM.

I think that's where our connection lies—in pain. He's been through it. Battled it. The evidence is clear in his emotional scars. The sterility. The harsh communication.

We're two tortured souls who've found each other by chance. And maybe all I need is to get my fill of him so I can cut this connection and go on my merry way. I only want what's between his thighs. The cheap thrill. That hard, generous length. And I bet my life he feels the same about my snatch.

Once this hot and sweaty masterpiece takes place, I will pull his ripcord and fast-track him in the opposite direction.

Toodaloo, motherfucker.

No emotion. No more attachment.

His lips curve, his growing smirk alluding to that slight dimple in his left cheek. My fingertips scratch over the rough stubble of his jaw. Harsh, yet too damn inviting.

My tongue snakes out, gliding over my tingling lower lip. My body is out of control. My heart vibrates beneath my ribs, my pulse pounds, my stomach flutters with a mass of tickling butterflies.

I release his throat, my fingers gliding over his neck, his chest, before dropping to my side.

I can't do this.

I can't continue, and I can't stop.

He steps back, kicking off his shoes, then grips the hem of his sweater and tank, and pulls them over his head, exposing more sculpted flesh. Not only muscles, but scars. His body is a canvas of brutality, with inch-long lines of puckered skin across his rib cage and a circular mark above his right hip.

He watches me watching him, wordlessly, almost breathlessly.

"You're accident-prone," I murmur.

"I guess I am."

"But still not the violent type, right?" I meet his gaze.

"Definitely not." His eyes glimmer with the slightest tease. "I hate the stuff."

I'd be a blind fool not to pick up on his sarcasm. It's there. *Right there.* In his grin, in his intensity, in the almost scary way he controls me without even knowing it.

Oh, God. I'm dancing with the devil.

And I love it.

He's dangerous. There's no doubt. And those *non-violent* scars around his ribs look awfully similar to stab wounds. The circular mark above his hip speaks of a bullet injury. Or maybe that's just my imagination talking, and they're only construction injuries. Laboring accidents.

Either way, I should pull his ripcord now. I should seriously give him a merry finger-wave as I boot his ass out the door.

I should. I should. I should.

Instead, need wraps itself around me, pulling my limbs,

crushing my chest. For once, I feel... I just *feel*. I'm not hollow. I'm not adrift. This man has me tethered to something, his presence keeping my feet on solid ground.

"Come here," he growls.

There are mere feet of space between us, but he demands my submission. He wants me to succumb.

I can't deny his request. I inch forward, my chin lifting to keep our gazes connected.

"Good," he purrs, slicing a hand around my hip to drag me into his body.

I gasp, and he steals the sound with his mouth, his lips overtaking mine, his tongue delving deep. He kisses me into mindlessness, those strong arms wrapping around me, his hands gliding down my back to cup my ass. He lifts me in a callous jerk, positioning my pubic bone against his hard cock.

I spread my legs, wrapping my thighs around his waist to grind against him. Warmth flood my pussy, my body eagerly preparing for pleasure. There's never been a better feeling. A greater sensation.

I wrap my arms around his head, tangling my fingers in his hair. His scent is seduction, rich from aftershave and etched in sweat and virility. His kisses are strong, and yet there's a slight glimmer of softness. The most delicate swipe of affection.

My heart hurts. I don't want it to, but it does. It clenches. It weeps.

"Fuck me," I demand into his mouth.

He growls and strides toward the other side of the room. My bed. He climbs onto the mattress, still holding me, still kissing me, then guides me to lie down as he kneels between my spread thighs.

The sight is profound. His eyes are wild. Carnal. His

broad chest heaves with energized breaths. Veins pulse from his carved arms.

I visualize his dick again, the generous size taunting my mind. I'm going to be disappointed. I just know it.

He shoves down his shorts, his underwear, and his thick cock is revealed. The length is above average, but the girth... My God.

I suck in a breath and my pussy clenches. Nope, not disappointed at all. I want to learn every inch of that hardness. I want it everywhere. Anywhere.

"You got protection?"

I nod and swallow to ease my drying mouth. "Top drawer."

He leans over me, pulls open my nightstand, and retrieves a loose condom. He's efficient. There's no hesitation. No reluctance. He rips open the packet, sheaths his length, and stares down at me. "Take off your clothes."

I ponder a protest. Playing hardball could be fun, but I'm too far gone for games. I tug the long-sleeve top over my head and wiggle my ass out of my tight sports pants to lie before him in my underwear.

"I said, take it off before I rip it off."

My stomach flips, and again, I contemplate dissent. This time it's for my protection. To keep a buffer between me and all the feels. I want him too much. Not only his lust, but the distraction. The connection. The reprieve from reality.

"Fine. Keep them on." His hands snake up my inner thighs, reaching my black lace panties. He grips the crotch, his fingers prodding, tugging, until the material tears. He stares down at me, his nostrils flaring, his teeth digging into his lower lip in a show of pure restrained aggression. "I hope you like it rough."

I shudder. "And what if I don't?"

His gaze glides to mine as a lone finger parts my slick folds. "Then I'll enjoy changing your mind."

That finger breeches my entrance, sliding inside me. It's a tease, the slightest penetration leaving me anticipating the considerable size of his dick. His free hand slides over my stomach, the callouses on his palms scratching, marking my skin.

He grasps the front of my bra, yanking the cups to the sides. I'm exposed to him, the dislodged material plumping my breasts, creating a mass of impressive cleavage.

"I'll have fun breaking you in."

I push to my elbows and clench my pussy around the lone digit. "You're too late to break anything."

His brows furrow, and I lean up to wrap my arm around his neck, pulling him down to me before he can question my response.

"Fuck me," I whisper in his ear and lick his neck. He's salty, the lingering sweat sinking into my tongue like an aphrodisiac.

He snarls and jerks his hips, the head of his cock finding my entrance. I feel his hand down there, positioning his length, then in one harsh thrust, he's deep inside me, stretching my muscles, blinding me with pleasure and the slightest twinge of torture. I moan, clinging to his neck as he shoves into me. Pulse after pulse. Slam after slam.

"*Fuck.*" His curse is ferocious, his movements merciless. He rests his forehead against mine, looking me in the eye. "Who are you?"

"Your fantasy," I tease with a kiss, digging my nails into his shoulders.

"No shit." He bites my lower lip, then sucks it into his mouth. "A fucking nightmare, too."

"I sure am." I chuckle.

He grins, exposing his dimple, and a softness in his eyes

I've never seen before. It's beautiful. Frighteningly so. For a second, I pause, taking in his complexity. The calm of his smile against his hard penetration.

"I thought you were going to be rough."

He bites my lip again, this time harder. "I thought it was better not to scare you."

"Or you turned into a pussy."

"Yeah?" He raises a brow and slams into me. "You really think so?" He snakes his hand behind my neck and grips my ponytail, tugging my head back. My breasts thrust toward him. My eyes roll.

Pleasure. So much pleasure.

His mouth trails a path from my cheek to my shoulder, then my chest. His kisses become stronger. Harder. I squeal as he sucks on my skin. *Shit*. He's leaving marks, tattooing me with his domination.

"Too much for you? 'Cause I haven't even started," he murmurs against the side of my breast, his hips still bucking, fucking the life out of me. Or maybe he's fucking life back into me.

I don't want that. I don't want change. I need this sterile existence. "No. Not enough." I need the harsh detachment to keep me sane.

I shove at his chest and buck my hips, encouraging him to roll. We tumble, switching positions, me on top, his muscled body beneath me.

"Better?" He raises a brow in question.

I nod. His cock sinks deeper, stretching me farther. "Mmmhmm."

He cups my breasts, his fingers digging into flesh. I ride him, my hands splayed on his hard chest. All my muscles are tense, taut from the build of bliss. Then my foot twinges. A cramp strikes. "*Shit*."

"What?" He scowls.

"I've got a cramp."

"Not my fucking problem." His words are rough, but his lips curve in a tease.

No, it isn't his problem, but he pushes to sit, his hand sliding over my thigh, my calf, my heel. He curls my toes in his fist and the pain increases. He doesn't stop fucking me; he continues the rhythmic pulse of his hips, the stimulation gradually fighting back as the cramp subsides.

"Better?" His eyes hold something that threatens to weaken me. Something that cracks my ribs apart in an attempt to touch my heart.

"Yeah." I glance away and bury my head in his shoulder.

His hands find my ass as he continues to sit, our chests plastered together, our sweat mingling. He guides my movements, making me grind against the dick nestled deep inside me. The friction teases my clit, the pleasure pulsing through me from my core, to my stomach, to my breasts.

"For a fucking temptress, your pussy is as tight as a virgin's."

I close my eyes and smile. "You're so sweet."

He chuckles, digging his fingers deeper into my ass. Tomorrow, I'll have a roadmap of marks on my body. A treasure trove of carnal memories.

He leans down, his mouth latching onto my nipple. He sucks. He grinds. He thrusts. Every movement catapults me toward an edge I'll happily dive over.

"Tell me your name. I want to shout it when I come."

I shake my head. I'm already close. I need to focus.

He growls, "Tell me." The rough texture of his tongue swipes my breast, trailing my areola.

"Oh, God, don't stop." I want more. I need more.

"Then tell me."

71

I pulse faster, my orgasm within reach. He groans, and the delicious sound acts as a trigger.

My pussy contracts, pulsing over and over. Wave after wave of ecstasy pummels me from the inside out. Drowning and re-energizing at the same time. I moan, longer, louder. "Yes. Yes. *Yes.*"

"Damn you," he growls, pistoning his hips.

I slowly blink through the shattering peak, my mind and body tangled in a delicious web of delirium and euphoria.

Each change in his expression becomes a memorable snapshot I vow to never forget. He shouts his release, his fingers creating scars—emotional and physical. That beautifully rugged face contorts. Sweat beads his skin. Wisps of hair cover his eyes as his forehead scrunches.

I watch, enraptured, as his pleasure takes hold, and I thrive on him succumbing. For once, he's not in control. He's weak. He's human.

My chest tightens in excitement, as if I've won a battle. But what could I have won other than a temporary distraction?

His shoulders slump, and his grip loosens. The emotionless face I've grown accustomed to returns along with his steady breathing. I stare at the stranger poised between my thighs, unable to look away from the lazy intensity staring at me.

"Who are you?" he murmurs, resting back on one hand.

I snap out of the lust haze and command myself to focus. "I've already told you."

"You haven't told me a damn thing."

"Then maybe it's none of your business."

His nostrils flare, and I'm equally annoyed and turned on by his anger. "Is it a crime to want to know your fucking name?"

Yes. He shouldn't need to know. I certainly have no interest in learning his.

"It's Emma." I scowl. "You already know that."

"Bullshit," he grates.

I pull back with the evaporation of ecstasy. So much for a distraction. The memory of how I got here floods back. The images of Dan assail me, creating revulsion.

I crawl off him, my body immediately missing his, and move to sit on the edge of the mattress. I lean over, massaging my forehead as my mind rambles unwanted thoughts.

How did I get here?

I was happy once. Loving. Optimistic. I didn't have a care in the world. Then Jacob changed everything, instigating a domino effect I had no control over. I functioned with continued detachment. I lived for one thing, and one thing only. And this is what I've become.

All the fulfilment I experienced moments ago washes out like a tide, and hollow disgust flows in with the force of a tsunami. I've just had sex. Mind-blowing, limb-shaking sex. Mere minutes after finding out I'm a murderer.

Who have I become?

"You should leave." My statement is strong, belying the already fractured parts of me which fragment into tinier slivers.

I stay silent, waiting for a protest that doesn't come.

The mattress jolts with his shifting weight, then he's gone, moving away from the bed, his padded footsteps retreating. His clothes rustle. His shoes thud against the floor.

"Emma... Stephanie... Whatever the hell your name is, I want to see you again." Each word is growled harsher than the last. "Tonight. At the bar."

I grab my pillow and drag it to my chest. I won't

succumb again. I need to pull my shit together, not spread it out for the world to see. I have to figure out what to do now that I'm one of those people I usually fight to punish. And now, more than ever, I have to gain retribution for what has been done to my family before I become the focus of someone else's vengeance. Or worse—trapped behind bars.

"Do you hear me?" he asks.

I nod. "Yeah. I hear you."

But hearing him doesn't mean I'm listening.

8

HER

I don't meet him that night. Or the next. Or the one after that.

Too many nights pass with me sitting by the window watching him enter Atomic Buzz. But he's always there, always looking up at my window before he walks inside, and always glancing toward my position in the shadows when he leaves hours later.

I've tried to focus. I've pulled out all the memories I have on Jacob from the box hidden beneath the floorboards under my bed. I've scattered the newspaper clippings, the grainy photos, the family tree, and covered my living room floor, my coffee table, and the sofa.

Those papers have lain untouched for days.

I've attempted to find dirt on the name Dan mentioned —Vaughn. Zeke or Zander or Zack. Nothing comes up. Jacob York had successfully disappeared, and this new Vaughn alias is a ghost. Or maybe the lead was a lie.

Either way, it cost Dan his life and has now trapped me in a tighter cage of paranoia. I haven't left my apartment in days. I'm constantly alert, always on the lookout for anyone suspicious approaching my building. I reach for my gun whenever my phone vibrates with a notification that my door surveillance camera has been triggered. And sleep... Well, let's just say sleep and I aren't friends anymore.

I need to get a grip, but there's no grounding here. Each day that inches closer to Dan's funeral compacts the emotional instability clogging my veins. I've followed the investigation. Doctors say he suffered a dissected carotid artery from a blunt force trauma that led to a blood clot being carried to the brain.

The blunt force trauma was from me.

His death was a result of the injuries I'd inflicted.

He literally died at my hands, and as I look down at my palms, I can see the damage I've caused. My fingers seem savage. Less feminine, and now tarnished with brutality.

His funeral will be held the day after tomorrow, and I can't stomach the mental images my overly creative mind conjures. All those people who will mourn a depraved man. All the tears. All that misplaced heartache.

He should've lived to endure his punishment.

I drag my gaze back outside and stare at Brent's bar. Thoughts of the mystery man are the only thing capable of temporarily wiping away the anger. Even when he's not there, I can see him walking through those doors, glancing up at me.

I need to get a grip. *No.* I have to escape and clear my head. Even if just for a day.

I shove from the window ledge, grab my coat, and leave my apartment for the first time in days. I linger in the lobby, stalking the sidewalk like a deranged mental patient as I scan the roads and sidewalk for police. A suspect hasn't been announced yet, but that doesn't mean they don't have one.

I could be on any number of radars—authorities and Dan's family.

I slip outside, the weight of a million stares on my shoulders even though fewer than ten people are in sight. I hustle across the road, my jacket collar high and my head low as I enter Atomic Buzz.

Inside, I'm relieved there's only two of the regulars drinking away their sorrows. I approach the bar and slide onto a seat. "Hey, Brent."

He pauses in the middle of stacking racks of glasses on the far counter and turns my way. "You're back twice in one month. What did I do to earn the honor?"

"I actually came to ask a favor."

He places the rack down and dusts his hands. "What's up?"

A lump forms in my throat. I hadn't realized asking for help would be difficult. Favors build connections, and I seem to be making too many of them lately.

"I know it's late notice, but can I borrow your car tomorrow?"

"You heading back to Seattle to see your family?"

The lump grows, increasing the need to swallow.

He remembers. Of course he does. He listens to every word I say. He cares about me, even when he shouldn't.

"Yeah. Just a quick day trip. I'll have your car back before you close tomorrow night. I'll make sure to fill it with gas and give you cash for the cab rides you'll need while I'm gone."

"Don't worry about the money. You know you can borrow anything you want, whenever you like."

I nod and lower my gaze in an attempt to ditch his lingering stare.

"You look tired," he adds. "Is everything okay?"

"Yep," I answer without thought. "I just didn't want to

rent a car at late notice. By the time I get to the lot and find—"

"I'm not talking about the car."

I assumed as much.

I paste on a confident smile and lift my gaze. "Everything is super-dooper perfect. I couldn't be better."

Go hard or go home, right?

His eyes narrow, not buying my bullshit, and I hold the expression like a motherfucker, unwilling to lose this battle. I can't handle his concern on top of everything else. I simply can't.

Eventually, he nods. "Have you seen that man of yours is hanging around a lot? I think I've doubled my income this week because of him alone."

I scowl. Maybe I should've held more interest in learning mystery man's name because calling him 'my man' isn't a trend I'm down with. "He's not mine."

Brent shrugs and grabs a liquor bottle from under the bar. He pours a nip, then grabs another bottle and another, finally filling it with soda before he slides the concoction toward me. "It sure looked that way when he left your building last week."

Last week? Geez, I've been hermitting my life away for longer than I thought. "I kicked him out the night we left here together."

"I know." He gives a conniving smile. "He told me."

"He did?" I shuffle forward, not realizing my mistake of showing my piqued interest until it's too late. And now I can't be bothered hiding my intrigue. "What did he say?"

That smile turns to a grin. "He told me he likes you. That you were different. But he also said he wouldn't apologize for carrying a gun because he was here to protect his family."

"He told you about the gun?" *Christ*. The guy acts as if every word he utters is a secret, yet he happily blurts the details to Brent. Maybe the whole recluse act is just that— an act to hold my interest. "I don't believe it."

"What part don't you believe?" he asks.

I don't want to believe any of it. I don't need to think about him liking me when he's already become my only comforting thought through this hellish week. I don't want my opinion of his gun to change, either. I've made a lot of my judgements about him based on his sinister intent with a deadly weapon. I've branded him dangerous because of that firearm.

If he only carried to protect his sister...

If he truly is a non-violent man...

"*Fuck*," I mutter under my breath.

"What now?"

"Nothing." I grasp the drink and sip. Tomorrow can't come soon enough.

"He seems like a genuine guy."

Genuine? In what? To me, the guy seems genuinely bad news. Genuinely toxic to my concentration. Genuinely a huge fucking mistake with his overly inquisitive nature.

I transition from a sip to a gulp, chugging the alcohol until it's all gone. "This isn't a conversation we're going to have." I push my glass toward him and slide off the chair. "Is it still okay to borrow your car?"

Brent chuckles and retrieves a set of keys from a hook on the back wall. "Sure." He lobs the prize at me. "Drive safe."

I catch the offering, along with a relaxing sense of relief at the enabling escapism. "Thanks."

I pull out the cash I've stashed in my jeans and place it on the bar. "For the cab rides and the drink."

"You know I don't want your money."

"And you know I don't want to hear your protests." I kinda love this guy. He's my only friend, no matter how disillusioned he is by the lies I've told. "I'll return the keys as soon as I get back."

"Don't rush. I can deal without a car if you need it longer."

"You're too damn good to me." I wink at him and make for the door, energized to get out of this city for a while. I'll leave before daybreak, clear my head with the three-hour drive, lick old wounds while I visit my family, then return home with a plan for the future.

I push open the door to the street, and the heavy glass falls away under the hand pulling from the other side.

"Hey." The deep, familiar voice slays me. Grips me. Punishes me.

I ignore the temptation to fall into lust and continue onto the sidewalk, only chancing a brief glance at my mystery man.

A brief glance is all it takes for his image to sear my retinas—worn, ripped jeans, a black jacket with the cuffs hitched a few inches up his tanned forearms, and a white T-shirt beneath that hugs his chest. "You're drinking earlier than usual tonight."

He releases the door, remaining outside as I pivot my attention toward the curb and watch for traffic. The light crunch of his steps follows me. Intuition tells me he's a foot away. I can feel him. Sense him. His interest raises the hair on the back of my neck and makes me shudder.

"You been watching me, princess?"

Fuck. *Fuck.*

"It's okay," he murmurs. "I don't mind the attention."

I roll my eyes and turn to face him. "I've gotta go."

In a blink, the subtle humor glistening in those hazel

irises is gone, and a delicious scowl takes its place. "You're not going to join me for a drink?"

"Not tonight." Not any night. Not when my stomach turns in knots whenever he's close. I step onto the road, wait for a passing car, then jog to my side of the street. I'm yanking at my own ripcord, trying to fast-track my departure, but my heart is thumping in excitement, ignoring the inevitable crash and burn that will happen if I don't get out of here.

"Then when?" The question comes from right behind me. "What's got you in such a hurry to leave...again?"

Shit.

"I've got a big day tomorrow. I need to get up early." I reach my building and enter the pin code into the keypad. The panel beeps, the lock clicks in release, and I pull the door wide, only to have his fierce hand push it shut.

I stiffen, all my muscles frozen and humming as I drown under his intense stare.

"What are you doing tomorrow?" he asks.

I sigh and fight the good fight, trying not to lick my lower lip to give him the encouragement we both crave. "I'm heading out of town."

"Oh, yeah?" He raises a brow. "Where are you headed?"

Far away from his questions, his interest, and his temptation. I can't keep encouraging the distraction. As much as I want to deny it, I thoroughly enjoy his attention. I'm suffocating in my need to breathe him deep, and not just into my lungs—into my life.

I shouldn't have to remind myself it's imperative to lay low and focus. The police are looking for me, whether they know it or not. And I have to find Jacob before karma deals me a heavy punishment.

But this man sees more than he should. Those hands

touch more than I want to allow. And whatever is going on in that mind of his is sure to create havoc.

No more.

I hitch my chin high. "I'm visiting my boyfriend."

How do you like them apples?

The tight clench of his jaw is a blatant sign he doesn't like my apples at all.

"Is that right?" he snarls.

"Yep."

His nostrils flare, and he licks his lower lip in such a delightfully slow roll of predatory intent that I have to squeeze my thighs together to stem the growing throb.

"And this boyfriend of yours, does he mind that you're fucking me?"

Chills. So many chills.

"Fucked," I clarify. "We did it once, and it was a mistake."

He steps closer, looming over me. "That's not the vibe I'm getting."

I squeak internally. On the outside, I stare like a mother-fucker. "Really?" I inch into him, straightening my shoulders, raising my chin. "You're looming over me, glaring. To me, the only vibe here is threatening."

He flashes a smirk. "And I bet you're wet as hell because of it."

Touché, asshole.

I turn my back and re-enter the pin code into the keypad. "I'm sorry, but I'm not interested."

The panel beeps, the lock releases, but he's pressed into me before I can reach for the door, his thighs nestled behind mine, his chest against my back.

"Say it to my face," he demands.

My heart races, the rapid beat out of control. I swallow,

knowing a believable declaration will be difficult to achieve. Hard, because this prick has my ovaries in his tight-fisted grip, but not impossible.

I turn, my brows raised in superiority. "I. Don't. Want. You."

I plaster myself to the wall, hoping for distance. He's hot. Scorching. Every inch of his body pressed into mine is an inch of heavenly connection.

He leans closer, his breath warming my lips. "Bullshit."

I want to succumb, to surrender to his erotic distraction but...

He strips the decision away from me, charging forward, taking my mouth with his. He steals my breath, his tongue swiping my lips to demand immediate entrance.

Goddamnit.

I can't deny him. I can't deny myself. I'm going down with this ship. Going down faster and harder than a cheerleader on prom night.

I grip his jacket, kissing him as if my life depends on the enthusiasm I place into our contact.

He growls, the rumble of his chest vibrating through me. He pushes me harder into the wall and grips my hips, his fingers digging into my jeans. His erection grinds against my pubic bone, making me want to beg.

No matter how risky or careless or insane, I want this man. I need him, if only to uplift me for those few short moments before I come crashing back down.

He retreats, retracting his devilish affection in a slap of withdrawal. His heavy breathing brushes my lips, my chin, my cheeks. Those fingers continue to dig into me. The light from inside highlights the flecks of color in his eyes, the greens, the browns as he stares at me with such sweet bewilderment that I know he thinks this is crazy, too.

I've kicked him out of my apartment and thrown his gun out a window. I've vomited in front of him, then launched into attack mode, before falling into bed in a mass of our tangled limbs.

This doesn't make sense. It's not what attraction is supposed to be. But attraction is what it is.

"Lie to me again," he murmurs. "Tell me you don't want me."

My heart climbs into my throat, restricting, suffocating.

"Yeah, I didn't think you could," he taunts, releasing my hips. His fingers find the waistband of my jeans, unclasping the button, lowering the zipper. A hand delves into my pants, beneath my panties, sliding straight to my pussy.

I gasp, not in shock, in undiluted pleasure. Everything tingles. Vibrates.

"For someone who doesn't want me, you sure are wet."

His fingers plunge inside me, two or three, I'm not sure. I'm too focused on grasping his shoulders to stop myself from crumpling to the floor. He twists, pulses, strokes. He pulls no stops in his masterful manipulation as he peers down at me, stalking my expression.

I want to succumb, not just physically, but emotionally, too. I want to admit how I feel. To tell him the tiny morsels of time in his presence are like a feast to my starving soul.

I sink my teeth into my lower lip, caging those words inside.

"You fucking want me," he snarls. "I bet you want me more than any other guy."

I close my eyes and grip him tight. Those talented fingers don't stop moving. The heat of his stare doesn't fade.

I'm falling, yet soaring. I'm hurting, yet drowning in the most exquisite pleasure. There's no life. No past. No future.

There's only now. Only ecstasy. Only sexual possibility. We should take this upstairs. We could. If only my secrets weren't scattered over the floor in a mass of devastation.

The door swings open in a swoosh of noise and displaced air. I snap my eyes open and freeze when I see a woman standing there, gaping.

Mystery man shoves his shoulder into the wall, plastering his body to mine. He covers me, hiding what he's doing without stopping the pulse of his fingers for even a second.

"Get out of here," he snarls at her.

Protective. Oh, so protective.

I could swoon. Instead, my body trembles. I know nothing about this man, and yet he slays me. "Tell me your name."

His fingers plunge deeper as he holds my gaze. "Why? You've never shown any interest before."

I pant, my breathing fractured. "Well, I'm interested now." I need something to call him. Something other than '*my* mystery man.' I have to dissociate him from being mine at all.

He releases a barely audible chuckle. "If I tell you my name, will you promise to scream it when I make you come?"

I shake my head. "No." No way in hell. I'm out in the open, probably in view of Brent and those drunks who would be getting the show of their life. Not to mention the current state of my soaked panties is already a big enough compliment to satisfy even the largest ego. "I won't."

His fingers stop moving in a harsh threat. "Then whisper it for only me to hear."

Oh, God. My restraint snaps, and I moan in agreement. There's no will to deny him. Not when it's a mere whisper of surrender.

"Promise." His thumb flicks over my clit, igniting a pulse of wildfire.

"I will," I blurt. "I promise."

"Good." He leans closer, the rough stubble of his cheek brushing mine. His lips gently slide over my ear. "You can call me Hunter."

I whimper.

Hunter.

What a fucking seductive name. So much better than Jim or Jeff or Bill.

He twists those fingers, deeper, faster, the pad of his thumb pressing harder on my clit.

"Hunter," I whisper in warning. I'm close, nudging the precipice.

He inches back and gazes down at me, his eyes intent, his lips tight. God, I want to fuck him. I want to pull him close and kiss and kiss and kiss until I feel my soul return.

"What, princess?"

"Hunter." I can't say anything else. I can't think anything else. "Oh, God, *Hunter.*"

I close my eyes and rest my head against the wall as my pussy clamps tight. My core contracts over and over, the height of bliss hitting me as he leans his body into mine to keep me upright.

He doesn't stop fingering me. Those digits pulse. His thumb continues to work my clit.

I cling to him, my mouth finding his neck, my teeth digging into his flesh. I taste. I feel. I become invigorated. All because of this man.

The realization lessens the bliss, guiding me down from my peak in a gentle descent. I whimper as he holds me in one arm, his other hand still filling me.

"You done?" he murmurs.

My voice is lost to pleasure, my throat too tight to speak.

I nod and meet his taut expression, noticing the wild, restrained lust in those harsh eyes.

"Good." He pulls away and steps back. His jaw ticks as he adjusts his cock, the thick outline of his erection bulging at his zipper. Then, without a goodbye, he turns and walks away muttering, "Tell your boyfriend I said hi."

9

HIM

I STRIDE ACROSS THE STREET, HOLDING BACK THE NEED to shove my fist against something that will break bone. She's playing me, I know that, but I still listen to her lies like a man starved of sound.

Problem is, I can't tell what's the truth and what's bull-shit. Decker couldn't get a trail on her. Her apartment is owned by Brent Hendrix—the fucking bartender. Even the utilities are in his name. There are no ties to a Stephanie or Emma Stephens. She has to be paying him in cash to make sure she doesn't leave breadcrumbs.

But I'll find one.

Tomorrow.

I would bet my left nut she's not going to Seattle to meet a guy. I refuse to believe she's fucking me with a boyfriend a few hours away. But even with my nut on the line, the slightest doubt has furious jealousy streaming through my veins.

I want to kill this lover of hers. Real or imaginary.

The feel of her body against mine has become torture. The vanilla scent of her, too. All sweet and feminine. She's pliable to my touch, molding into me like butter, yet tough as nails at the same time.

So many conflicting aspects. A fucking kaleidoscope. Or maybe that's what she wants me to see. Smoke and mirrors.

I storm inside Atomic Buzz, slap my palms on the bar, and demand, "Scotch."

Brent glowers at me and prepares the drink. "Bad day?"

"You could say that." Every day has been a mix of heaven and hell since this woman walked into my life. I can't stop thinking about her—who she is, what she does, and why we've been brought together.

"Have you ever heard her talk about a boyfriend?" The question escapes my mouth without thought, making me sound like a needy little bitch.

"Steph?" Brent frowns.

"Yeah." I guess we'll stick with that for now because I don't believe her real name is Emma, either.

"No. Not at all. She doesn't share that shit with me."

So, having another dick on the side is a possibility. Great. Fucking perfect.

He hands over my scotch.

I throw down some bills before snatching the alcohol from the bar to go sit in the far corner of the room. Yeah, I'm sulking. For fuck's sake.

I need to leave, but I'm stuck here maintaining the charade that I showed up to get a drink, when I was actually stalking a woman who just left her apartment for the first time in days.

Impeccable timing is my only advantage, which Decker gained by hacking the video surveillance outside her apartment door. It seemed to be the only hole in her secretive existence—she logs into her online feed via her neighbor's unsecured internet.

So I have nothing on her—no name, no insight, no

fucking clue—but I get notifications when there's motion around her door and a crystal-clear, black-and-white view of when she comes and goes.

Like right now. My cell vibrates in my jacket, and I already know it will be her. I tap into the video app to see her standing in the hall of her building. She enters the pin code to her apartment and releases the locks. I clench cell as she opens the door, then she walks inside, out of sight, but still visible enough in my mind to make my dick pulse.

I should be doing a million other things. I should be on the other side of the city, preparing for an impromptu trip to Seattle.

Fuck.

I'm over a week late getting back to Torian. I've dodged his calls for days, which means I'm a heartbeat away from a gun-barrel prostate exam if I don't pull my shit together.

I gulp the cheap scotch and flick through my cell screen to call Decker. It's time to level-up our game.

He answers on the second ring with a chipper, "How can I be of assistance, fuck face?"

"Listen up." I'm not in the mood for his shit. Not that I ever have been. "I need you to be on the road tomorrow."

"Okay... Where's the party?"

I scan the bar, making sure nobody is paying me attention, and lower my voice. "Seattle."

"Who are we dealing with?"

Her. The woman who drives me mindless with curiosity and hunger. "We're still on the same project. Nothing has ch—"

"Are you serious?" He chuckles. "Torian is right. You're slipping."

Every muscle snaps taut. "When did you speak to Torian?"

"He called a few days ago wanting an update because you won't answer your cell."

Fucking hell. "What did you say?"

"What could I say? You haven't told me shit."

If Torian took the time to call, he would've pushed, demanded, threatened. He wasn't the type to walk away empty-handed.

"What did you tell him?" I repeat, my tone lethal.

"I said you were following some lead on a woman. That she's tied to Dan somehow… Which is only an assumption at this point, because it marks the time you dove headfirst into this weirdness."

I suck in a breath and hold it until it threatens to break my restraint. "Did you give him any specifics? Did you say anything that could lead to her?"

He gives a derisive scoff. "How is he going to find out who she is when I can't?"

Jesus. It's not about finding out who she is. Torian won't give a shit. If he knows about her, he'll do what I should've done days ago—get the information she has via whatever means necessary.

"Look," Decker starts, "I thought I was covering your ass. What was I supposed to do? Fabricate a story when I have no clue what's going on? We both know he'd lose his shit if he found out I was lying. And as much as I love you, buddy, it's not enough to take the fall when it comes to that crazy motherfucker."

No shit. Why does he think I didn't answer my phone? I don't need the drama.

I down the remaining scotch and breathe slowly to lessen the aggression pounding at my temples.

"What's going on, Hunt? Who is this chick?"

"I don't have a clue." It's the truth. "I know she was in

that hotel room. She beat the fuck out of him, and I'm pretty sure she gained our information while doing it."

There's a pause. A silent criticism. "Why the hell didn't you tell me?"

Good question. The jury is out on that one. "Why did I need to? Would you have worked harder? Have you half-assed the background check because I didn't give you enough info?"

I'm a weak prick, trying to distract him from the more important questions, like, why didn't I get what I needed that first night? Why didn't this end back then? And why did I let it continue?

"I've done everything I can," he grates. "I don't half-ass anything, asshole, and you know it."

I do. But I don't regret the diversion. "Then you don't need specifics. You need to work with what I give you and remember who pays you. *Me.* Not Torian."

"Please tell me you're not sleeping with her." His plea is almost inaudible and followed with more criticizing silence. "Fuck, Hunt. You are, aren't you?"

I rest my glass on the table and massage my temples between my thumb and middle finger. I can't answer him. *No.* I don't need to.

"Are you still there, asshole?" he snaps. "What the fuck is going on?"

I don't know. I'm so lost in her I can't tell when common sense ended and obsession began. It wasn't supposed to go down like this. It started as a bit of fun. I was messing with the cocky bombshell with the sassy mouth. Then she flipped the fucking board on me and started to beat me at my own game. She had me chasing my tail and second-guessing myself.

I *never* second-guess myself.

"You need to sort this out," he says. "And fast. Torian isn't going to wait forever."

"I know." I fucking know. "I'm going to call him." I have no other choice. "I'll get in touch later with specifics for tomorrow."

"Yeah. I'll be waiting."

I shove from my chair and walk from the bar, not acknowledging Brent, who tracks my steps with his gaze. As I get outside, I glance up at her window, unable to break the habit.

She's there. I can feel her staring down at me, watching my movements with the same dedication I've shown watching hers.

I reach the end of the building, turn down the side street to my car, and start dialing Torian's number.

The call connects, and he greets with a, "About damn time you called." His tone is level, calm, but the man could turn on a dime.

"You got time to talk?" I ask.

"I'm at Devoured."

The call disconnects. One minute, conversation. The next, silence. It's not a bad connection. It's a demand to meet in person.

Fucking great.

I climb into my car and drive across town to his father's restaurant. I slow as I pass the front windows and see Torian inside, standing amongst a crowd of his family while he holds a young girl on one arm. His niece. His sisters are there, too, while a million other kids run around with balloons and streamers.

A private family function.

Fucking perfect.

I park my car and stalk inside, ignoring Carlos at the

door, who quickly glances at Torian for approval to let me in.

The man of the moment inclines his head and grins at me as I approach. The slimy fucker is dressed in his typical designer suit, his brown hair immaculately styled, his face clean-shaven. The guy is young. Too fucking young to have the amount of power he carries under his belt. But he owns it, taking the authority in his stride.

I bypass his attractive younger sister, along with the small army of children who have made his father's restaurant their bitch, and stop in front of Torian and the girl.

"Hunt." His smile remains in place, charismatic yet undeniably fake. I can see the anger hidden beneath the calm facade. I can sense the frustration, too. "I expected to see you sooner. You don't usually make me wait."

I ignore the little girl staring up at me and return his grin. His intimidation techniques don't work on me. They never have. Threats are only successful if you have something to lose, and Torian is well aware I've deliberately cut ties with anyone of value. "I told you I'd get in contact once the job was done."

"Why does it sound like you're about to tell me something I don't want to hear? Do you have what I need or not?"

"I'm still working on it."

His smile increases. Ignorant women would fall to their knees for that playboy charm, but I know the meaning of his expression. I know, and I refuse to give a shit. He leans down, placing his niece on her feet. "Go play with your friends, Stella."

"Okay, Unkie Cole." The girl skips away, her skirt swishing with every bounce.

He watches her, always smiling, always smug. "How are you still working on it when Dan is dead?"

"There was someone with him. A woman. I think she could be a lead to—"

"I didn't ask for a fucking lead. I asked for a name. *One* name. It wasn't a hard task."

I clench my teeth and look away in an attempt to control my temper. I'm not a failure. I won't accept being treated as one. "She beat him." I lower my voice. "Aren't you interested to find out why?"

"I'm only interested in the name. Why would I care about the whore who was with him before he died?"

"She's no whore."

"That's not what the detective tells me."

My pulse spikes, but I can understand where he's coming from. I'd assumed the same thing to begin with. "With a body like hers, she'd be stupid to work in a neighborhood well beneath her physical appeal. There has to be more to it than that."

She doesn't need to slum it for money. One look inside her apartment and I could tell she had cash. If she wanted to sell her body, she could easily do it with deep-pocketed men.

"Why are you wasting my time with assumptions, Hunt? Admit you've failed, and we can deal with the consequences."

"It's not an assumption, and I haven't fucking failed. She tortured him. And she's on the road tomorrow to meet someone in Seattle. I think she has contacts there." I drag my gaze back to meet his unfaltering stare. "If she was trying to keep him quiet, don't you want to know why? Don't you want to know if there are more players in this?"

Torian's eyes narrow. His lips flatten. He stares at me for long moments, scrutinizing, obviously strategizing. "Why do you care?"

"Money." That is the only acceptable answer. For me

and him. "I'll get you more valuable information, and you can pay me for the extra work."

He laughs, long and hearty, as if I'm a fucking comedian. "Now that makes more sense. You've always been a money-hungry bastard." He inches forward to place his hand on my shoulder and guide me toward the front door. "And I appreciate you thinking outside the box. But do I need to reiterate how tired I am of waiting for a resolution on this?"

"It won't be much longer." I have no foundation for my promise. I'll just have to make it work. I'll have to move faster.

"Maybe you need help."

"No." I plant my feet and glare. "You gave this job to me, and I work alone."

"Really?" He taunts me with a smirk. "Does Decker know that?"

Decker is different. He helps from the outside. I never rely on him; I only ever lean. "Speaking of," I growl, "he's off-limits. You call him again, and we'll have a problem."

He laughs, but this time the facade cracks. The sound is sinister. Angered. "I wanted answers, and you wouldn't return my calls."

"Well, you have your answers now, so back off."

He squeezes my shoulder, the touch another threat. "I have nothing but your assurances, which mean little to me. In fact, I think I need to insist on someone else assisting you. I'll send Carlos to tag along."

I snap my gaze to those kids laughing and playing. I stare. I glare. I make sure they're at the front of my mind so I don't lose my shit. "You put a tail on me, and whoever it is will wind up face down in a dumpster."

A threat for a threat.

Torian chuckles and releases his hold, raising his hands

in an act of surrender no sane person would believe. "Okay. Okay. I get it. You're invested in seeing this through. I can appreciate that."

"Thanks," I snarl.

We have worked together for years. We have been through more than most family members endure. But I have no doubt this man would cut ties in the blink of an eye. He also knows I'll do the same if pushed.

"I'll call you when I'm done." I stride ahead, a cautious throb tickling the back of my neck. I need to be finished with this job. I need to be done with it. With her.

"Hunt," Torian calls over the sound of celebrating children.

I stall, the cautious throb now taking over my limbs as I turn. "Yeah?"

"You've got forty-eight hours."

10

HER

I take Brent's car and head out of Portland before day breaks.

It's an easy drive tainted by the itch of paranoia. I stalk my rear-view mirror and pull over numerous times to make sure I'm not surrounded by the same cars. I also drive below the speed limit in an attempt to stay off the radar of any highway patrols.

Once I reach the outskirts of Seattle, I start to relax, and autopilot kicks in. I don't think about where I'm going until I'm in a familiar neighborhood, passing memories with each block.

Nostalgia tickles my senses as I slow through my old stomping ground. My elementary school looks the same, the brick building barely having aged over time. There's the track field I ran on. The mall I used to hang out at with my friends. My kindergarten teacher's house.

They all seem the same, and for a moment I feel the same, too.

The past engulfs me, returning me to another life where I was a different person. Back to the days when my only concerns were good grades and which party I would go to on the weekend.

I continue through traffic lights and streets, not stopping until I'm staring up at the thick metal gates which block my view from the prestigious property my family used to own.

It isn't the same vertical wrought-iron design my father installed. They've been replaced with horizontal ivory slats that attempt to cut me off from my childhood, but I still remember.

I can't forget how my sister told me to climb the property wall if I ever wanted to sneak out at night. I remember the smell of wisteria that lingered in the breeze every spring. I remember how my brother would run down the hall early each morning, waking me up with his enthusiasm to start the day.

I remember it all as if it were yesterday, even when it sometimes feels like a conjured fantasy. I want to get out and touch those walls that once encased a wealth of happiness, to peek into a yard which created laughter. But I can't.

I need to be careful. I won't risk being seen by people from my past. Not when they could drag my focus away from my goals with greater efficiency than Hunter already has.

I've started craving comfort again. Even the slightest human interaction. After a few brief encounters with a man I barely know, I've become foolishly charmed by the possibility of more.

Disconnecting from extended family has always been my hardest task. I've broken ties with anyone who previously took care of me. The aunts and uncles. The cousins and friends.

Leaving them behind was necessary for focus. I couldn't second-guess my end-game or the steps it would take to get there. I've become strong and determined with the sterility. I have no distractions.

The only things that matter are my parents and siblings, and the building fire they created inside me. They stoked the flames of retribution. That is why I am here. I need them to remind me of the promise I made ten years ago.

Them and only them.

I start the engine and continue along the road, passing the place where I fell off my bike and broke my arm, and the corner where I had my first kiss. After a quick detour for cheap takeout, I drive to the next suburb, toward the people I cherish most and love even more.

As I approach, remorse mixes with the digesting hamburger and fries now seated in my stomach. I've neglected my family for too long, and there's no excuse.

I approach another set of gates, these not quite as ostentatious as the last. They don't fit my mother's demand for flamboyance, or my father's appreciation for security. But the rich grass is immaculate, and I know Mom would love the scent of approaching rain in the air.

I pull over and climb out to face the devastating reunion. I keep my head low and try to ignore the uncomfortable scratching sensation at the back of my neck as I pass the first row of graves, then another, and another. I stop when I reach the seventh, and that hamburger threatens to make a comeback at the sight of the four identically shaped headstones standing before me, each with different text.

Stanley Carmichael. Emma Carmichael. Stephanie Carmichael. Thomas Carmichael.

I raise my chin, paste on a smile, and pretend I've got this.

"Hey, Mom. Dad." I scan the cemetery to make sure I don't have an audience to my one-sided conversation. Apart from a gray-haired woman yards and yards away, I'm alone. Like usual. I should be used to that by now.

"Sis. Baby Tom." My younger brother hated that nickname. He didn't like being seen as little or small. I'd only taunt him because it gave us the opportunity to tussle.

God, I miss tussling with him.

I kneel before them, my heart so heavy each beat feels certain to be my last. This is where I belong. Well, not exactly here. A few feet to the left, in the reserved space beside my brother. "I fucked up."

I swallow as a whisper of a chastisement brushes my mind. I hear their words, their voices, or maybe it's the approach of psychosis. I guess I'll find out sooner or later.

"I messed up bigtime." I stretch out along the grass and turn onto my back. I lie between them, my mom to my left, my dad to my right, as I blink up at the heavy clouds and let the chill of the ground seep through my coat. "I killed someone in my search to find Jacob."

Silence presses down on me, blanketing me in loneliness. It becomes hard to think. To breathe. To live. "I took his life, and now I know it's a race against time before karma catches up with me."

More whispered words fill my mind. Words of comfort and support. I have to believe it's them. I need to convince myself they're here, listening.

"The funeral is tomorrow." Dan will be laid to rest. His family will crumple, his friends will sob, and I have to accept the guilt.

My heart freezes beneath tightening ribs. I glance over my shoulder to my family, who have been reduced to stones amongst lush grass, and swallow through overwhelming dread. "I've become Jacob. I've done exactly what he did. And I don't know how to forgive myself."

Silence.

There are no comforting messages this time. I can't hear them. I can't feel them.

The bitter cold of loneliness digs deeper, and I curl into the fetal position, letting the frigidity take over. My stomach tumbles. Roll after roll of building self-loathing.

This is what I need to focus. I can't forget what I'm fighting for, what my goal is.

I close my eyes and focus on the image of Jacob in my mind. Young, blond, athletic.

I'd give anything to make him suffer. To restrain him the same way he did my family, and set his house on fire. I'd watch those flames melt his skin, and I wouldn't feel an ounce of remorse. I'd hear his screams, and I would smile. And he would scream. I know he would, just like I know my family did as they burned to death.

Bile launches up my throat.

I can't go back there. Not that far. It's too hard to leave.

I squeeze my lids tight and focus on relaxing. I have to calm myself. Think positive thoughts. I picture each muscle, one at a time, willing them to loosen. Toes. Calves. Thighs.

This is why I rarely return to Seattle. It took all my energy to commit to the future and not dwell in the torment of my past. Years dragged before I could break the habit of spending days in bed, cuddling my pillow as I sobbed with the need to wake up from this nightmare.

Relax. Hips. Stomach. Chest.

But I'd been so naive with Jacob. Entirely innocent. We'd been together for months. The perfect power couple—the jock and the loved socialite. I'd selfishly enjoyed the additional attention, not only from a dedicated boyfriend, but from my classmates who all decided they wanted to be me.

They didn't notice the changes in him like I did. They

didn't see how his devotion turned into obsession. They didn't acknowledge his growing aggression.

Then again, even I found it hard to come to terms with him being capable of his horrific end game. And the actions of his wealthy parents who helped him escape police custody. I'm one-hundred percent certain his entire extended family assisted in the efforts to hide him from his punishment for all these years. That's why I won't feel shame or guilt at wanting him dead. He deserves it, and his family deserves to mourn the loss.

Fuck, woman, concentrate. Arms. Face. Mind.

My head becomes heavy, tempting me with sleep. Or maybe dragging me into approaching nightmares.

I never would've thought one simple, careless deception could cause such devastation. That a few simple words could be the difference between life and death.

I can't go to the party with you, Jacob. I have plans with my family.

I can taste the lie in my mouth, can feel it curl and twist around my tongue. I want to break up with him. I just don't know how. So, instead of going to that party, I walk to my best friend's house in the hope we can figure it out together.

I ignore his ten phone calls. I pretend he doesn't exist. But he ensures I'll never forget him.

The sound of wailing sirens follows me on the stroll home. Smoke billows in the distance. By the time I reach the bottom of my street I'm running, sprinting toward the bent and battered gates at the front of my property.

I search the yard, looking past fire engines and firemen in an attempt to find my parents and siblings. It's Friday night. My father always leaves work early. Stephanie is grounded for sneaking out to see her boyfriend. And my mom and Thomas are inseparable.

They're all home. But there's nothing to worry about

because we have smoke alarms. Dad pays the alarm company to check them every spring. They would've gotten out. I'll find them around here somewhere. Maybe even in the back yard.

They've already located four bodies restrained in one of the downstairs rooms.

My heart lurches at the murmured words. I don't even know who they come from. The statement is just there, ringing in my ears, tearing at my soul.

No. I run for the front door, heat licking my skin, only to be dragged back. I scream. I sob. I crumple.

Don't be in there. Please, God, don't let them be in there.

I'm hauled onto the grass where some nameless, faceless woman yaps at me until I'm catatonic. *It will be okay. You're not alone. Do you want me to call a friend? A relative? Are you cold? Hungry?*

I remain still. Frozen in stone. I can already feel it—the isolating detachment, the brutal desolation.

I watch, in a daze as men rush around me, attempting to put out a blaze that burns my world to the ground. The fire crackles. Windows shatter. The sight before me doesn't make sense, not even the sense of overwhelming loss.

It's going to be okay, princess.

The familiar tone eats up my sorrow, and I snap my gaze to the left to find Hunter seated beside me. He's dressed in fireman's clothes. His face is smudged with soot. His skin is beaded with sweat.

Relief overwhelms me. There's no rhyme or reason. Not when hell has erupted around me.

What are you doing here?

I frown as he gives me that look of his. The one built of power, intent, and determination. I feel strengthened from the sight of him, from his mere presence. All I want to do is sit on his lap and curl into his arms like a child. To be protected and cared for. But I'll never be foolish enough to act on my desires. I'm already weak enough. The only way to grow strong is to detach myself from anything of value.

No car, no house, and definitely no loved ones.

Hunter, why are you here?

I repeat myself, over and over, as he sits there in silence. There's no more burning building. No dying family. The flames dwindle. The devastation evaporates. Everything fades. There's only him. Only me. Only faith and building assurance.

He leans close, his knee brushing mine. He reaches out a hand, his fingertips skimming my cheek. The zing that always accompanies his touch pummels my insides. I can breathe again. I can smile.

Tell me, I whisper. *Tell me why you're here.*

He smiles, sad but sure, those hazel eyes filling with promise and conviction.

I'm here because that's where you need me to be.

11

―――――

HIM

I CROUCH BEHIND THE HEADSTONE FOUR ROWS BACK and listen to her mumble in her sleep. She's been lying on those graves for more than an hour, dead to the world. No pun intended.

My phone vibrates from the grass beside my thigh, the screen alighting with a notification from the walkie-talkie app. I shove my wireless earpiece back into place and click the button to make Decker's responses play automatically on arrival.

"Hunt, now I understand why you're so into her. She's morbid as fuck."

Prick.

From first thing this morning, this so-called friend has been a pain in my ass. He's commented on her tight jeans and the coat that apparently starves his view of her tits. He's criticized her driving, her mental stability, and her judgment for sleeping with me.

He's ogled her, made dirty comments and filthy promises. He's poked, teased, pushed, and I've withstood it all. But pretty soon I am going to break—his neck.

I press the response button on my screen and whisper, "Concentrate, motherfucker. Have you noted the names on those gravestones?"

"I'm all over it. Once we get home, I'll have answers for you."

Good. I'm running out of time.

"Do you think her tits are real?" Deck asks. "I've only seen her with a jacket on, but she looks too top-heavy for her figure."

I don't know where that piece of shit is hidden, but I raise a hand over my shoulder, above the shelter of my hiding place, and shoot him the bird.

Laughter echoes into my ear. "I think I've discovered a new favorite game. Teasing you about this chick is fun as hell."

I press the response button and mutter, "Teasing me will get you killed."

I chance a glance over the thick stone resting place of Doug Smith to find her lying in the exact same spot from ten minutes ago. She hasn't budged, only the cadence of her mumbled words has changed.

She's having a nightmare, and if she doesn't wake up soon she'll get soaked by the approaching black clouds.

"How long are we going to sit around playing with our dicks?" Decker asks.

I slump against the headstone and massage the bridge of my nose. "If you're playing with your dick," I whisper, "maybe consider cutting communication for a while."

"You know what I mean, lover boy. I'm happy to support your somnophilia, but I'm going to draw the line at spending the night in a cemetery."

"Somnophilia? What are you—"

"Hunter." Her voice cuts off my question.

I freeze. Not moving. Not breathing.

"*Hunter.*" This time it's a scream.

"Don't panic," Decker says in a rush. "She's still asleep… probably balls-deep in a nightmare about your tiny dick."

I ignore his blatant death wish and scour the ground for something to throw. I have to wake her up. Not because of the nightmare. Not because of the impending rain. I have to wake her because… *Fuck.* Just because.

I crawl to fetch a pebble a few feet away, then turn and launch it close in her direction. The projectile hits a nearby headstone with a thwack, and her legs jolt.

I slide back against my hiding place and wait as a drop of rain hits my cheek.

"Stay down. She's awake," Decker mumbles. "She's getting up."

Water hits my nose, my jacket, my jeans, the drips falling with lethargic frequency.

I clench my fists, fighting the need to see her, to read her expression and get a clue as to why she called my name. Was it really a nightmare? Does she know of my intentions? Can she feel me nearby?

I remain hidden, every inch of me on alert, as the rain settles in.

"She's on the move. Headed toward her car," Decker adds. "I'll be right behind her."

I hear a rush of footsteps, the release of a car door, and the thwack of it closing. There's the purr of an engine, then the crunch of loose asphalt.

I grab my phone and press the button to talk. "You better be all over her. Don't let her out of your sight."

"My pleasure."

Fucker.

I wait until the sound fades, then dash for my car parked outside the fence on the other side of the cemetery.

I'm behind the wheel within minutes and speeding through the streets seconds later.

Adrenaline makes me her bitch—pounding heart, racing blood and all. I'm so entirely fucked up because I know this shit will end badly, and yet I still love the game of cat and mouse.

The trill of an incoming call from Decker hits my speakers, and I connect via Bluetooth. "Where are you?"

"She's driving toward the I-5. I think we're going home."

"Okay." *Fuck.* She hasn't met with anyone. Not even a goddamn boyfriend. "Stay on her, and let me know if you run into any trouble. I'll make sure to keep my distance."

I end the call and sink into my seat. This excursion hadn't been the epiphany of information I'd needed. I have the address of the house she stopped at when we first arrived, and the names on the headstones. But I expected revelations.

And now I have to rely on Decker to do more digging. He'll have less than a day before I have to quit playing nice with her to ensure I get the answers Torian needs.

She will hate me. Fight me. And I'm a perverted motherfucker for the way my cock pulses at the thought.

Over the passing miles, Decker keeps in contact, giving me updates when necessary. "We've reached the highway." "We're at Tacoma." "I just passed Olympia."

I follow, along with rain that switches from a light dusting to a heavy downpour and back again. I play out the conversation I'm going to have with her once this turns sour —the threats, the lies, her physical abuse.

My dick appreciates the mental stimulation, even though I'm not thrilled to be sporting wood on the I-5 with no relief in sight. Not for a few hours, at least. By then I'll be back in Portland in the shitty bar, waiting for her to arrive with Brent's keys. I just have to pass her somewhere in between now and then.

I have every intention of spending the night in her bed. I'll beg, borrow, and steal to get between those sheets. Or more accurately, I'll bluff, intimidate, and manipulate.

Old habits die hard.

Night descends, and boredom grows. The taillights in front of me brighten the highway like a switchboard, and I become tired of the radio silence. I haven't heard from Decker in more than forty minutes, which isn't normal.

I dictate a message, press send, then wait some more. Once another five minutes pass, I succumb to the update deprivation and place a call. "What's going on?"

"I'm not sure. I'm a little on edge thinking we might have a problem."

"What is it?" I press down on the accelerator.

"We could have a tail."

"And you didn't think to call me?" *Fuck.* "Where? What car?" I scan the passing vehicles, even though I have to be miles behind him.

"It's a black Mercedes. I noticed it a while ago, but it hung way back. Now he's being obvious. Every time she slows, he slows. If she speeds up, he's right there behind her."

"Have you got eyes on the driver?" I pass car after car, exceeding the speed limit without any shits given.

"I'll take a closer look."

There's silence, nothing but the slush of water beneath my tires.

"Damn it," he snarls.

"What?" My chest pounds, and I grip the steering wheel tighter.

"He's got tinted windows. I can't see dick. But he's retreating now that I'm riding side-saddle."

"Don't hound him. Keep back and watch. I don't want her thinking she's boxed in. I'm going to make a call and see if I know who's responsible."

"Torian?"

Yeah, fucking Torian. "I'll let you know."

I disconnect and make the new call.

"Good evening, Hunter."

"Have you lost your fucking mind?" I suck in a breath and let it out slowly. "You've got eyes on me, don't you?"

He laughs, and I have to force myself to remain calm. Decker comes into view up ahead, his white suburban in the middle lane, the fucking Merc farther ahead.

"You promised you wouldn't follow," I snap. "You gave me forty-eight hours."

"I made no promises. In fact, I think you were the one who made a pledge during that conversation. Something about a dumpster, if my memory serves."

"Did you think I was joking?"

"No, but I thought I'd send Carlos to investigate anyway."

"Well, your investigator is about to run my mark off the road."

"Maybe he's there as a friendly warning, too."

Breathe. Just fucking breathe.

"I get it, okay? You want answers, and you think I'm dragging my feet. Believe me, I understand. But this will pay off. You don't need to send your bitch to play hardball."

"Are you sure? Carlos says she hasn't met with anyone yet. I'll be interested to hear his full report once he returns."

"After all these years, you don't trust me? Come on, Torian. You either let me do this my way or you're on your own." I'm bluffing. I have no choice. "Commit to the forty-eight hours you gave me. Let me do my job."

The Merc's brake lights grow smaller with its gaining

speed, and he cuts into the middle lane in front of Decker, closing in beside Steph.

"Torian…" My chest pounds. My temples, too. "You're going to blow this, and I'm so fucking close." To her. To this. To insanity. "What's the plan, anyway? You're losing your fucking mind if you want to run her off the road."

"Maybe that's necessary."

"For what reason?" I snap.

"To send a message. Or do you already get the picture?"

"I've got the fucking picture. Do I have forty-eight hours or not?"

"No. Now you're approaching twenty-four."

The line disconnects.

"*Fuck.*" My shout reverberates through the car. I can't get any closer. Not without letting her know I've been trailing her. All I can do is twiddle my fucking thumbs as this son-of-a-bitch veers closer and closer into her lane.

I call Decker.

"What do you want me to do?" he asks. "This guy is going to ram her."

"I know." And all I can do is watch. One look at me and the game is over. She can't see me here. I could claim it was a coincidence we ran into each other whenever she left her building. But being in the same place, more than an hour from her home, is a fucking stretch. "Slow down. Maybe he'll back off if you do."

"Okay. Got it."

The Merc veers for her again. Slow. Slow. Then fast, almost ramming into her. She swerves, the car fishtailing along the slippery road as her brake lights beam bright.

"*Stop,*" I yell at Decker as I rapidly approach.

She hydroplanes, sliding one way, then the other, taking over the middle lane, then the third.

I slow, but I can't stop.

I can't fucking stop.

"Help her." I hold my breath as Decker slows in front of me, hanging back to stalk her movements.

I approach, getting closer and closer, while she careens off the road, along the soaked grass and puddles that spray water in every direction.

"Make sure she's okay." My pulse spikes as I pass. I'm fucking shaking. In anger or fear, I don't know.

"You've really got a thing for this chick, don't you?" Decker asks.

"Pretend I do and make sure you act accordingly." I stalk my rear-view mirror, watching as he pulls up beside her. "That means you touch her, you die."

He chuckles. "Although I'd love to make promises, sometimes the charm can't turn itself off."

"Touch her and die," I snarl.

"You're such an easy target these days."

His laughter echoes through the car until I disconnect the call.

I have to get over this shit. I'm nobody's bitch. Not hers. Not Torian's. And definitely not this fucker in front who thinks he can mess with my assignment.

I shove my foot against the gas, and the car kicks up a gear. Decker and Steph disappear in the distance of the mirror, and I force myself not to look back.

I crank up my music and let the rhythmic thump of rage take over. I'll catch up to this motherfucker and teach him a thing or two about road safety. I'll also ensure Torian doesn't get that report he's waiting on and make it clear I always fulfill my promises.

12

HER

I CAREEN OFF THE ROAD, PANIC CLOGGING MY THROAT. I jolt in my seat as I bump along the grass median strip, hitting puddles that douse my windshield. The car slides sideways, completely out of control, along with the frantic beat of my pulse. I release the brake and try again, shoving my foot down hard.

The brakes grip. Tight. I keep my foot planted as I'm flung forward. The seatbelt finally locks, burning my neck and holding my chest in place. My forehead hits the steering wheel. Pain consumes my skull, and the world blurs.

For a moment, there's nothing. No movement. No sound. No panic. Just a blur.

"Jesus Christ." I close my eyes and breathe. Slow, calming breaths.

The rhythmic thump of the windshield wipers returns to my awareness. The light patter of rain, too. Cars pass, slushing water.

I'm safe. I'm safe. I'm safe. I chant the words over and over in my mind.

It was a careless road accident. A stupid goddamn mistake. That's all. There was no malicious intent. No hidden agenda. No asshole trying to kill me.

I open my eyes and swallow the need to crumple. For once, I wish I could be weak. I want someone else to fix my mess. To make everything okay again. I want the guilt over Dan to be gone. The pain over my family to ease. And I want Hunter.

I want him now.

Come on, bitch. Focus. Get your ass out of here.

I place the car in reverse, and a shadow creeps into my peripheral vision. A large, looming figure approaches my door. I lunge for the glove compartment and yank it open.

"Are you okay?" a man asks.

I pause in my reach for the gun hidden beneath road maps and glance over my shoulder. A guy stands at my window. His image is distorted through the droplets of rain against the glass, but I can still glimpse a relatively handsome face full of concern.

"I saw everything. Do you want me to call the cops?"

"*No.* I'm good." I straighten and wind the window down a crack, letting the chilled wet air gush in.

He smiles at me as rain hits his smooth honeyed skin and chocolate hair. "You sure? That old guy shouldn't be on the road."

"Old guy?"

He nods. "hair, thick glasses, golfer hat. He almost cut me off a few miles back."

The tightening in my lungs loosens. I can deal with the thought of an old-timer. It's the other possibilities that poke at my paranoia. "I didn't see who was driving."

"I don't think he saw much of anything either." He chuckles, but the humor quickly fades under his narrowing brown eyes. "You've got a bump." He points to his forehead. "Are you sure you're okay?"

"I'll be fine once I get back on the road."

He retreats a step and glances along the side of the car, his gaze low. "That might be a problem. Those wheels look pretty deep."

Shit. *Shit.* "*Shit.*" My frustration comes out in a rough shout. This is the karma I expected. The starting phase that will slowly morph into something big enough to drag me under its suffocating wing.

He flashes a sexy grin. It's gorgeous, filled with oozing amounts of charm. "Don't worry. I'll get you out of here. Why don't you put it in reverse and give it a try?"

A shiver runs down my neck. Not a welcome one. As physically appealing as this guy is, I don't want to be reliant on him. But being stuck on the side of the highway, in the middle of nowhere, is even less of a preference.

"Yeah..." I nod and wince at the renewed pain pounding through my head. "Okay."

I place the gearshift in reverse and slowly lower my foot on the accelerator. The wheels spin, whirring and sliding without traction. "Damn it."

"I'll give you a push."

He stalks for the front of the car, and I can't help my usual cautious analysis. He's tall. Way taller than I am. Thick arms, broad shoulders. In an attack, overpowering him would be difficult. In all honesty, it would be almost impossible without a substantial eye gouge or knee to the groin.

He stands before the beaming headlights, places his hands on the hood, and meets my gaze through the windshield. "Give it another try."

"Hold on a sec." I reach across the car, grab my gun from the glove compartment and my coat from the passenger seat. I hide the weapon inside the thick material and place them both in my lap.

I don't believe this guy's selfless act. I don't care that he's attractive, or kind, or charming. I'm not even sure I buy his account of the old guy not seeing me. I have no choice but to question everything.

"I'm ready now," I call out the window. "How about you?"

"Go for it."

I inch my foot down on the pedal. The wheels spin, whir. I hold my breath, my pulse increasing with each passing second. I can't stay out here. I can't wait for a tow. The piece-of-shit car has to move. There is no other choice.

Please, please, please.

The man roars as he pushes, his expression pinched, the material of his long-sleeve gray shirt growing damp and sticking to his biceps.

The car slides in and out of traction, moving sideways, farther and farther, before finally gripping. I exhale in a gush of relief and steer through bumpy, soaked grass.

The man follows, running after me, still pushing, until I pull the car to a stop parallel to the highway. He grins at me through the windshield, his chest heaving as he straightens, exposing more muscles hugged by his shirt and the faint hint of dark tattoos beneath.

He walks around the hood, shaking his feet, and returns to my window, his lips quirked in smug satisfaction.

"Thanks." I glance down at his soaked shoes and wince at the pants drenched from his ankles to his knees. "I'm sorry about your clothes."

"You don't happen to have a towel, do you?" He leans forward and looks in the car, scoping out the front and the back.

The chill returns, sliding down my neck, my spine. I

slip my hand into my coat and palm my weapon. "No, unfortunately, I don't." I shouldn't be this jumpy, not when he clearly needs a towel, but distrust comes with the territory.

"No problem." He waves me away. "Where are you headed, anyway?"

None of your damn business. "Portland."

"Me, too. Do you want me to follow you in case you have any problems?"

"I'll be fine." My response is unintentionally growled, which only increases his grin.

"I'm not looking for a gratitude blow job, if that's what you're thinking. It's just that the roads are slippery, and it's harder to drive at night. Your wheel alignment might be messed up, too."

"I don't have much farther to go. And if I run into any problems, I have someone I can call."

"Okay. I'll get out of your hair, then." He reaches out a hand to shake.

I stare for longer than necessary, my heart pounding as I release my gun and clasp his offering. "Thanks again."

His palm engulfs mine, and he's warm despite the rain and cool temperature. He also grips my hand gently. Not weak, but not overpowering.

Those dark eyes turn somber, and I can see sympathy staring back at me. Or maybe it's an apology. I don't know either way, but he stares for longer than he should, his attention stealing parts of me that I want back.

I pull my hand away and paste on a smile. "It was nice meeting you."

"Likewise." He inclines his head and gives me a two-finger salute. "I'll see you around."

He walks away, and I watch my side mirror until he's inside his car. I wait. Then wait some more. He doesn't make a move to leave before me. In fact, he flashes his lights, instructing me to go first.

"Damn you." I pull onto the highway, trying to watch the road and the Good Samaritan who can't take a hint as he follows.

I pump the brakes to make sure they're in working order, then I press my foot down on the gas. I stop worrying about highway patrols and breaking the speed limit, and focus on ditching the guy behind me.

I reach Atomic Buzz within fifty minutes and park in the alley out back before walking inside.

Brent is behind the bar with Hunter perched on a seat in front of him.

They both look toward me at the same time, and I shiver. It's easy to ignore Brent's gentle smile; I've seen it so many times before. What I can't tear my gaze away from is Hunter and the concern tightening his brows. His eyes narrow, taking me in, head to foot. The air in my lungs becomes heavy. My sternum throbs. I raise the collar on my coat in a vain attempt to shield myself.

Why does he have this effect on me? How does he have any affect?

I left town to gain distance from him, yet the physical miles seem to have brought me emotionally closer. My dream, and the fucked up message my subconscious tried to send, have me on the verge of weak, pathetic girliness.

"Thanks for the loan." I continue forward, forcing my attention to Brent, and lob the keys at him. "I appreciate it."

"No problem." He places the keys back on the hook. "How did the old girl run?"

"Like a dream." I lick my lower lip, trying to relieve the scorching heat of a predator's stare. "She's parked out the back. I even took her through the car wash so she looks all pretty." Truth be told, I'd had to hose off all the caked mud and grass to hide the evidence of my off-road adventure.

Hunter slides off his seat, and I stiffen as he approaches. Every inch of me is aware of him—my nerves, my pulse, my intuition.

"Are you okay?" His voice is low, yet strong.

That's what I need right now—strength, and lots of it.

What I wouldn't give to be a person who could crumple into a pool of exhausted tears and dramatic sobs. To have the freedom to be vulnerable and allow him to gather me in his arms and whisper words of comfort.

Like in the movies.

Like in a dream.

I grind my teeth, grinding away the weakness at the same time. "Yeah. Of course." I step back, needing distance from the eyes that narrow on my forehead. "Why wouldn't I be?" I lick my lower lip, then curse the action. "On second thought, don't answer that."

I need to break this... whatever it is—attraction, distraction, complication. "I've gotta go."

"You're not staying for a drink?" Brent asks.

"No, not tonight. I'm exhausted." I give them a lazy finger wave and turn for the door. Then I hear it—his footsteps. Hunter's pursuit.

My heart trembles with giddy excitement, and I wish it didn't. I wish I had some glimmer of control. But I'm completely lacking.

I reach the door, push outside, and stop as soon as I feel him approach behind me. "I can't do this tonight, Hunter. I'm too tired."

"Relax." He settles into me, his legs brushing the back of my thighs, his arm wrapping around my waist to place a gentle hand on my stomach. "I'm not looking for sex."

I don't move. I can't. I'm starved for his touch, my appetite too demanding to ignore.

"Are you hurt?" he murmurs.

I frown in confusion. "Why would I be hurt that you don't want to have sex with me? I just told you I'm too tired to deal with you tonight."

His breathy laughter sweeps over my neck, and he walks around to face me. His hand raises, slow and sure, his fingers pushing the hair from my forehead. "I'm talking about this." A gentle touch glides around the tender bump in pure, heart-melting torture. "But if you want to keep talking about sex..."

"No." I nudge him out of the way and walk to the curb to check for traffic. "I'm completely exhausted."

"Too exhausted for sex?" he asks. "I guess we skipped the whole dating thing and slid straight into being a married couple."

I can't hold back a smile. "Don't be a dick."

"Then don't be a pussy."

My humor fades. He's right. I need to toughen up. "Good night, Hunter."

I walk across the road and hitch my handbag higher on my shoulder.

The crunch of his steps follows. "I'm worried about you."

It's not the words that slay me. It's the tone. The pure concern. Ten years have passed since anyone has uttered words like that to me. Ten long, painful years.

"I bumped my head." I reach my building and face him. "It's no big deal."

He nods and his focus lowers, the seductive trail moving over my cheek, my jaw, to my neck. His brows snap tight, and his jaw ticks. "*Fuck.*"

"What?" I place a hand on my neck, to the place where

the seatbelt had burned me. "Is it bad?"

"It's bad enough." He nudges my wrist away and scrutinizes the area. "What happened?"

"Nothing. Just let it go."

I continue to the building entrance and enter the pin code. The lock releases, and he pulls the door wide.

"Let *me* go," I clarify.

"I will. Once I check you over and make sure you're really okay."

I stand there, caught between two options, one sensible, one indulgent. "It's my neck and my head. That's all."

He nods. "Good. That means it won't take long."

He lathers me with his concern, pulling at the thinnest fibers of my control. He's figured me out and determined how much I crave him. He knows he's my weakness.

"You've got five minutes."

He smirks, and the sight should have me retracting my offer. It should...but it doesn't. He follows me into the elevator, down the third-floor hall, and into my apartment.

Oh, shit.

The box of my life secrets is still open with the pages scattered across the floor, over my coffee table, and along the sofa, like a mass of dirty laundry. I shoot a glance at Hunter and he's staring, taking it all in with those scanning eyes.

"Sorry about the mess." I dump my handbag on the floor and take slow, measured steps, forcing myself not to rush forward. "Help yourself to the coffee machine, or get whatever you want from the fridge."

"I'm good." He follows, stopping at my sofa to peer down at the skeletons now outside of my closet. "Do you need a hand?" He leans over and picks up a piece of paper.

"No." I lunge and snatch the newspaper article away. "It's confidential."

He infuriates me with a dubious raise of his brow.

I lose all pretense of calm and scramble, shifting the pages into piles to cover them from view. "I do research work for a university professor. He doesn't like when we discuss projects with outsiders."

"Outsiders?"

Shit. I sound like an idiot. "Yeah." I shrug. "He studies criminal psychology but already has enough issues of his own, ya know?"

He nods and focuses on the piles I've created, his neck slightly craned to peek at the information. "Seems interesting enough."

"Not really." I grab the last of my secrets from the floor and stack them on top of those on the sofa, then those on the coffee table. I shuffle until they're in a neat pile and then place them back in the box.

"There." I dust my hands and will my pulse to settle. "All done."

He continues to nod, lazy and contemplative.

"Now, where were we?" I wiggle the coat from my shoulders and drape it over the sofa. "You wanted me to prove I was fine, right?" I spread my arms wide, then tap my nose with each forefinger and do a twirl. "See? I'm perfect."

Again, he gives me a lethargic nod, and this time a smirk is added to the mix, as if he's agreeing that I'm perfect. "How did it happen?" He approaches with predatory steps. "Was it your boyfriend?"

I swallow, my mouth tingling. I want to lie. I want to lie so damn bad and tell him this fake boyfriend hurt me. *He hurt me because of you.*

Would Hunter care? Would he vow to protect me?

I suck in a deep breath and stand tall. I'm not going to succumb. Not again. "I had a slight car accident. I ran off the road."

He stops in front of me, almost toe to toe.

123

"I adore Brent, but his car is a piece of shit. The seatbelt didn't lock fast enough, and I hit my head on the steering wheel."

He remains calm. Always in control. "Are you hurt anywhere else?" His gaze scans me, across my hairline, along my jaw, down to the small V of my thin cotton sweater.

"I'm not hurt at all."

He grips my sweater and begins to lift.

"Hunter." I place my hands on top of his. "I'm not doing this now." No matter how adamantly my body voices a protest.

He meets my gaze, those hazel eyes strong and true. "I know."

He continues to lift my sweater, taking it over my head and dropping it to the floor. He captures my stare as he unbuttons my blouse from the top. I hold my breath as his knuckles brush the inside curve of my covered breasts, and I can't fight the need to swallow.

He glances down, and his jaw tenses.

I'm caught in a daze, transfixed by the way his hair falls gently over his forehead, as a lone finger streaks a line from my shoulder to my cleavage.

"You're hurt worse than you thought." That finger continues strumming my desire with its delicate caress. "Are you sure you're okay?"

"Hmm?" I glance down to the light pink line marking my chest. An extended war wound left from the seatbelt. "It's nothing. It doesn't even hurt."

My attraction is much more painful.

He ignores me, those fingers trailing farther along my buttons, this time leaving them in place. He reaches the hem and lifts, exposing my stomach.

I notice everything he does, the soft blinks, the slight

narrowing of his stare. Every inch of me is in tune with every inch of him, the gentle rise of his chest, the bite of teeth into his lower lip.

He's beautiful. Harsh, yet stunning.

The pad of his thumb swipes my abdomen, the touch trailing above the waistband of my jeans in exquisite lethargy.

It's so light.

Too light.

Barely enough.

"There's the slightest mark here. You'll probably bruise tomorrow."

I don't care. Right now, I wouldn't mind if the morning brought the end of the world, as long as he didn't stop touching me.

"Is there anywhere else I need to check?" he asks.

Mmmhmm. There sure is, doctor.

"No." I clear my throat. "Is there anywhere on *you* that I need to check?"

His light chuckle is like melted chocolate and scented candles—the absolute perfect prelude to sex.

His eyes darken, growing devilish. "Maybe." He slides his hands over my ass, gently pulling me closer to grind into me.

I withhold a whimper, caging it inside my throbbing chest.

All I can think about is sex. Lots and lots of sex. Tangled sheets. Sweaty skin. Glistening muscles. Moaning. Screaming.

Oh, God, I could come already.

"You distract me," I admit.

"From what?"

I blink to awareness, realizing my stupidity. I've fought

to keep him away from my secrets, only to stumble with the simple grind of his dick.

I'm slipping.

"Nothing." I shake my head.

He growls, his fingers digging into my ass. "I should've known better than to assume you'd ever share any insight into your life. You won't even tell me your fucking name."

He doesn't stem the aggression in his tone. I see it. I feel it, too. The threat should scare me. Instead, I crave it. I want more. "You know my name."

"Yeah." He scoffs. "It's Emma. Steph for short."

He retreats a step, and his withdrawal leaves me chilled. Icy. I want to reach out, to grasp, and tug, and pull. Instead, I hold my ground as he begins to pace.

"When are you going to tell me something real?" His question is a plea that hits the weaker parts of my resolve. "I want to hear the fucking truth for once."

I lift my chin, battling his emotional onslaught.

Don't falter. Don't break.

"Who are you running from?"

I shake my head. "I'm not running from anyone."

"Bullshit."

"It's true." I keep my hands at my sides, even though I want to reach out and reconnect. "I'm searching for someone. I've been searching for almost ten years."

His brows pull tight. He's assessing me, attempting to sift through the truth and lies. "Who?"

"An old friend. A boyfriend."

He releases a derisive laugh. "Another one?"

"No. Not another one." I inch back to rest my hip against the sofa when all I want to do is move toward him. Into him. "I lied about Seattle."

"Yeah?" He narrows his gaze. "Why?"

More stupid. So much stupid.

Stupid. Stupid. Stupid.

I look away. I can't do this. For normal people, this might be simple, giving answers to menial questions. For me, it's slicing open a vein and letting my soul rush out.

He advances, eating up my vision to cage me against the furniture. "Why?" he growls against my ear.

"Because I can't want this. You shouldn't be here."

"I don't want to be here either, Emma." He leans in, brushing his lips against my neck. "Steph..." He does it again, the next kiss lower. "Princess..." And lower, devouring the sensitive spot where my shoulder meets my neck. "I have a million things I need to do right now, and the only one I plan on doing is you."

He keeps his mouth in place, and each second is a dose of pleasured pain. A temptation and a punishment.

"Do you love him?" he murmurs.

My heart drops at his raw emotion. "Who?"

"This boyfriend you're chasing."

I clutch his shirt, twisting the fabric. Even the concept of loving Jacob makes me nauseated. "No. We have unfinished business. That's all."

"Then how can I help you find him?"

The nausea vanishes, the bile and hatred being replaced with the warmest gratitude. Then disappointment. "You can't. The only connection I had to him is now dead."

There's another pause, this one filled with tension. "The senator's son?"

I don't answer. He's seen enough of my dirty laundry for one night. "Can we talk about something else?"

He nods, scraping his teeth over my shoulder. Tickling. Teasing.

I breathe him in, letting the lingering scent of fading aftershave sink into my lungs. "On second thought, let's not talk at all."

13

HER

THE NEXT MORNING ARRIVES WITH ME HAVING TO claw my way out of the deepest depths of sleep. I sit up, the sheet falling from my chest to expose my nudity as sunlight bathes my room.

"Hey." Hunter clears his throat from beside me, his eyes closed. "You okay?"

"Yeah. Bad dream, that's all."

A nightmare.

I'd been at Dan's funeral, witnessing the pain I'd inflicted on innocent people as they stood sobbing around his grave.

I'd apologized, over and over, but nobody could hear me. The crying grew, building to a cacophony that pounded in my ears, until mourners began walking away. One by one, the crowd had dispersed, leaving a lone man to stand before the open hole in the ground.

Jacob.

"We're both the same now." He'd smirked at me. Fucking smirked.

I can't get the image out of my head. It's there, stalking me from every corner of my mind.

"Oh, shit," I whisper. It's a sign.

"What's wrong?" Hunter mutters.

"Nothing." I slide from the bed and tug my nightshirt from under my pillow. "Go back to sleep."

He groans and turns onto his stomach, planting his face into the mattress.

I pull the shirt over my head and stare vacantly across the apartment.

Jacob could be at the funeral. And yeah, maybe I am clutching at disintegrating straws here, but it is a possibility. One that makes my heart pound and my hands sweaty.

Could it be that easy? Could my actions toward Dan have led to what I've been searching for?

Maybe that's why he died. Dan had to so I could find Jacob. Instead of chasing him for the rest of my life, the asshole will come to me.

Fate and destiny have collided. It all makes sense now.

I could go to the church. *No.* The enclosed space will be tricky. I'll go to the cemetery instead and watch as the cars roll in. If I find my mark, I'll place a tracker on his vehicle and let the retribution begin.

I smile. I almost laugh.

Soon, I'll be free, and my family can rest in peace.

I rush on my toes to my wardrobe and inch the doors apart. I grab my handbag from the hook on the wall, place it on the floor, then kneel to open the plastic storage container stashed behind my coats.

I scrounge through the contents and pull out anything I might need.

GPS tracker—check.

Cable ties—check.

Silencer—check... Just in case.

I place them in my handbag and double-check my gun is there from yesterday.

Could I even pull the trigger at the funeral of a man I've murdered? *No.* I won't inflict more pain on these people. But I will arrive prepared.

I grab my black corporate dress off a hanger, then rush back to the bed and pull underwear from my drawer, along with my phone. With my handbag in one hand and clothes in the other, I sneak to the bathroom and close myself inside.

I do an Internet search on the funeral. The church service is at ten. *Shit.* I only have an hour before it starts, which gives me roughly an additional hour to get to the cemetery, right?

You'd think I'd know more about funerals, having lost my entire family, but I wasn't involved in planning that event. I'd been catatonic. All I remember is the walk down the aisle toward four matching coffins, each with a large adornment of lilies displayed on top.

My mother had never liked lilies.

Focus.

I dump my stuff on the floor, and have a record-breaking time trial in the shower. I spare five minutes on a rushed makeup attempt, two minutes for my hair, then I'm ready and pulling the bathroom door wide.

Hunter is seated in bed, his back against the headboard, his hands behind his head. I pause, gifting myself with the briefest visual indulgence. I fell asleep in those arms, against that Hulk-like chest, and I can't deny I want to do it again.

"Good morning." I grin, unable to hide my appreciation for last night's orgasm extravaganza. Hunter has a way with me, one that rocks my womb and has probably destroyed me for any other man.

"Morning." He takes me in with a visual sweep, over the

stiff black dress that shadows every inch of my skin, from knees to collarbone to shoulder. It screams sophistication, but I can tell he sees the sex appeal. "You look nice."

"Thanks." I'm not a giddy person—at least, I wasn't until he showed up in my life. Now, I'm not so sure. "You look well rested."

"I am. For once." He jerks his chin at me. "Come here."

I struggle not to comply. My wants and needs wage war. "I can't. I have to leave."

His gentle appraisal transforms to tight scrutiny. "Where are you going?"

He flicks back the sheet, exposing his divine lower half before he slides from the mattress. He approaches, entirely naked, completely aroused, and I force myself to hold his gaze. "Where?" he repeats.

"A funeral."

The hint of fear slides through his features, a brief snap of flaring eyes and parting lips before he masks his concern. "Why?"

"I don't know," I lie. "For curiosity. For closure."

"You're talking about Dan Roberts, right?"

"Yeah..." I don't appreciate how intuitive he is. "How do you know him?"

"I knew *of* him. Everyone does. He was the crooked son of a senator. He had links to drugs and solicitation, among other shady shit." He stops in front of me, unabashed and unapologetic. "People who associate themselves with men like Dan are dangerous. They aren't people you want to be around. Even at a funeral."

"I don't plan on handing out business cards or networking with those in mourning. I just need to go. For me."

For my family.

He steps into me, draping his arm around my waist. "I

131

don't want you there." He speaks against my lips, gifting me with light butterfly kisses until his words sink in.

I pull back and meet his gaze. There's no remorse over his dictate, no shame visible in his features. Only determination.

"You're overstepping," I whisper.

This thing between us, whatever it is, doesn't carry a noose. I'm not his woman to leash. I never will be.

"Then let me come with you. Let me drive you there. I don't even have to get out of the car. I'll just be close if you need me."

I shake my head. "I can't." I need to lay low. Not draw any attention. Police will be there, looking for the murderer, and I don't want to ping any radars.

"Let me put it this way, I'm going whether you like it or not." He steps back and walks for his clothes piled beside the bed. "We can do it the easy way, in the same car. Together." He snatches his jeans off the floor and tugs them on sans underwear. "Or you can be stubborn and get there on your own."

I ignore how he has to fold his dick like a full-grown anaconda to shove it inside his pants. I ignore and ignore, because at a time like this I shouldn't be thinking about him pretzel-ing his dick.

"Whatever you decide," he growls, "you won't be there alone."

No. "I need to do this on my own."

"And you will." He pulls his shirt over his head and straightens the material with the repeated brush of a hand. "I'll wait in the car."

"Don't push," I plead. "This is for me, Hunter. It's personal."

He tugs on his boots, rough and full of aggression. "I said I'd wait in the damn car."

I want to hate him. I probably would if the ride didn't make the travel component of my plan ten times easier. I'll have a base to spy from, unlike being left in the open if I catch a cab.

He strides for the door and pulls it wide. "You coming?"

I glare, not appreciating how he's manipulated the moment to become the offended party. He's the one stepping on *my* toes. Not the other way around.

"Yeah." I sigh and grab my coat from the rack. "I'm coming."

W e travel in silence. Hunter broods, while I plot.

I don't want anyone else affected by my actions. No one but Jacob. Which means I can't make a scene.

I need to focus on finding his car. That way, I can track him to his house, where the possibilities will be endless. I'll have more time to scheme. I'll have innumerable opportunities to make this perfect. And revenge will be so much sweeter if I don't rush.

I'll get my chance to make him suffer. To make him pay for stealing my family from me. For hurting them. Torturing them with flames and agony.

I dig my fingernails into my palm to distract myself.

I can't go back there. Not today.

Guilt tries to haunt me with each approaching mile toward Dan's final resting place. But I don't let that penetrate either.

It's time to step up to the plate with my A-game.

We approach the open black gates of the cemetery ahead of time, and I point to the side of the road. "Can you pull over here, please?"

"Outside?"

"Yeah. Just for now."

He veers to the curb and turns off the car, the silence growing thicker. He taps the steering wheel, winds down his window, and turns the radio on, then off again.

"Have you got something you want to say?" I ask.

He puts his arm out the window and drums his fingers against the door. "You know you can talk to me, right?" he mutters.

I sit forward in my seat as the hearse comes into view at the end of the road. "About what?"

"About anything."

Dan passes in front of us, the black coffin in full view. I swallow, my heart trembling. This is the first funeral I've been to since my family died. And the first where I've been the cause of the festivities.

I scan the passengers in the vehicle procession, searching for a familiar face.

"Did you hear me?" Hunter growls.

"Yeah. I heard you. But you're pushing too hard, too fast." In other words, I'm falling, too far, too soon. "You need to back off."

His response comes in the form of a white-knuckled grip around the steering wheel.

"Look... I don't do this." I wave a hand between us. "Ever. Not relationships. Not sleepovers. I'm used to being alone."

His jaw ticks. "I'm not familiar with fairytales either, princess. I'm trying my best here."

My lips curve at the description—a fairytale. If only. "Give me time, okay?"

He scoffs. "Yeah. All we need is time." He starts the push-button ignition and puts the car in drive. "Do you want me to follow?"

"Yeah... Thanks."

We pull in behind the last car and weave along the narrow, curving road through the cemetery. My pulse increases the farther we go, until we stop behind a mass of parked cars.

Mourners walk across the grass, the crowd milling around a grave in the distance. I can't distinguish faces from here. There are too many.

"I'm going to make my way to the burial site."

Hunter glares through the windshield as I open my door and slide out. He's angry with me, and I understand the frustration. But I can't let it get between me and Jacob.

"Wait," he grates. "Are you sure you're happy to go on your own?"

I should crack a joke. I want to. I've done everything on my own for so long that his question is comical. "I'm good." If only his concern didn't leave me thirsty for more. "Thanks for caring."

His nostrils flare, those fingers still gripping tight. I shake off the excess guilt, tug my handbag higher along my shoulder, and pull my sunglasses down to partially cover my face. "I'll be back soon."

I close the door and keep my head tipped toward the ground. I don't raise my gaze until I've inched my way into the outer ring of the intimate crowd.

Large framed pictures of a dead man are placed on the other side of Dan's coffin, which is poised above the hole in the ground. They stare, smiling, mocking, unsettling me. Two rows of seated guests whimper softly, the senator seated on the end, his head high, his face impassive.

The reality of my crime hits me, the blow landing heavy against my chest. I created this pain. I'm the cause of the heartache experienced by each and every one of these guests.

I let out a long breath and close my eyes. I'll pay for my

sins soon enough. I know I will. Until then, I can only hope to drag another deserving criminal down with me.

I dance my gaze over the mourners as the priest begins the burial service. I pass over the sniffling women who dab their eyes and the array of men who barely show an ounce of emotion.

Kind words are spoken about an honorless man, lies are shared, and here I stand, searching for hope with none in sight.

I can't see Jacob. Not even anyone vaguely familiar to the teenager who has since grown into the man in the picture with Dan. I lean to the left to see hidden faces, then again to the right.

He's not here.

But he has to be. I can feel him through the building tension in my bones, my stomach, my heart. This moment is going to be the culmination of everything I've worked for. The years of searching and plotting. The nights of tears and torment.

He has to be here.

He has to be.

I inch forward to gain a better view of the people closest to me and scan the outer row of mourners. I swoop my gaze in a swaying arc, back and forth, until my attention latches onto a familiar profile to my left.

My heart stops.

I freeze.

But it's not Jacob. It's the Good Samaritan from yesterday. The one who helped me on the highway. His head is bowed, not in grief, but in conversation. He's talking to a GQ model-type on the far side of him, their lips moving in lazy chatter.

I pretend to focus straight ahead and watch from my peripheral vision.

The crowd becomes restless. The sobs and sniffles grow. Then I hear the mechanical whir of the coffin being lowered, and people break into category-three mourning.

The Samaritan and the hottie straighten, doing a half-hearted job of paying attention. They're definitely not close to the deceased. So, why are they here? Business, maybe? Are these the type of men Hunter warned me about?

I inch back. One step... Pause... Two.

The Samaritan's gaze lazily swings in my direction, then makes a direct hit.

I stiffen, and so does he. His lips part and his eyes widen, and I'm okay with the shock, because I feel it, too. But then he glances away, the action quick and panicked.

Why is *he* panicked?

A sudden case of vertigo hits, my world tilting. Is he a cop? A detective?

I rush to scour the mourning faces again, this time with more scrutiny. Am I being watched?

I place a protective palm over my handbag.

Oh, fuckity fuck. I'm in big trouble. Even bigger trouble than normal, seeing as though I have a handbag filled with premeditated craziness.

I glance over my shoulder to Hunter. He's getting out of the car, his gaze still on me as he shuts the door.

He knows. He can tell something is wrong. I'm not being paranoid anymore.

I take another step back, and the suspicious stranger turns away from me, as if trying to hide. Or at least pretending I don't exist.

It's too damn late for that, buddy.

I know he's up to something. I just don't know what that something is.

Mourners murmur amongst themselves, while others hug or stroll to their car.

137

I'm trapped in indecision, ready to run, but prepared to fight. I can't go down without Jacob. If this is the end of my freedom, then I need him to be right here with me.

I chance another glance at Hunter and find him striding toward me, shoulders back, chin high. He looks ready for battle, and that's exactly what I need. I want him to know how petrified I am. That I need him. That I'm ready for him to save me, today and from now on.

He slows as he approaches, his face set in stone, but when he reaches my side, he bends down and scoops something off the ground. "Excuse me, ma'am, I think you dropped something."

I frown as he straightens. There's no familiarity in the way he speaks to me. Surely, he can't still be holding a grudge from our earlier conversation.

He reaches out a closed hand, and instinctively I offer him my palm.

He places the clicker to his car in my hand and clasps his fingers over mine as he whispers, "Pretend you don't know me and get out of here. I'll find you later."

All I can do is blink, my heart hammering, my mind racing.

"Go." His touch falls and he walks away, toward the Samaritan.

I stand in stunned silence, growing colder and colder with each of his departing steps. I'm caught between the need to run and the need to understand. The desire to chase after him and the fear making me want to flee.

He keeps walking straight toward those men, and I can't look away. Not when he stops beside them. Not when he inclines his head in greeting.

And definitely not when one of them addresses him by name.

14

HIM

Her hand has the slightest tremble as I tell her to leave. I put that tremble there. I'm the cause of the slightly parted lips and the wide eyes I'm sure she's hiding behind those dark sunglasses.

I can feel Torian watching us. Watching every single thing I do.

I never should've brought her here. I should've faked a car breakdown or gotten us lost along the way. The only reason I didn't was because I needed to know who she was looking for. That one clue could've saved me. Saved *her*.

At least that was what I thought, until I found Decker and Torian standing less than a few feet away from her.

I walk toward them, trying to act casual when my insides are wound tight.

"Hunter," Torian greets. "Fancy seeing you here. Did you know the deceased?"

I ignore his poor excuse for a joke and turn my attention to Decker. "I guess the attendance today is a surprise for all."

His jaw tightens. He knows he's fucked up, but there's anger in that expression, too.

"Have you checked your messages lately?" he grates.

No. My phone has been in the car glove compartment since we returned from Seattle. "You know I rarely have my cell on me."

"That's true." Torian nods, unconcerned by the underlying tension in our conversation. "But it's a weak excuse for poor communication. I'm still waiting on an update on what happened yesterday."

I itch to glance over my shoulder and check to make sure Steph has gone. I know better, though. I can feel her attention burning the back of my neck. The good news is that Torian hasn't latched onto her. Carlos mustn't have taken any photos, and no photos means no familiarity or cause for concern. Yet.

She's in the clear. As long as I can figure out a way to keep her safe, while also extracting the information I need.

Once we get out of here, I will sit her down and have the tough conversation. I'll explain what's going on, and we'll clean this mess.

"I assumed you already had an update from Carlos." I flash Torian a cocky smirk. "How is your little bitch boy doing this morning?"

His left eye twitches the slightest bit. "I'll let you know once I hear from him."

"Yeah." I chuckle. "You do that."

Decker clears his throat. "Can you two measure your dicks somewhere else? This isn't the time or place."

"You're right." Torian watches as mourners move around us, walking to their vehicles, while a small group remain around the burial site. "We will discuss this later. I should go and give my condolences to the senator."

Relief expands in my chest as I wait for him to leave.

Then something nudges my arm and the reprieve turns into panic as Steph steps into my periphery—the beautiful blonde hair, the smooth creamy skin.

She stops between me and Decker, and the guy stiffens. I can't help doing the same as she raises her sunglasses and gives a friendly smile.

"Fancy seeing you here." She pats us both on the arm. "Small world, right?"

Decker clears his throat and glances to me for guidance.

I have nothing. No direction. No response. Only dread.

"You all know each other." Her statement is calm and collected, belying the furious warrior I see flash in her eyes.

"Yes, sweetheart, we do." Torian reaches out a hand. "I'm sorry, I haven't had the pleasure of an introduction."

"I'm Steph." She raises her hand for him to shake and uses the other to lower her glasses into place.

"Steph," he repeats, letting her name linger between us like a warning. "I'm Cole, but call me Torian. It's lovely to meet you." He grasps her hand and looks at me as he brings her knuckles to his lips. "How do you know Decker and my Hunter?"

My Hunter.

He's digging my hole deeper, burying me.

"Oh, we go way back." She releases his hand and places it against her bag. "Don't we, Hunter?"

Torian glances between us, back and forth, putting puzzle pieces together.

"Yeah, I guess we do," I growl.

"We met when he came into town to look after his sister and nephew." She looks at me, and I can imagine those eyes glaring from behind her glasses.

She's pissed. Really pissed. And I could strangle her for it.

"Your sister?" Torian raises a brow. "All this time and I didn't know you had family in Portland."

She nods. "Oh, he definitely does. And he's very protective. Big and macho and mean. But..." She raises a cautionary finger. "He's *not* a violent man. Isn't that right, princess?"

Okay, now she's being downright derisive.

Torian breaks out in laughter, long and loud, not giving any respect to the people behind him who have just buried a loved one. "I like this woman. I really do." His gaze snaps to me. "I understand now."

No, he doesn't. He can't. Not when I struggle to understand it myself.

"Understand what?" She leans into me, shoulder to shoulder, all chummy and shit.

Torian continues to chuckle, making me well aware I've played right into his hand. "Hunter has been distracted lately. Now I understand the cause. You should've told me it was your family."

"Yep. Nothing but family," she drawls.

I dig my fingers into my palm, forcing down my anger while I try to determine if she's truly dim-witted or just has a death wish.

"Well, I better not waste any more of your time." She places her hand on my back, my gun. The touch is a message. A clear warning. "I'll leave you boys to your conversation."

I nod, one quick jerk of fucked up acknowledgement.

I want to grab her, keep her at my side, and never let her go. But she walks away, leaving me with a friend who looks as if he's having a heart attack and a man I'm beginning to want to see six feet under.

"She's a spitfire," Torian muses.

"Stay away from her." I keep my gaze trained on her

until she stops at my car and opens the passenger door. "You're not going to touch her."

A dark brow raises over the frame of his sunglasses. "Is that so?"

"Yeah. That's so. As far as you're concerned, she's off-limits. I'm sorting this out."

His humor finally fades. "We had an agreement, Hunter. One you didn't fulfil."

"I still have a few more hours."

He inclines his head. "You're right." He flicks out his arm to check his watch. "But let's agree that once your time is up, she'll no longer be yours. She'll be mine."

I keep my mouth shut. I have to. I'm smart enough to know more threats won't work, and I can't find the composure to say anything else right now.

"I'm off to see the senator." Torian smirks in farewell. "We'll speak later."

I remain silent as he walks toward Dan's family, between the white outdoor chairs to the other side of the burial site.

"You should have called me," Decker mutters. "Now you're fucked."

"Thanks for the insight, asshole." I start walking backward, needing to get to Steph. "Why the fuck are you even here?"

"If you checked your phone, you'd know. I called over fifteen times."

"I left it in the car while—"

"—while you were fucking balls-deep in her snatch."

I clench my teeth, unable to deny the truth.

"I'm right, aren't I?" He raises his voice with the building distance between us. "Jesus Christ, *Hunt*. Fucking call me."

There he goes again, trying to make my name sound like cunt. "I will. As soon as I'm done with her."

I turn and stride toward Steph when all I want to do is run to her.

She's seated in the passenger seat, watching, waiting. She has to know what's coming isn't going to be pretty. The next instalment of this shit show is going to be epic, and she has front-row seats.

I reach the car, open the driver's door, and sink behind the wheel.

I don't look at her. I don't mention our fucked up situation. I don't say a word—not about the men I'm sure she's curious about, and not about the silenced gun she has in her hand, pointed in my direction.

15

HER

I'M FUCKED.

And not only am I fucked, I'm a goddamn idiot for thinking this Decker guy from the highway could be a cop when it now seems clear his intent was much more sinister.

My hunter, Torian had said.

He made it sound like a description, not a name, which made my blood run cold with possibilities. It hadn't been a slip of the tongue. His focus had been trained on me, waiting for a reaction. And he'd gotten one—a heart-palpitating, soul-screaming one I hope I was able to hide.

Hunter slides into the car, starts the engine, and doesn't acknowledge the weapon in my hand as he veers onto the narrow road and drives from the cemetery.

He's not daunted by the threat. He's probably used to it.

The detachment only increases the chill sinking into my bones, freezing every inch of me. In a perfect world, this would be the part where he divulged all his lies and begged for my forgiveness. But my world isn't perfect.

There is no knight in shining armor here.

I have to save myself.

He drives through the busy streets and onto the highway with neither of us breaking the silence. The voices in my head are already too deafening.

This is bad. This is so horribly, terribly bad, and I don't know how to make it stop. How could I have missed so much? I've probably missed everything. All the signs. All the clues.

He pulls onto an off-ramp, and I tap my heel against the floor, unable to hide my panic. The time for pretending I have this under control is gone. "Where are we going?"

"Somewhere we can talk." He continues into a rural area, his eyes trained on the road.

I glance around, to the diminishing houses and lack of cars. There are miles and miles of nothing but trees and long grass. Not one witness in sight. "Pull over."

"In a minute. It's not much farther."

My hand trembles as I raise the gun and place the barrel against his temple. "Pull. Over."

His fingers tighten on the steering wheel. I can't tear my gaze away from the palpable fury evident in his tight jaw and the rapid pulse in his neck. I'd known he was dangerous, and still I'd ignored the threat. My intuition escaped me, and I was left vulnerable to his manipulative charms.

Not anymore.

I press the gun harder and brace for him to snap. I'll pull the trigger if I have to. I have no choice. He'd said it himself—only dangerous people would be at Dan's funeral.

The car slows and veers onto the shoulder, the tires crunching under gravel. We stop. But it's not just the forward momentum. I cease breathing. Thinking. There's only white noise and the monotonous reminder of my mistakes.

"Get out." I withdraw the gun and point it at his chest, bracing for any sudden movement.

"You're not going to shoot me."

I laugh, and my stomach drops at how wrong he is. I won't stop fighting now. I won't let my heart mess with my objectives.

"*Out*," I snarl.

He glances at me, his eyes bleak with concern, one brow raised in condescension. A conflicting expression. Two warring emotions, despair, and disdain.

I have to focus on truth and not let the lies sway me. This man holds no concern. Not for me. Not for my life. And certainly not for the vendetta I have to achieve.

I divert the barrel to the right, one inch, maybe two, then squeeze the trigger.

Noise explodes around me, the burst of audible violence filling the confined space even with the silencer firmly affixed to the barrel.

Glass shatters his window and he jerks away, his eyes wide, wild, and threatening. The condescending brow disappears. His lips move, but I can't hear him. I can't hear anything apart from the deafening ring in my ears.

"*Out*." I hide my building hysteria behind a curl of my lip and open my door, the barrel now trained back on his chest.

His jaw ticks, all that rough stubble shifting while wisps of hair frame his eyes in an untamed mess.

He's still gorgeous. Brilliantly so. But I see through it now. I'm beginning to understand my self-sabotage and how far I've fallen.

He turns to get out, and I take the opportunity to pull the gun from the back of his jeans and throw it at my feet. He doesn't flinch, just slides from the seat, and closes the door behind him.

I follow on my side, round the hood, and fight the need to massage my aching temples.

He shoves a finger in his ear, wiggles it, then does the same to the other. "You're fucking crazy, do you know that?"

"Thanks for noticing." But he's wrong. I no longer feel crazy with my energetic lust for revenge. I'm hollow. The emptiness is irreparable.

"Oh, I fucking noticed, all right. And no doubt I'll have the friendly reminder for the rest of my life in the form of *damaged goddamn hearing.*" He stretches his jaw, working it from side to side. "Don't ever do that again."

I want to laugh, to ridicule the concept that anything at all will happen between us ever again. Not sex. Not betrayal. Not backstabbing. But he'll learn that soon enough.

"Who are you?" I demand.

He straightens, growing taller as his lips press tight and his chin lifts. He tries to stare me down, and I don't understand how he can look at me like that. Without remorse or regret.

My throat constricts, growing tighter and tighter. Maybe his silence is a sign of guilt. But it's not enough. I need more. I need *something.* He played me. Humiliated me. Betrayed me. All the while seducing me with his strength and confidence.

"*Start talking.*" I almost scream the words, and still he doesn't answer. "Otherwise, we do this the hard way." I lower the barrel, aim at his feet, and squeeze.

Bang.

He doesn't shift as dirt dances at his toes. Not a jump or a flinch. He's not scared of me. Not scared of guns or bullets or death.

"Goddamn it. *Tell me who you are.*" I raise the gun and storm toward him, aiming at his chest.

148

Still, he doesn't cringe, or cower, or recoil. He doesn't do anything. Not a damn thing, and it's killing me. Voices scream in my head, demanding answers, demanding punishment. I need him to react to what he's done. I need an acknowledgement of the devastation eating me from the inside out.

"*Tell. Me—*"

He lunges, grabs the silencer, and yanks down with a hard twist. I had a split second to pull the trigger, but I didn't.

I fucking didn't.

I squeal as my hand follows the movement, bending awkwardly. My fingers lose grip, and the weapon is wrenched from my hand. From powerful to powerless in the space of a heartbeat. In the blink of those menacing hazel eyes.

I retreat with quick backward steps that could easily turn into a sprint if I think he's going to shoot. I wait for him to turn the tables, to place me in his sights. Instead, he flicks on the safety and slides the gun down his leg, assisting it as it falls to the ground before he kicks it away.

We remain frozen in a stony standoff, matching each other glare for glare.

"You first," he mutters.

"No way in hell."

He runs a hand through his hair. "Fuck, you're stubborn about your stupid secrets."

"I can deal with being stubborn." What I can't deal with is being fooled by another man who only wants to hurt me. "You know, earlier, when I first saw the recognition between you and that guy I met yesterday, I thought you might be a cop." I swallow to ease my emotion-filled throat. "I thought maybe you'd been watching, waiting to arrest me, but you're not a cop, are you?"

He laughs, flashing his too perfect teeth and too perfect smile. "You're looking on the wrong side of the law, princess."

My throat threatens to close. Swallowing is no longer an option. "Okay..." I can figure this out. "Obviously, you know Dan Roberts. So, I assume you're a criminal. Maybe a lowlife dealer."

Or a pimp? A thief?

"I'm worse than that." His eyes harden, and I believe him.

He walks toward me, and I sidestep, making sure not to place additional space between me and the gun.

"A member of the mafia?" I ask.

He plants his feet and glares. "I'm the guy who finished the job you started."

I keep moving, walking in a circle as his explanation runs through my head. Over and over. He's deliberately playing more mind games, dragging this out to lengthen the torture.

Either that, or I'm truly not as smart as I once thought.

"Think about it, Steph," he taunts. "What were you doing the night I met you?"

No. I frown and shake my head. I'm not going to allow that train of thought to make sense. I can't.

"Come on now, princess," he murmurs. "You can say it."

I don't want to.

He steps forward, once, twice. A slow, sure stride that intensifies my panic.

"You killed him," I whisper.

I don't know if it's a question or a statement. It should be an adamant declaration. X marks this map like a neon sign in the dead of night. But I need it to be a question. And I desperately want the answer to be 'no.'

There's a slight pulse in his throat. The briefest glimpse of a hard swallow.

"Oh, my God." He *did* kill Dan.

I stand before him, legs numb, chest heavy, heartbroken. Relief doesn't flood me. I don't feel vindicated. Instead, bile churns in a mass production in my stomach because the harsh man I've fallen for isn't harsh at all. He is horrific.

"Why?" I'm still shaking, but now it's not just my head. It's my hands, my arms, my foundations.

I inch closer to the gun. It's right there, three feet to my left.

His gaze drops to the weapon, then returns to my face. "Don't do it."

I need to. I have to. He isn't going to let me walk. Obviously, I am stupid, but not *that* stupid.

He's poised to strike, every muscled inch of him taut and ready.

I lunge to the side, my hands sliding through dirt, my fingers grating over gravel. He dives after me, grips my ankle, and pulls. I scream as he drags me backward, then to my feet, and into his arms.

I'm plastered to him. Back to chest. Ass to crotch.

"I told you not to do that," he growls.

I kick. I scream. I thrash.

His hold tightens and he rushes forward, eating up the space to the car to press me into the cold metal. He smothers me, choking my strength under the heavy weight of memories.

He made me feel safe. He made me feel wanted. He made me *feel*. That is the worst part of all.

"Why?" I demand. "Why did you kill him?"

His breath brushes my neck. He's so close, he's under my skin. "Dan had a habit of finding useful information. But instead of handing it over to my contractor, he kept blackmailing for bigger sums of money. The guy was in a perfect position, hearing whispers from the police through his father. He could've gone far. Instead he got greedy."

"And greed deserves death?" I snarl.

"Greed, and assault, and rape, among other things." The growled words vibrate through my ribs. "I don't feel guilty in the slightest, princess. So don't try that shit on me."

"And what about framing me? Do you feel guilty about that?"

He stills. "I didn't frame you. I've done this enough times to know how to cover my ass. Nobody else has to take the fall."

Again, it isn't what I want to hear. I picture dead bodies at his feet. Innocent faces. Vacant eyes.

He steps back and I remain still, clinging to the car like it holds the answers to my problems. And maybe it does. The ignition fob is in the center console. Starting the engine and getting out of here is a button-click away.

"Look at me," he demands.

No. Not going to happen. I refuse to look into the eyes of a cold-blooded killer and feel attraction. And that's exactly what would happen if I met his gaze. I wouldn't be able to help it. I wouldn't be able to stop it.

"Steph, I need you to listen."

"I'm listening."

He sighs. "I didn't get the information I needed from Dan. I followed you instead, and by the time I went back to the hotel, he was already too fucked up to talk."

"What does that mean?" I stare out at the vacant fields, the miles of space between me and safety.

"I heard you interrogate him. I just didn't get specifics. I now need the information he gave you. And I need to know why you wanted it."

"I didn't get any information." Nothing his merry murderous crew would find useful, anyway.

"Don't lie to me." He grabs my elbow and tugs, making me face him. "He had the details on an informant, and I heard you asking him for a fucking name."

He presses into me, thigh to thigh, hip to hip. His hands land on either side of my head, a threatening stance, if only those eyes weren't slaying me.

I cluck my tongue at him. "That looming thing doesn't work anymore. Last time you did it, I got an orgasm, remember?"

His lips kick, slow and subtle. "You can this time, too. All you need to do is give me the name."

I fight a shudder. Fight and fight and fail. Tingles wrack my body, from collarbone to nipples and stomach. "No. Thanks."

"Come on, Steph. What did he tell you?"

"*Nothing,*" I snap. "I didn't get a damn thing."

This man has already stripped me of too much—my dignity, my strength, my confidence. He won't steal the secrets of my past, too.

"Please." The plea is pained, almost believable. "I'm not joking. They're going to come after you. That man you met earlier—Torian—is a bad guy. Worse than Dan. Worse than me. Worse than any motherfucker you've ever met. But if you talk, I can help you."

I roll my eyes. "So this big, bad motherfucker lets me walk free if I talk?"

"I can protect you."

"Oh, goodie." I release a derisive chuckle. "Is this where I'm supposed to swoon?"

"No. This is where you tell me the fucking truth so both of us walk away from this unscathed."

I chuckle again, and this time it hurts. Pressure

consumes my chest, moving higher, wider, deeper. "Too late," I whisper.

He lets out a heavy breath and leans in to rest the side of his head against mine. I want to fight for space, for freedom, but I can't when everything inside me still aches for proximity.

I need to believe in his torment. That the pain he's wrapping around me in tightening ribbons is real.

"I never meant for this shit to happen between us. I never meant to want you," he admits. "And now we're in a fucking mess, and the only way out is for you to tell me what you know."

"Then trust me when I say whatever information you're after, I didn't get."

"That's for me to decide."

He leans closer, those lips a breath away, his hips pressing harder. The thick length of his erection nestles against my pubic bone, and I freeze in disbelief.

This fucker is horny. And damn it, the thought of his arousal has the same effect on me. My nipples tingle. My pussy tightens.

"Tell me," he whispers against my neck.

His mouth trails my skin, leaving a path of goosebumps in its wake. He's a murderer. A killer. And I still want to kiss him. Taste him. Devour him.

I hate myself for the war waging inside me. The battle between sanity and stupidity. A ragged breath escapes my lips and he leans closer, our mouths almost touching.

"I'll protect you. I can promise that."

I crave the truth of those words, even when he's played me so many times already. I can't help bridging the space between us to sweep my mouth over his in a gentle glide.

He relaxes, all those muscles losing their tension. I don't

want to enjoy this, but I do. The bliss sinks under my skin, flutters my heart, and warms my limbs.

I want more. I want everything.

Stupid. Stupid. Stupid.

I break the connection and pull back, sinking my teeth into my lower lip to stop the tingling throb.

"If I tell you, will you really protect me?" I ask.

"With my life."

I smile through my heartache and raise my hand to his hair. I guide the strands away from his eyes, brush my fingertips along the rough stubble of his jaw, then launch the heel of my palm into his Adam's apple.

He buckles, hunching over in an instant.

I give him a shove to escape the confinement of his body. He coughs, splutters, and swings out an arm, trying to catch me. I slap away his touch and run for the gun, leaning over to scoop it up before twirling back in his direction.

"Move away from the car," I yell.

He clears his throat, chokes, swallows. "Don't do this." His voice is raspy as he shakes his head.

"I'll shoot you if I have to." I flick off the safety and jerk the barrel in an instruction for him to move. "And this time I'll aim higher."

He backs away, the hand at his side balling into a fist as the other holds his throat. He continues to cough, to splutter. "They'll kill you."

"They'll have to find me first."

I'm good at hiding. I can do it a little longer. Then once I finish the unresolved business with Jacob, I'll run, because I'm good at that, too.

I open the driver's side door and slide inside, keeping my gaze on him the entire time.

"Don't be stupid." He hunches, hands on knees, looking

over at me from beneath his lashes. "There's an easier way out of this."

"I appreciate the concern." I close the door, start the ignition, and shove the car into drive. "But I can look after myself."

16

HER

I don't know how I get back to my apartment. The drive is a whirlwind of adrenaline and hysteria until I'm sitting in his idling car in the loading zone in front of my building.

I cut the ignition, leave the key fob in the console, then sprint inside. That asshole deserves to have his car stolen, and so much more.

I enter the building pin code, shove open the door, and skip the elevator to sprint up the stairs two at a time.

Once I'm inside my apartment, I focus on getting back outside as soon as possible. My knife is placed in a leather holster and attached to my bra. A switchblade is inserted into my left boot. Mace goes into the right. My gun is shoved into the pocket I've sewn inside my coat.

I grab the stack of cash from the ice-cream tub in the freezer. Another from the sealed bag in the toilet cistern. Then the last from the hidden panel inside the bedside table bottom drawer.

Anything of value goes into my backpack. My laptop, my money, a change of clothes, and most importantly, the few treasured items from my family that I sifted through burning embers to find. The rest has to stay.

I place anything else I might want later—electronic devices, more weapons—into purple garbage bags and shove them down the disgusting trash chute in the hall. I can only hope they are still in the dumpster when I chance coming back to retrieve them.

I'm not going to hang around and load a damn truck. I don't even give myself five seconds to say goodbye to memories. Hunter isn't messing around, and neither can I.

I haul the pack onto my back and lock the door on my way out. I even grab my portable surveillance camera in the hall to take with me.

I run three blocks, catch the first cab I find, and ask the driver to take me as far away as possible. He cuts across town, and I get him to drive in circles for almost an hour to make sure I'm not being followed before I get out.

The sun starts to set as I walk miles and miles until I find a cheap motel with an easy escape route, pay cash in advance, and ask for a room that backs onto the alley.

The click of the door is deafening as I close myself into my new home. I don't bother to unpack. All I remove from the backpack is the surveillance camera, which I place in the window, the lens pointing outside.

Coiling tendrils of self-loathing wrap around my ankles and hold me in place. Failure threatens to drag me under.

All I can see is Hunter. All I can feel is his presence— his breath on my neck, his hands on my skin.

"Fuck you," I scream. "*Fuck you. Fuck you. Fuck you.*"

Someone bangs on the wall from the next room, and I scream louder. "*Fuck you, too.*"

I drag my feet to the bed and slump onto the mattress. My dress tightens around me like a straitjacket, constricting and choking. I yank at the zipper, drag it down, and throw the material across the room.

Sitting in my underwear doesn't help either because I still feel dirty.

Used.

God, I hate him. I hate his lies. I hate what he stands for. And most of all, I hate that I can't truly hate him at all. My building emotions aren't born of anger. They're weaker than that. I'm consumed with betrayal and pathetic heartbreak.

"Damn it to hell. I'm not this woman." I flop back on the bed. I *can't* be this woman.

Someone this weak and useless won't succeed in gaining revenge on the man who murdered her family. *No*. This woman will get herself killed by distraction. It's a certainty.

I shove a hand through my hair and stare at the ceiling.

At least I'm not a murderer. My conscience is clean in that regard, and yet the relief hasn't arrived. It felt so much better to have killed a man while another warmed my bed than it does now when I'm innocent and alone.

How pitiful is that?

I don't even know myself anymore.

I shake my head, but I'm unable to shake the train of thought.

I crawl up to the pillows and try to ignore how he's made me feel. I still have to get back to my apartment to retrieve the bags in the dumpster. I also have to get rent money to Brent somehow.

For now, though, I need to rest and recharge. I didn't sleep well last night, which is probably why I'm overly emotional.

I roll to my side and close my eyes. On instant replay, all the time I spent with Hunter comes rushing back. His face, his comfort, his promises.

All lies.

Every single breath he took in my presence was fake. And I am no closer to Jacob, either. Everything has turned to shit.

I drift, sleep dragging me under, then spitting me back out, over and over on a continuous loop. I dream about him. His voice murmurs, the words hazy. His mouth presses against mine and his lips curve in a smile while a possessive grip lands on my hip. I moan and clench my thighs.

I want you. God, why do I still want you?

He drifts away, disappearing into darkness.

I dream of my family. Of the past. Of the Samaritan— Decker—and the other threatening man from this morning —Torian. I toss and turn and finally give up hope of ener- gizing rest when the sun begins to pound the back of my lids.

I groan, snuggle the pillow to my chest, and open my eyes.

Bright light beams down on me from the partly opened curtain. I sit up, frown, and narrow my gaze on the surveillance camera now pointed in my direction.

What...the...

I push onto my elbow. There's no way I focused the lens on the bed. I hadn't been *that* tired. I faced it in the other direction. Outside.

I flick back the covers and search for my phone. "Shit." I should've had it right beside me.

A sheet of paper swoops off the mattress, floating through the air with menacing grace as I cease moving. It drifts down to the pillows, laying gently beside me like a threatening plague.

I glance around the room, my senses heightened as I search for anything out of place. There's no movement, no unnatural sound. Nothing nudges my senses, only the camera bearing down on me and the note taunting me.

I reach across to the pillows and retrieve the paper to read the neat script—*Stop messing around and find a better place to hide.* I snap a hand over my mouth to hold in my fear.

He found me. He was in my fucking room.

I scamper from the bed and do another scan of my surroundings, over the television, across the windowsill, my gaze pausing on the door. A steak knife protrudes from the wood, a piece of paper stabbed beneath the blade. I rush toward it and pull the note free.

You're beautiful when you sleep.

My heart kicks, and I hate it. I hate it so much my tummy tumbles.

I crumple the message in my fist and throw it to the floor. I scramble to collect my belongings, the video camera, my phone, my dress. I pull on the only set of clothes I packed—a pair of black workout leggings, a loose top, and an even baggier hoodie.

I don't waste time hanging around. I get out of there and rush to catch the bus pulling to a stop at the end of the block.

"Please drive. Quick," I beg the middle-aged man behind the wheel. "Someone is following me."

The damsel-in-distress gig works most of the time, and now is no exception as the driver hastens to close the door and pull away from the curb.

Three people are on board, all of them watching me from their spaced positions throughout the rows of seats. A teenage girl. An elderly man. A woman in a business suit. I remain in the front of the bus, on a seat parallel with the aisle and close to the door.

I can keep an eye on my surroundings while I pull out

my phone and log into my surveillance account. The damn device has been silenced since the funeral, which means I didn't get a notification when Hunter approached my room around four in the morning. He tested the door handle, then walked out of view.

I fast forward the video until the image tilts, turns, then I'm in the picture, half-naked on the bed. He walks away from the camera, toward me. I don't flinch in my sleep. I don't even stir as he looks down at me, without malice or anger. He stares, watching, waiting, while I lie vulnerable and exposed.

My heart crumples at the longing I see in his expression, even though I know it's not really there. It's a hallucination. A mirage. I glide my finger over the screen, touching what can no longer be truly touched and hate myself for the pathetic gesture.

Why didn't he hurt me? Why didn't he tie me up and demand the information he wants so badly?

He leans in, and I hold my breath as I watch him press his lips to mine.

"Holy shit." It wasn't a dream. He kissed me in my sleep, and I kissed him back.

Why? I don't understand his intent. Am I supposed to believe his actions are some sort of truce? Did he change the camera angle to showcase his incredible acting skills?

He places his notes around the room, not tiptoeing, with casual self-assurance, then he glances at the camera and those eyes meet mine.

Why is he doing this to me? Why am I letting him?

He keeps reeling me in, sinking his hooks into the vulnerable parts I thought I'd strengthened.

"Pull over at the next stop, please," I instruct the driver.

I log out of the feed, delete the app, and place my cell

on the seat as the bus veers to the curb of an unfamiliar street.

"Thank you." I haul my pack onto my back and stand, leaving my phone behind. If Hunter placed a tracker in my cell, he could enjoy the excursion the day would bring, because I have no plans to participate in his game anymore.

I need to feel whole again. Free.

And so I run.

17

HER

I run for months. Well, it's actually only four weeks, but it feels like forever. Every time I crash in a new location, he finds me, and he always leaves a note.

Most of the time his messages are playful—*You're not good at this, are you? I like those pajamas. I'll see you tomorrow.*

And sometimes his words cut to the heart of me—*When this is over, you're mine.*

The dictatorship isn't as offensive as it should be. Nothing about this seems as offensive as it should be. Yet again, I've become a willing participant in his game.

I fall asleep each night with growing anticipation. I wake every morning to heart-pounding excitement. I search for his messages like an attention-starved fool, and each and every time I find one, my stomach soars.

At least it had, until five days ago.

That was when I extended the playing field and fled to a small bed and breakfast in Eagle Creek. He didn't follow. There hasn't been one note. Not a single word.

He's either lost interest, or something or someone made him stop.

"Are you thinking about him again, pet?"

I glance to my right, at Betty, the elderly lady who owns the bed and breakfast. She's kind enough. Smart, too. But her intuition is on-point, which makes the hair on the back of my neck stand on end. If she didn't cook like a master chef and feed me like I'd been homeless all my life, I would've cut and run after my first night.

"I'm not thinking about anyone." I rest my elbows on her porch railing and glance out at the glowing lights of Eagle Creek. It's nice here. Quiet. Which makes it difficult to dodge thoughts of Hunter.

"Have it your way." She moves to stand beside me, taking the same stance—elbows on the railing, her gaze straight ahead staring out into the night. "You've lost your hope, though. I can see it in your eyes."

Damn woman can't even see my eyes at the moment. It's dark out, and I'm not looking in her direction. Still, she's right.

What if Hunter has grown tired of playing?

The answer shouldn't matter. I shouldn't even ponder the question. Only I do. On repeat. All day. All night.

"Who needs hope when I can smell blueberry pie?" I shoot her a glance and raise a brow. "Hmm? You're going to feed me again, aren't you?"

She chuckles, her face gaining a mass of enviable laugh lines. This woman has experienced a lot of joy. Every single one of those wrinkles is a testament to her happiness. "I certainly will... If you promise to try to find that hope you showed up here with."

I sigh and turn back to the night. "It wasn't hope. It was a game." A silly challenge I spent too many nights playing.

"I know hope when I see it, and yours wasn't the type to

revolve around a career or family. It was the type of love-filled hope that can only be inspired by a man."

Love?

Now *that* is a word capable of slamming the brakes on any conversation, as far as I'm concerned. "Did you get lost in the liquor cabinet again?"

She snickers. "Maybe. But I'm right, aren't I?"

"My life is too complicated for love. Or hope, for that matter." In my chest, there is a void where both emotions should be. An abyss. "It's just not for me."

"With that attitude, I'm sure you're right." She pats my shoulder with a gentle hand. "Now, how about that pie?"

"Yes, please." I'll agree to anything that will get her meddling insight out of my life. "Want me to make the green tea?"

"No, I've got it." She starts for the front door, the aged wooden planks creaking under her steps.

This place feels like a home. The constant delicious scent of food, the warmth, the conversation, and the inbuilt security of a German shepherd guard dog in the back yard and the tiny yap-yap Maltese inside. I didn't even bother setting up my camera here. Nothing could escape the attention of the canines.

It would be a great place for me to stay a while. To find that clarity and focus I need. But no matter how homey it is, I can't shake the uncomfortable feeling that I need to be somewhere else.

I *want* to be somewhere else.

I'm sure it's as simple as missing my apartment. And not having Brent nearby in case I get smothered with loneliness. I owe him rent money, too, which I really need to resolve. I never even got back to my apartment to fetch my belongings from the trash.

Or maybe I have to stop kidding myself and admit I'm

growing insane without an update on Hunter. I need answers, and I want the good night's sleep I'll finally get once I have them.

I don't know if he's lying in wait, about to strike. I don't know if he's hurt or if he found someone else to play with. I don't know if Torian gave up on my so-called information.

"Betty." I walk after her and pull open the front door. "Do you mind if I use your phone?"

Brent will know something.

Maybe Hunter is still hanging around at the bar or scoping out my apartment.

"Are you calling that man of yours?" She raises her voice from the kitchen down the long hall.

"Of course. You know I always listen to your advice and jump to respond."

"You're a horrible liar."

No, I'm not. At least not when I want to be.

"Go ahead and use it," she calls "Just throw a few dollars in the jar on the table if it's long distance."

"Thank you." I stride for the small wooden stand beside the staircase leading to the second floor. The corded phone sits crowded among pens, paper, the money jar, car keys, receipts, and mail. It's the only place in this house that isn't immaculate.

I dial Brent's number from memory and lean against the banister while I wait. When the call connects, I straighten and stare down at the one-stop dumping ground of knick-knacks as I picture his face.

"Atomic Buzz," Brent mutters.

My stomach tumbles at the sound of his voice. "Hey. It's Steph. How are you?"

The lengthening silence makes me wince. I can't blame him for not speaking to me. I've been a selfish bitch who only thinks of herself.

"I'm sorry," I whisper. "I know I left without a word, and that I'm late with rent money." He doesn't have a generous bank account like I do. And still, he's never been anything but generous to me. "I shouldn't have checked out without telling you. But I'm going to try to get back there to fix you up for what I owe. I just—"

"No. Don't." He cuts me off. "Forget it. I don't need it."

My chest squeezes. We both know he's lying.

"Please, Brent. I know I should've called sooner. I had to get out of town real quick. I didn't mean to fuck you over."

"Like I said, forget it," he growls at me. My only friend. My only connection to kindness and support.

"I get that you're angry. I deserve it. And I don't expect you to forgive me. But I'll travel back into Portland tonight." I'd have to find a ride available in the early hours of the morning for safety's sake. I can't go back now. It's only a little past ten, and people would be out and about. But I can return to Portland to make the delivery. No problem. "I'll get there after you close and slip the money under the door."

"I said *don't*." His tone is gruff. "I don't want to see you here again. Do you understand? Don't—"

His words are lost to rustling over the line. I hear a grunt. A muttered curse. Then more rustling.

"Brent?" I lower my gaze to the thick maroon carpet and stare blankly as I focus on sound. "*Brent?*"

"Forget what he said, pumpkin," another voice croons in my ear. A voice I can't pinpoint. It isn't one of the bar regulars. It isn't Hunter. It's someone else.

"Who is this?" I demand. "Put Brent back on the phone."

"Your bartender friend is unavailable right now. I think it's best if you come here and speak to him in person."

I swallow over the throb building behind my sternum. Someone is threatening Brent to get to me, and the stupid son-of-a-bitch tried to protect me. Save me.

"Are we clear?" the man asks. "Get back here now. No weapons. No cops. You've got an hour."

The call disconnects, leaving me with nothing but white noise and building panic. I drop my arm to my side, and the receiver slips from my fingertips to fall to the floor.

Is this Torian's doing? Or someone else?

I focus on the mess scattered across the small table. The pens. The receipts. The car keys. I have to get to Atomic Buzz, and I can't wait for a driver.

I shoot a glance down the empty hall, toward the sound of clattering plates and the clink of cutlery. I have to leave. Right now. I can't go upstairs for my few belongings. I can't say goodbye. The knife attached to my bra will have to be my only protection, because I don't want to ponder the danger it will put Brent in if I bring a gun.

I place my hand over the BMW car keys and clench my fingers around them.

Then I walk from the house and don't look back. Not even when the dogs start barking announcing their intuition of my betrayal.

The shiny black sedan is parked in the carport, the moonlight reflecting off the dark surface. I click the lock release, slide inside, and reverse out of the driveway, like stealing a car comes naturally to me. But it doesn't.

Remorse eats away at my chest. My lungs ache. I can picture the joy in Betty's features evaporating. The woman who provided me with a safe haven is now being punished.

"Goddamn it."

I drive to Portland, the miles passing as I break every speed limit. I reach my street and drive past the bar. It's almost eleven, well within open hours, but the lights are out and the closed sign hangs on the front door.

I continue forward, pretending someone's life isn't resting in the palm of my hands, and turn down a nearby side street. I flick off the headlights, inch into the darkness of a suburban driveway, and park behind a family wagon.

Whoever lives here will wake up to find Betty's BMW. They will have to report the incident, and get the car towed to be able to move their own vehicle.

The plan isn't foolproof, but it's the best I can come up with to get Betty's car back to her safe and sound, and as soon as possible.

I get out, lock the car, and creep toward for the street. I walk a block and a half until I reach the alley that leads to the back door of Atomic Buzz.

I don't have a plan. I don't even have confidence. All I have is the necessity to help someone who always helped me. Brent offered me his apartment years ago, when he had planned to move in there himself. He shared his life with me, when I never even told him my name. He gave me patience and generosity. He gave me friendship and solace.

It's time to repay the favor.

I inch across the back wall of the businesses along the alley and blend into the shadows. I take cautious steps, walking on the tips of my sneakers. I watch for litter and glass, making sure I don't make any sound when the crunch of a distant footfall comes from the street I just walked out of.

I slink deeper into the darkness and don't move. Another step approaches and another, becoming faster, harder. I shoot a glance over my shoulder to find a man running toward me, tall and broad, dressed in black with a baseball cap pulled low to cover his face.

Fuck.

I don't think. I sprint.

I make it ten steps before he hauls me off the ground by an arm around my waist while a hand slams across my mouth to cut off my scream.

"Shh," he whispers. "It's me."

His hard body presses into me. I recognize the scent, I remember the warmth, and for a second I feel safe.

My traitorous body relaxes, and Hunter removes his hand, tugging me toward the wall of the building. My chest hums at the reunion. I'm stupidly relieved to see him. Happiness wouldn't even be a stretch.

"What are you doing here?" I cling to the little hope that comes with his familiar face.

"I heard what was going on."

"And you're here to what? Thwart my efforts or help?"

He tugs me toward the opening to the alley, the street-lights exposing me to anyone who may be in the area.

"There's no helping this situation," he whispers. "If you go in there, they'll kill you."

"Who's they?"

"Torian and his men."

"Aren't you one of his men?" I ask.

"I'm a contractor. Big difference. He wants the information—"

"Then I'll tell him to his face that I don't have the name he needs."

"And he'll tear you limb from limb until you change your mind or die in the process."

My pulse pounds erratically in my throat. "Why is that your concern?" He gave up on me days ago. He cut and run.

"Quit the shit, Sarah. This thing between us isn't over."

Sarah.

He knows my name. My real name. The one I haven't uttered in years.

I release a silent breath of a chuckle, because if I don't, I'll crumple.

"It took a while, princess." He reaches for my hair, stroking the stray strands from my cheek. "But I finally figured you out."

I jerk away, unwilling to succumb to his allure even though that's all I've wanted to do for the past few weeks. "You're lucky, because I still know nothing about you."

"All you need to know right now is that I'm here to help. I'm going to get you out of here."

I frown. "What about Brent? How will you get him out?"

His lips press tight, and it's all the answer I need.

"No." I step back, toward Atomic Buzz. "I'm not leaving him."

"He's as good as dead, and you know it."

His comment slaps me across the face. Hard. I keep moving, hoping to distance myself from his words. From everything. I refuse to believe there's no way out. "I won't lose him, too."

"Shh." He follows, gripping me around the waist in a one-armed grab. "He's already gone."

"They gave me an hour," I argue. "I've still got time."

"To do what? Beg? Plead? They're not going to give a shit when you don't have the informant's name."

I keep shaking my head. I won't believe him. I refuse. "Then I go down with him." I couldn't die with my family, but maybe this is an honorable alternative because I sure as hell won't let another person die because of my decisions.

"Like hell," he growls, all protective and animalistic. He wants to help; that much is clear. I just need to convince him to do it my way.

"Please, Hunter." I grab his jacket, curling my fingers in the leather. "Help me."

His brows pull tight, and I see the conflict he tries to battle.

"*Please.*" I clutch tighter. "I'll do anything."

He lifts his chin as if accepting my terms and steps back to retrieve a phone from his jeans pocket. "Let me send a message to Decker and see if he can get his ass here."

Decker—the guy from the highway. I don't trust him. Then again, I don't have the luxury of trust at the moment.

"Okay." I nod, my hope building.

He presses buttons, then places his phone in his jacket and meets my eyes with a sad smile. "I guess we have to wait and—"

A bang splits the air. A pungent, ear-splitting gunshot that travels from the vicinity of Atomic Buzz.

I suck in a breath, but the air doesn't penetrate. I can't breathe. I gasp, trying to cling to positive thoughts, which flitter away in the chilled night air.

"We need to get out of here." Hunter steals my hand and pulls.

I hear him, yet the words don't sink in. They're distant. Faded. Everything is a mile away while I stand here in solitude, bathed in sorrow and drowning in guilt.

"Sarah." Hunter gets in my face and clutches my arms. "Look at me."

He's there, *right there,* and still, I can't focus. All I can see is Brent. Dead. Because of me. Because of what I've done.

"I n-need to get in there." I move to walk around him, only to have his hands grip tight.

"It's too late."

"No." I push at his chest. "He might not be dead. He could be hurt. We have to call the police... An ambulance."

He gives me a shake. "*It's too late.*"

I waiver like a rag doll in his grip. I can see the truth in his black eyes. I can see the pain and brutal honesty of what has happened.

"No," I whisper. Then louder with a thump against his chest. "*No.*"

His eyes widen and he spins me, hauling my body against his to drag me backward down the alley. I can't protest, not in movements, only in words. "*No. No. No.*"

He claps a hand over my mouth, holding me tighter. I tremble, my limbs shaking violently as shock takes over.

"I'm sorry," he whispers. "But we can't stay here."

Why not? My life no longer has value. All I do is hurt people. And although I may not have been responsible for Dan's death, Brent's blood is on my hands.

"Why?" I plead. "Why would they do this?"

"It doesn't matter right now." He speaks softly in my ear, in full control even though destruction follows our every step.

He takes me from the alley, where I finally find my feet, then holds my hand as I jog beside him. I'm not thinking. I can't. Otherwise, I'd be moving in the opposite direction. Toward Brent. Toward help. We go around a corner, onto the street I used to walk down to get my groceries, and he stops beside a car I've never seen before.

"Tell me you won't run back to the bar."

I meet his eyes, those deep, penetrating eyes that now hold a wealth of sympathy.

I shake my head. "I shouldn't leave him."

"He's already gone. You know that as well as I do." He implores me with a look filled with so much conviction I want to fall to my knees and sob. But I won't. I don't cry anymore. I haven't in ten years.

"Let me get you in the car." He slides a hand around my waist, as if I might fall, and leans to the side to open the passenger door. "Quick. The cops will be here any minute."

He guides me forward, into the seat, and fastens my belt in place. "Promise me you won't take off as soon as I leave your side."

I stare at nothingness while he hovers, unmoving.

"Where would I go?" I murmur. "I have nowhere left to run."

And no will to do it either.

18

HER

Hunter closes me in the car, rounds the hood, and then slides into his seat. He's gunning the engine in seconds, speeding through streets I can't bring into focus.

"It's going to be okay." He breaks the silence. "I'll make sure it is."

I hear guilt in his voice. The same strangling guilt that tightens around my throat.

"How did he know?" I ask, my gaze straying from one passing streetlight to the next. How would anyone know of my friendship with Brent? I rarely went to Atomic Buzz. I shared a few drinks once or twice a month. I paid rent in cash. Nobody knew how much that man meant to me, not even the man himself.

"Torian?" Hunter asks. "It wouldn't have taken much. Especially not when you borrowed Brent's car to go to Seattle."

"That's how you worked out my name, isn't it?" I drag my attention from the road and face him. "You followed me?" To Seattle. To my childhood home. To the cemetery.

"Yes."

One word. No elaboration.

I nod, no longer shocked by the depth of his betrayal. "Were you the asshole who ran me off the road?"

"No." He hits me with a two-second scowl, then returns his focus to the road. "I'm the asshole who showed that piece-of-shit a thing or two about manners."

"You killed him?" I can't find the will to care. I'm devoid of emotion. Completely lacking concern.

He remains quiet, shielding me from the truth.

"Hunter?"

"No, I didn't," he growls. "I could've. I should've. I even promised I would. But then I remembered how you reacted to Dan's death, and I didn't think you'd appreciate me taking a guy's life, despite what he did. I only inflicted the pain and threats necessary to make sure he wouldn't give Torian any valid information about you."

I frown, my brain taking too long to process any coherent thoughts. "Am I supposed to be flattered? Should I say thank you?"

He releases a derisive laugh. "No. Don't thank me, princess. I fucked him up enough to make him wish he was six feet under."

My chest loosens. Why?

I refuse to be charmed by his brutality. I won't be seduced by violence. And yet a part of me is comforted by the thought of his protective savagery.

I'm so irrational right now it's scary.

I glare and return my attention to the road, letting the hollow ache sink back in. He drives onto the highway, takes a familiar off-ramp, and then onto a desolate street.

"Where are we going?" I rest the side of my head against the glass. "Is this another ploy to get me away from civilization so you can kill me?"

"Yeah." He nods. "I trail you for weeks to make sure

you're safe, save your ass from getting killed, only to slit your throat on a back road in the middle of nowhere."

"Smarter men have done stupider things."

He sighs. "I'm not going to hurt you, Sarah."

"Anymore, you mean?" The taunt slips from my lips without permission.

"Yeah," he murmurs. "Not anymore." The promise is barely spoken, yet filled with solemn conviction. I believe him. At least, I want to. I *need* to.

I have nobody. Nothing. And God, I'm beginning to hate it.

My immediate family is dead. My extended family are so distant they wouldn't even recognize me after all these years. My one friend has just been murdered. And tonight, I stole a car from the only other person who has acknowledged my pathetic existence.

"Why did you stop chasing me?" I ask, exacerbating my pitiful situation.

The car slows as he looks me in the eye. "You don't know? I thought you must have figured it out."

"No. Why would you think that? I've had no clue this entire time. I always used cash. I don't know how many times I got a new phone, only to throw it away days later. But you always found me. At least until I went to Eagle Creek."

"Because you stopped using your video surveillance." He turns his attention back to the road. "Without the feed, I had no idea where to look."

My mouth gapes. "You hacked my feed?"

How the hell did he do that? *When* did he do that?

He glances at me, and his lips kick at one side.

"You think this is funny?" I accuse.

He smirks. "No, I'm thinking that I'd love to slam my mouth against yours to taste your shock."

My heart stops, drops, and rolls. I'm burning. Blazing.

"Decker gained access to your account not long after we first met. It gave me the ability to track whenever you left your apartment."

"But…"

"You always stayed in cheap hotels with a window that faced the road. Without fail, you would point the camera at something Decker and I could search online. Either a road sign, a business name, or a landmark. You made it easy."

Until I moved into a bed and breakfast and started relying on Betty's dogs for security instead of my camera. "I thought you'd given up on playing games. I didn't think I'd see you again."

"No." He shakes his head. "I hadn't given up."

If my stomach wasn't currently in a battle with grief and attraction, I'd slowly devour the delicious bowl of his determination.

He flicks the car lights to high-beam, illuminating a stretch of road I recognize.

"Is this…"

"The place you shot at me?" he taunts. "Yeah."

"Why are we back out here?"

He slows, approaching a dirt drive with a dilapidated wooden mailbox to the side, the faded number thirteen partially covered by overgrown shrubs.

"Who lives here?"

"I do. This is where I wanted to take you the day of the funeral."

"Why?" Surely, taking me to his house will expose vulnerabilities for a man with his profession. How does he trust me so easily? Or is this knowledge a bigger vulnerability for me? "Do you plan on keeping me here?"

"Keeping you?" He scoffs. "Can you stop assuming the worst for a second and focus on what you already know?"

"Which is?" I scan the front yard, with its imposing trees covering the ground in a canopy of black.

"I was supposed to hurt you, okay? But I didn't. I should've, and I chose not to. After wasting weeks sidestepping my contract, I'm not going to change my mind now."

"That's comforting," I drawl.

A house comes into view, the roof bathed in moonlight, along with the front porch that gives a slight hint to the wall of windows behind.

It looks nice. Modern and tidy, with no garden, only manicured lawns and sensor lights that flick on and temporarily blind me.

"Shit." I squint through my adjusting vision while he pulls into the garage.

The car turns off, and I sit, waiting for answers to questions that multiply. Why did he bring me here? Why did he save me tonight? What happens next? And the most poignant of all—"Why did all this happen, Hunter?" My voice is soft as I stare at his vacant garage wall. "Why didn't you ask me for information on day one? Why didn't you force it from me?" I turn to face him. "You're this cold-blooded killer who doesn't care about hurting people, so why didn't you use that against me?"

He focuses straight ahead, not meeting my gaze. "I don't know."

"Bullshit," I whisper. "You have an agenda. I know you do. I'm just not sure what it is."

"Come inside and I'll explain." He unfastens his belt and opens the driver's side door.

"Why? Why can't you do it here?"

"Because we both need a drink to settle the adrenaline." He slides from the seat and closes the door behind him. He walks around the hood, opens my door, and holds out a hand. "Come on. I'll tell you everything. Whatever you want to hear."

"Whatever I want to hear?" I raise a brow and swing my body around to face him. "Or the actual truth?"

"The truth. Okay?" He implores me with beseeching eyes, kicking me in the girlie parts with the thinly veiled emotion in his words. "I'm not going to lie to you again."

I tilt my head in scrutiny and my tongue sneaks out to moisten my dried lower lip. He watches the movement, his focus turning predatory in a snap. I can't resist that shit.

Why the hell can't I resist that shit?

"I'll follow you inside once you admit that Hunter isn't your real name."

"That's it?" He chuckles. "That's what you want to know first?"

I nod. It's a start.

"Okay. You got me. Hunter's not my real name."

"What is it?"

He hitches a thumb over my shoulder, pointing toward the door. "Follow me inside and I'll tell you."

"No." I glower. "Your name first."

He crouches between my bent legs, places his hands on my knees, and peers up at me. "It's Luke."

He could easily lie. I wouldn't know any different. But I believe him. I swear to God he's telling me the truth.

"You're not lying."

"No, I'm not, but nobody else around these parts knows my name. Not Decker. Not Torian. I'd like to keep it that way. Okay?"

"Then why tell me?" Why bring me here? Why do any of this?

"Because I want there to be trust between us."

I frown, not appreciating the momentary dip in my pulse. "I don't want to trust you."

"And I don't blame you for that."

His honesty is seductive. I guess seeing a major change in a man will have that affect. Or maybe it's like he said—I need to settle the adrenaline.

I scoot closer, his palms hitching higher up my thighs. My chest pounds with the need for comfort. My lips tingle at the thought of his kiss.

"I'm ready to go inside now," I whisper.

He nods and pushes to his feet, offering me a hand. I place my fingers against his and wince at how good it feels. There's strength in our connection. It doesn't make sense. But it's there. Buzzing. Tingling.

He leads me to the door, down the dark hall, then stops to flick on a light. A massive living area is exposed. Sofas, a dining table, a large television, and a sparkling kitchen. It's clean, stylish, and uncharacteristically homely.

I release his hand and take a few steps ahead, letting it all sink in. "Your home is nice."

"You sound surprised." He walks by me, into the kitchen to pull open one of the glossy white cupboards.

"I'm not familiar with the murderer stereotype. I guess I didn't expect it to be so..."

"Normal?" He grabs two scotch glasses and places them on the island counter. "I don't fit a stereotype, Sarah. And I'm not the horrible person you think I am. Not entirely, anyway."

I hope that's true. In fact, I'm banking on it.

"What do you want to drink?" He moves to a high cupboard above the stainless-steel, double-door fridge. "Scotch? Gin? I think I've got some vodka in here some-where, too."

"No, thanks. The last thing I need is alcohol."

He frowns at me over his shoulder. "How about coffee?"

"Caffeine isn't a good idea either. I'm fine, really."

He grabs a bottle of scotch and returns to the island bench.

My grief returns, not only for Brent, but for myself. This murderous, manipulative man has a comforting, tidy home to return to. He has his shit together. He functions better than I do.

It isn't fair.

Nothing in this world is fair.

"I don't know what to do for you." His admission cuts me to the core. "Tell me what you need."

"I don't need anything," I lie. The reality is, I need everything. Anything. Something.

He places the bottle down on the counter and walks toward me. My heartrate increases with every step. I don't want him close. But I also want it so bad it hurts, ripping and slicing me to shreds from the inside out.

He stops in front of me, and I fight the need to touch him. To reach out and steal his strength. He raises a hand, his fingers drifting close.

"Please don't," I plead.

That hand descends, my heart falling along with it.

"Is that a directive for tonight?" he asks. "Or forever?"

"Forever would be the smart answer," I admit.

"But it's not what you want." This time he raises his hand and doesn't stop until those fingers are tangling in the loose strands that have fallen from my ponytail.

I turn my head away and his touch moves to my cheek, my jaw. He burns a trail along my skin, devastating my senses.

"He's all I had." I face him, his sympathy sinking its teeth into my ribs.

"You've got me."

"The man who kills for a living." I release a derisive laugh. "You know, I've actively tried to take down people like you." And yet I can't step away. Not even an inch. "You have no respect for life."

"That's not true."

"How can you say that with a straight face?"

His jaw hardens, and his nostrils flare. "Don't judge me until you know me." He stalks back to the kitchen, pouring himself a generous glass of scotch.

"Then tell me." I follow, slower, more cautious. "Have I got this murderous thing all wrong? Was Dan the only man you killed?"

He raises the glass, drinks the contents in three heavy swallows, then slams it down on the counter. He glares and pours himself another.

"Well?" I ask.

"He wasn't the first," he snarls. "And he won't be the last." He raises the glass again, this time staring at me over the rim as he takes a sip. "And what about you, princess? How innocent are you? I saw what you did to Dan. And what do you have planned for Jacob? I can't imagine you want to catch up on the good ol' days."

Of course he knows about Jacob. How can I still be surprised?

"Dan abused women habitually, and Jacob killed my family. Neither one of them is innocent."

He lets out a harsh laugh, then raises his brows and his glass, as if in toast. "Well, at least we have the same work ethic."

"Are you trying to tell me you've never hurt anyone innocent?"

His jaw ticks. "That's exactly what I'm saying. I may have killed a lot of people, but none of them were good."

"What about children?"

"Jesus Christ." He smacks the glass down and runs a

hand through his hair. "I've never killed a fucking kid. I never will."

"Women?" I ask.

His chin lifts, almost imperceptibly, and he scowls at me. "One. Indirectly."

"How indirectly?" My pulse thunders in my throat as I wait for a reply.

A myriad of emotions flicker across his features—annoyance, regret, determination. "I killed her husband. A week later, she killed herself." He takes another sip, watching me. "Is there anything else you want to know?"

Yes. Everything.

"For now, I've just got one more question." I swallow. "Why did you save me tonight?"

19

HIM

I CAN'T LIE TO HER ANYMORE. I'M DONE PLAYING games. "I was there tonight because I needed to see you. I had to make sure you were all right."

Her gaze rakes over me, probably trying to weigh the truth against the fabrication. Her attention is like a touch— A slight sweep of gentle fingertips against my skin.

This is what I've missed, the addictive sensation that follows wherever she goes. Her scrutiny is like a drug. Without it, my insides scream and claw, begging to be sated.

"But you had no intention of saving Brent."

I stare her down, determined not to lie. "My first concern was your safety."

"Did you even message Decker to ask for help?"

"Yes." It was the truth. Kind of.

"And you left him to show up to an ambush?"

"No. I messaged him after I got you in the car." Again, truth. "A rental, I might add, seeing as though mine was stolen and stripped. Thank you very much."

Her lips kick at one side, but the satisfaction doesn't

reach her eyes. It touches my dick, though, makes it fucking throb.

She lowers her gaze and stares at the kitchen counter. "So, that's it?" She shrugs. "You just wanted to start the cat-and-mouse chase all over again?"

"No. We're not doing that anymore. You need to stay with me until things die down."

She turns her back and faces the room. "And when do you think that will happen?"

My preference? Never. But the time for the finer intricacies of the truth will come later. "I don't know. Maybe a few months."

She doesn't respond with a sharp quip like I expect. Instead, she remains silent, her arms moving to wrap around her waist.

"Will you stay?" I round the island counter, edging closer. She's turned me into a needy little bitch, and I hate it. I hate every fucking minute of it, and still, I can't ditch the hold she has on me.

"I've got nowhere else to go," she murmurs. "The police will be looking for me by now."

"Because of Brent?" She doesn't need to worry about that.

"That..." She nods. "And the car I stole in an effort to get to the bar in a hurry."

I raise my brows, impressed. "Did anyone see you?"

"No, but it's obvious. I stole it from the B&B owner where I was staying. One minute I asked to use her phone, the next I was walking out her front door with her car keys in my hand."

Her tone is full of regret, making remorse punch me in the gut. I stride for her, eating up the distance between us so I can place my hands on her waist.

She doesn't flinch, doesn't protest. She lets me touch her, and fuck, am I thankful.

"What did you do with the car?"

"I parked it in someone's driveway. I thought maybe the person who lives there would call the cops in the morning."

"That's good," I whisper into her hair. "No harm. No foul. Right?"

She releases a barely audible scoff. "Yeah. Maybe. But I took off without packing my things. I left everything there. The few clothes I had. My purse."

Shit. "Your I.D?"

"No. I don't carry it. Only cash. I placed a few valuables and some money in a locked box a week ago, but apart from that..." She sighs, her shoulders falling. "I literally have nothing."

I rest my forehead into her hair and breathe her deep. The scent of flowers and candy slaughters me. "Can I show you something?"

"Why not?" She releases a heavy breath. "It's not like I'm going anywhere."

I slide my palm over her wrist and lower it to entwine our fingers. "It's down the other end of the house."

She stares where our hands meet, and I wait for a protest to the connection.

"Okay." She nods and meets my gaze.

I could fuck her right here. On the floor. Clothes on. Face pale. Eyes filled with sorrow. I fucking could. But would I regret it?

I doubt it.

She wants this as much as I do. Needs it.

Instead of succumbing, I start for the opposite side of the room, toward the far hall. She keeps her hand against mine, warm and gently clasping, until I stop before a closed door.

"Go on." I jerk my chin. "Open it."

She frowns as she releases my hand and steps forward to grip the handle. I can't hear her breathe. I can't hear anything but lust and anticipation rushing through my ears.

She twists the handle and inches into the bedroom, her gaze scanning the furniture—her bed, drawers, mirror, and television.

"You emptied my apartment," she whispers.

"I thought I owed you that much. Otherwise Torian would've sent someone to ransack it." There is a slip of truth in there somewhere.

"Did you go through my stuff?"

"Yeah." I don't even pause. That won't be the worst admission she hears from me tonight.

"Everything?" She shoots me a glower over her shoulder.

"From the kitchen cupboards, to your bathroom supplies, and all those pretty pieces of lingerie that turned my dick to stone." I smirk, without an ounce of remorse. "There's a black leather item in there somewhere that I wouldn't mind seeing again."

There had also been other things she wouldn't have wanted me to snoop through. Not just the sex toys, but the information. I'd found her hidden box of articles on Jacob after walking over the only creaking floorboard in her entire apartment.

I'd read every word in my car as she slept in cheap hotels. There were details on her, too. Snippets of her life the Seattle newspaper had catalogued after her family died. There were details on the sale of her childhood home and her bank accounts. I know it all. At least everything that has been written down on paper.

She kicks off her sneakers, pads to the far side of the

bed, and pulls a pillow to her chest as she stands looking down at the mattress.

"It still smells like you," I murmur.

She shoots me an are-you-fucking-kidding look with one hike of her brow. "Smells a little like you, too."

I shrug. "I may have slept in here a time or two since you skipped town."

Her eyes narrow. "Liar."

"No lies here. I told you I missed you."

A flash of surprise passes across her features before she turns her back and slumps onto the bed.

"You don't believe me?" I start toward her, my steps slow.

"I don't know what to believe anymore." She buries her head in the pillow.

The need to bare my soul drags me forward. "I'm never going to lie to you again." It isn't a vain attempt to make her happy. It's a promise. A vow.

I had cause to lie before. Now my objective is keeping her here, and I know that will only happen if I give her the truth. The full truth.

She raises her face, and those pleading eyes are glazed, but she doesn't cry. Not one tear escapes. She's strong. Too fucking strong.

"There's something else I need to tell you, though." I force the words out, knowing this quiet moment will be over once I confess.

She blinks up at me and swallows. "I'm not going to like it, am I?"

"No, you're not."

She nods and lowers her attention to the floor. "Then don't tell me. Not yet. I need time to regroup or I'm going to break."

My chest hollows. I wasn't expecting to be denied. The

reprieve is too damn good to be true. Any additional minute with her at my mercy is a blessing. A fucking gift. "You won't break."

She lets out a derisive laugh. "I'm glad you're confident."

I grab the pillow clutched in her arms and tug until she lets it go. Her hands fall to the mattress as I move forward bringing us toe to toe, her knees to mine.

"I won't let you break," I pledge, grasping her chin to drag her attention back to me.

Her eyes are bleak, the grief ebbing off her in a continuous onslaught. All I want to do is pull her into me and fuck some life back into her. To make everything better.

She stares, barely blinking, barely breathing.

I see my future in those eyes. In this woman. It's fucking crazy and unwanted, but it's there. It's been there from the first night she fucked me over and threw my gun out a third-story window, to right now, when I'd give anything to see her smile.

I can't stop thinking about her. I won't.

"Do you hear me?" I drag my thumb along her lower lip. "I won't let you break."

"You must be one tough guy to stop that from happening." She reaches out, her fingers latching onto my waistband. Her gaze turns determined, seductive, and it takes all my strength not to slam my mouth over hers.

"I can be whatever you need me to be."

She grabs my belt and yanks at the clasp. She's looking for something to take her mind off Brent, and my dick is enthusiastic to run interference.

I'm hard already. Crazy with rapidly building lust. I want to taste her pain, her anguish. I want to be there with her, letting it drag us both under instead of me watching from the sidelines.

She lowers my zipper and tugs my waistband down over my ass.

"You sure you want to do this?" Once this starts, I'll have no will to stop.

"Are you really asking me that?"

"Yeah, I'm fucking asking, and once I get an affirmation there's no turning back."

She yanks my jeans lower. My boxer briefs, too. My cock stands between us, pulsing as she licks her lower lip. She pulls and tugs until my jeans are at my knees, then places her hands on my thighs. I hold my breath as she leans in, her greedy little tongue snaking out to taste the tip of my cock.

Fuck.

I groan. That simple touch...that brief brush of connection... Damn her. She's killing me.

I grab a fistful of her hair and she moans, her eyes rolling as I tug her head back. I pull until her chin lifts, and her attention is all mine.

"Are you fucking sure you want to do this?" I snarl through my weakening restraint.

"Yes," she whispers. "I'm sure."

I tighten my grip, and her chin ascends. "I'll make you feel good," I promise.

"I don't want to feel good. All I need is a distraction, and that's what you've been every day since you walked into Atomic Buzz all those weeks ago."

"A distraction?" I wrap her hair around my knuckles and yank.

She gasps, and it's the sexiest sound I've ever heard.

"I'll take pleasure in distracting the fuck out of you, princess." I shove my fist forward, pushing her head toward my cock. She smirks up at me, but the emotion doesn't reach her eyes. She's still hollow. Still grief-stricken.

"What's your favorite type of distraction?" I hold her a lip-lick away from my shaft. "Oral? Anal? Or will my dick make that sweet pussy its bitch?"

"All of the above."

Fuck. I won't last. I'm already wound tight, my balls throbbing, my dick pulsing.

Her tongue stretches out, gently gliding along my shaft from base to tip in a swipe of devilish torture.

I release her hair and bend down to grip her thighs. I tip her onto her back, yanking the tight leggings down her incredible legs. Her panties are already wet, the crotch bathed in her arousal. She smells like a feast. One I'm ready to devour.

I tug the pants off, then her underwear, and fall to my knees, leaving her in the gray woolen sweater that is far too cute for the dirty things I want to do to her.

With rough hands, I shove her knees apart and slide my hands under her ass to bring her to the edge of the mattress. She glistens, the puffy pink flesh of her cunt ready and waiting.

I sink my head between her thighs, my tongue leading the way to her pussy. The first lick straight down her slit has us both moaning. I do it again and again, making her writhe, sending me insane.

"More," she demands.

I pull back and remove one hand from under her ass. I swirl my thumb through her slickness, sink it deep inside. I do it again and again until my digit is drenched, then I let my tongue take its place.

I torment that greedy little cunt, while I move my thumb to her ass to swirl the lubrication over the puckered hole.

She groans, wiggles, squirms while my dick seeps with pre-cum. I press harder, breeching her ass to sink my digit inside. She jolts and shoves her hands into my hair to hold my head in place, demanding more.

Normally, I'd smirk at a woman this eager, but I'm right there with her. *No*, I'm surpassing her. The need to sink my dick inside her heat makes me fucking mindless.

I clench my free hand around the flesh of her butt. My thumb pumps her ass, while my tongue laps up a treat. I'm on the edge, and the briefest lapse in concentration will have me blowing against the side of the bed.

"Fuck me," she cries. "Hurry up and fuck me."

She rocks her hips like a sexual goddess as I move my mouth to her clit and rub against it with my lower lip. I watch her, wanting to deny her just for a little while as I enjoy the erotic display.

I've never seen a sexier woman. I never will again. With her top half entirely covered, she's still a fantasy brought to life.

"Fuck. Me. Luke."

Jesus fucking Christ.

I dump her on the mattress and shove to my feet, prepared to punish her for using my real name.

"Don't say that again," I warn. Not because I don't want her to, because I can't risk anyone finding out if she grows used to saying it.

"Sorry." She grins and leans up on her elbows. "*Luke*."

I grasp her knees and lift, sending her toppling backward as I position her drenched pussy right in front of my cock.

She holds my gaze, her chest heaving, her breathing ragged. I impale her, sinking deep, shoving so fucking hard I feel the pleasure all the way to my bones.

She clenches the quilt and gasps. "Oh my God."

I pound into her. Over and over. I have to close my

damn eyes because the sight before me is pure nirvana. But she's there, too, taunting me from behind closed lids.

I slide my hands along to her ass, lifting, arching her back higher, digging my fingers deep. Her scent is in my lungs, her taste is on my lips, and that perfect pussy is seconds from milking me dry.

"You're going to make me come," she pants.

I open my eyes, unable to deny myself. "Say my name," I demand.

"I thought you didn't want—"

"*Say my fucking name*."

I slam into her, over and over and over. Harder and harder and harder. She moans, the sound increasing while her thighs clench tight around my hips.

"Please, Luke," she cries out, her pussy massaging my dick. Pulsing and contracting. "I'm coming."

I shout as my release follows hers, my cum bursting free in relieving spurts.

I don't stop.

I can't.

I won't.

She keeps moaning, crying, those knuckles turning white as she grips the coverings. I've never wanted someone like this. I've never needed anyone like I need her.

I slam into her with each fading pulse of orgasm. Her pussy has exhausted me, chained and enslaved me.

I swallow while she pants, her gray woolen sweater tight against her breasts as her chest rises and falls. Her legs begin to relax. My thrusts slow. I've marked her thighs with my fingers and made her breathless from the way I fucked her. I've affected her, but it's not even close to the way she affects me.

"Don't say my name again," I murmur.

She nods, biting her lower lip, her lids heavy, her cheeks flushed.

I inch back, my cock leaving her heat, a trail of cum following in its wake.

Fuck.

Fuck.

Fuck.

"I'm sorry." I place her down on the bed and run a hand over my mouth. "I didn't mean for that to happen."

She frowns up at me, then awareness dawns and her eyes flare. "*Jesus. Fuck.*"

"You wanted a distraction, right?" I drawl.

Her glower is a great indication that this situation isn't something we can joke about.

"Why is everything a complete disaster with you?" she accuses. "Everything falls to shit. Every single time."

It isn't sunshine and rainbows for me either. Sarah has brought me nothing but trouble and mind-numbing lust.

"Why the hell are we still doing this?" She pushes to her elbows and looks up at me as if I have the answer.

I don't.

I have no clue.

"I wish I knew." I pull up my jeans to cover my ass and stalk from the room, returning moments later with a damp washcloth.

She flops back onto the mattress and rests an arm over her face as I slide a hand between her thighs. I wipe the slickness from her legs, her mound, her slit.

My dick throbs with the possibility of round two. That greedy motherfucker.

"I'll deal with the morning-after pill tomorrow," she murmurs.

"Right." What if I don't want her to deal with it? *Fuck.* Am I really that desperate to have her locked in my life?

I place the cloth on her bedside table and turn off the light. She crawls across the mattress then pulls back the covers, her movements visible with the slight illumination from the living room.

I ditch my shoes and clothes to climb naked onto the mattress. I don't offer to give her privacy or space. She won't get either from me. No matter how hellish this is, I can't drag myself away.

I want her. Not just her body or her secrets. I want her trust. I want more. I want everything. Every touch. Every breath. I want to know she's mine, and I won't stop until I'm successful.

I slide in beside her and place my palm on her stomach, my lips on her shoulder.

I listen to her breathing and feel her stomach rise and fall. Every so often she sniffs, and it's the most vulnerable, emotional sound I've ever heard. She's caged all her anguish inside, not letting it break free.

"Why did you keep turning the camera around?" she whispers into the darkness. "Was it a hint to tell me I was disclosing my location?"

She turns to face me, and I briefly close my eyes to bite back the bliss of her snuggling into my chest.

I've never had this. Not the woman in my home. Not the cuddling or the after-sex conversation.

"It wasn't that at all."

"Then what was it?"

I remember my vow of honesty and bite back the need to lie as I meet her gaze. "I had to see you. Those hours before you woke were all I had."

She lowers her attention to focus on my chest. There's no other reaction. She isn't happy for my weakness. She isn't latching her claws in, scrambling for more. "Why didn't you interrogate me for the name of the informant?"

"Because I know you don't have it. After the funeral, Decker filled me in on what he'd dug up on you now that we have the names from the headstones in Seattle. I read about your family, which led to Jacob. There was a photo of him with Dan in your apartment." I glance over my shoulder to the room. "It's around here somewhere."

I turn back to her sad eyes and lazy appraisal. My mind tells me to cut and run, but my lungs ache for more. It's a constant fight between want and need. It has been for weeks. I think it will be for a long time to come.

She's hypnotizing. Mesmerizing. She's a damn dream, or maybe she's a nightmare. Either way, I'm not ready to wake up.

She burrows into me, resting her cheek to my chest. "You never kissed me again. Not after that first night."

My pulse thunders. "Did you want me to?"

Her head shakes the slightest bit. "No."

She stabs me through the ribs with that one word, creating a hole where my self-respect should be.

"But no matter how much I told myself I didn't want it," she whispers, "I needed it more than anything."

20

HER

I STARTLE AWAKE TO THE SOUND OF A SHRILL, rhythmic beep coming from another room.

"What the hell is that?" I push from the cage of Hunter's arms and sit.

"Don't worry. It's just the motion detectors at the gate. Decker must be here."

"How do you know it's him?"

He slides from the bed and yanks his jeans on. "Nobody else knows where I live."

I ignore the monumental realization that I'm one of only two people trusted with this man's address, and glance over my shoulder to the bedside clock. "Why would he be here at three in the morning?"

"I don't know." He slides up his zipper and clasps the belt, the peaks and troughs of his abs highlighted with the gentle glow of light coming from the living room. "Stay in here while I deal with him."

He starts for the door, and my throat tightens at the thought of him leaving.

"Hunter?"

He pauses at the threshold and glances at me. "Yeah?"

"Can I trust Decker?" It's a stupid question. I can't even trust Hunter, despite my body being at his mercy. But I need his affirmation. In the quiet hours before I passed out, all I could think about was Brent and who, apart from me, was responsible for his death. "Could he have led Torian to Atomic Buzz?"

"No." His response is immediate, without contemplation. "You don't need to worry about him."

I clutch the sheet to my naked chest. "How can you be so sure?"

"We can talk about it later. When you're ready." He gives me a sad smile and closes the door behind him, imprisoning me with rabid contemplation.

If Hunter knows Decker isn't to blame, then he must also know who is.

I slide from the bed as the beeping stops, pulling my woolen sweater down to cover my ass. I hustle to the door, inch it open, and listen.

I don't hear anything. Not movement. Not conversation.

"Hunter?"

He doesn't answer.

My apprehension increases, tickling the back of my neck as I tiptoe down the hall and stop in the shadows before the opening to the living room. He isn't in sight. He's not inside.

Something flickers in my peripheral vision. I tilt my head to see him outside, shirtless, striding away from me across the lawn toward Decker, who gets out of the car I'd seen him in weeks ago on the highway.

I creep forward, not hiding, but also not making my presence known by positioning myself in line with one of the porch poles so Decker can't see my approach. I begin to hear words, some clear, some indecipherable. Nothing makes sense yet, not even when I reach the door and grasp the handle. Slowly, I plunge the lever, opening the door a crack.

"She's asleep," Hunter murmurs. "I don't want her disturbed."

Decker nods. "How did she take the news?"

"She doesn't know the half of it yet."

I inch to the side to see Decker's profile. He's frowning. No, it's a glare. "What half does she know?"

"It was her choice," Hunter snarls. "I was going to tell her, but she's been through a lot. It's her preference to wait until she calms down."

My cheeks heat at how weak I sound. They heat even more at the possibility of Hunter thinking I'm fragile. I shouldn't crave his praise, and still I itch to have him infatuated with me, the way I am with him. Mindless, crazed, and emotionally unstable, too.

Decker laughs, the sound caustic. "Do you hear yourself? I fucking know she's been through a lot. And you're too much of a chicken shit to tell her why. My God, man, when it comes to women, you're the dumbest asshole I know."

I push the door wider and tiptoe onto the porch, the chilled night air drifting under my sweater to touch the nakedness beneath.

"So, when are you going to tell her?"

"When she's ready."

"When she's ready or when you're ready?"

"*Jesus fucking Christ, Decker.*" Hunter runs a hand through his hair. "I said I would tell her, and I will."

I move closer, needing to be near him. That's all I want. I'm stronger when he's close. Even now, I grow emboldened, ready and capable of listening to whatever I need to hear as the door falls back to click in place.

Hunter stiffens. Decker pins me with a stare.

"You can tell me now." I walk across the porch, my uncovered feet tingling from the cold. "I'm ready to hear it."

Decker mutters something under his breath. A curse, maybe. But Hunter remains still, his back to me.

"What is it?" I walk down the three steps to the lawn. "What do I need to know?"

"Nice outfit." Decker clears his throat and stalks in my direction. "I'll meet you both inside."

"Why?" I ask. "Aren't you a part of this, too?"

"Oh, no." He raises his hands and shakes his head. "No, no, no. I follow orders. I don't make the plans. This is all on him."

I nod, trying to steel myself against the upcoming news. An ominous feeling creeps down my spine as he passes and goes inside.

Hunter doesn't face me. He stares into the darkness, silent in contemplation, or maybe it's annoyance over my interruption.

"Hunter?" I take one step, then another. "You can tell me now."

Finally, he turns, his head lowered, his gaze meeting mine through thick, dark lashes. "Torian wasn't in the bar with Brent."

My heart drops, and I force myself to nod. "Okay... Who was?"

His attention flicks toward the house. Toward Decker.

I swallow, coming to the conclusion that a predator is behind me. Inside the house. I move away from the porch, coming closer to my protector, and glance over my shoulder. "He killed Brent?"

"No. He didn't kill him."

"Then who did? And why was he there?" My words are garbled in a tangled mess as fear and the need for retribution rush through me.

"He made sure everything ran smoothly." Hunter straightens his shoulders as if preparing for an onslaught. "He controlled the situation for me from the inside."

He looks at me as if waiting for my comprehension to dawn, but there's no dawning here. I don't understand. I don't think I want to.

"I organized everything." His lips are downcast, his eyes grim. Everything about him screams remorse, and yet nothing makes sense.

"*You* arranged for Brent to be killed?" My tone is strong, belying the fissure cracking right through the heart of me.

He stares for long moments that drag on for an eternity. "Sarah, he's not dead."

Not. Dead.

A spark of excited relief bursts to life inside my chest. He's not dead. He...is not...dead.

I want to fall to my knees in thanks, but Hunter's unshifting look of stony remorse fizzles my relief. "Is he hurt?"

I retreat a step, needing space to think, only to freeze at the sound of the porch door opening. Decker walks outside, a large bowl cradled in one arm. He leans against the banister, watching me as his hand dives into the bowl, retrieving a pile of popcorn.

"*Son-of-a-bitch*," Hunter hisses. "We're not entertainment. Get the fuck inside."

Decker smiles, all toothy and wide, then snaps the handful of popcorn into his mouth.

Concentrate. Think.

Hunter arranged for Decker to be inside the bar.

"Is he hurt?" I repeat, standing my ground and squaring my shoulders. "I heard the gunshot. You wanted him dead."

"No. I wanted you scared. I wanted you vulnerable and in need of my help. When I told you I was messaging Decker, I did. I told him to fire a warning shot."

I snap my lips closed to stop a gasp escaping.

He wanted me back in Portland. He wanted me here.

"Is. He. Hurt?" I enunciate each word through clenched teeth.

"No." He shakes his head. "He's fine."

"A little pissed off that he got held at gunpoint," Decker clarifies. "And that I shot a hole in his wall. But yeah, fine."

"You're not helping," Hunter growls.

I blink slowly as rage and humiliation burn my eyes. "So much for no more lies."

He snaps to attention and takes a step forward. "I haven't lied since I promised you the truth. Since we arrived here."

What a privilege that must be to a snake like him.

I stand immobile. Heart heavy. Soul weary.

"I won't lie to you again, Sarah. Everything that has happened since we came here is real."

He means the fucking and maybe the brief admission that he wants me. But who doesn't want A-grade snatch?

Asshole.

My feelings had been more than that. So horribly, disturbingly immense.

"Say something," he begs.

That's a tough request, seeing as I'm tongue-tied with humiliation.

I owe him nothing. Not my anger. Not even my words. But I can give him one. "Goodbye."

I start for the house. I'll get changed, stuff a pair of clean underwear in my pocket, then run.

That's all I do now. Run. Flee.

Every step I've made since Hunter entered my life has been wrought with failure and disappointment. And yet I stupidly felt my emptiness lessen.

I take the three stairs onto the porch one at a time, calm and civil, while I scowl at Decker, who continues to eat popcorn like he's watching an Academy Award performance. I walk inside without a word, head straight for my doppelgänger bedroom, and change into a fresh pair of jeans from the clothes Hunter has stacked in the wardrobe.

I grab a few pairs of underwear from my bedside drawers, shoving them in my pockets, and lift my mattress to retrieve an old switchblade stored in a hole between the springs.

"You can't leave."

I straighten at the sound of his voice and lower the mattress back in place.

"You don't have any money on you. You don't have a phone."

I turn with a derisive smile and face him standing in the doorway. "No, and I don't even have my dignity, because you stole that from me, too. But I'll make it work."

He winces. "Let me explain."

"I don't want to hear it." I shove the blade into my pocket beside the already tightly compacted underwear. "All I want is for you to let me walk out of here without another confrontation."

"I can't do that." The words are murmured softly, in the deepest, richest tone.

I stride toward him—I'll stride straight through him if I have to—and he widens his stance, his shoulders broad, his arms hanging limp. He covers my escape.

"I'm not doing this with you again," I mutter. "Move."

He doesn't.

I continue forward and try to shove my way through. He stands like stone, his beseeching eyes tearing me apart.

"*Move.*"

"Ask me why."

I close my eyes briefly, warding off the insincere heart-break in his tone. "I don't need to."

I push at his arm, and he responds by getting right in my face. "Yes, you do. You need to know why I did it."

I pull away, thankful he allows the retreat. "I already know why. You love to play games. You love tormenting me. It's who you are. It's what you do."

He cringes.

"See?" I throw my arms wide and give a bitter laugh. "I'm right."

"Yeah. You are." He nods. "I loved playing our games."

My heart squeezes at the admission. I don't want to be right. No matter how obvious the answer, I wish and wish to be wrong.

"I lost you for five days. One minute, I knew where you were; the next you were gone." He leans in, but not toward my face. He moves to the side, his breath tickling my neck. "That first night, not knowing where you were...*Fucking. Killed. Me.*"

He enunciates those last words into my ear with such vehement passion my chest tightens. Sternum. Ribs. Lungs.

"I was scared." He moves closer. So close I can feel the heat emanating from his bare chest. "I thought you were hurt. Or that Torian changed his mind about the deal we made."

"What deal?" I pull away to meet his gaze.

"I practically sold my soul for your safety."

Lies. Lies. Lies.

I shake my head in disbelief.

"It's true." He looks me in the eye, undaunted by my

skepticism. "There's trust between me and Torian, no matter how temperamental. So, I vouched for you, putting everything on the line to convince him I believed you when you said you knew nothing. But I wasn't entirely sure he would leave you alone. Then you disappeared, and I thought he was responsible. My panic only increased the longer you were gone. I was mindless, Sarah. You've got no idea how crazy I was searching for you."

"So you fooled me into thinking my one and only friend was murdered?"

He clenches his jaw, raises his chin. "Would you have come home with me for any other reason?"

I open my mouth, poised to respond.

"Think about it," he demands. "There's no way you would've gotten in my car if I'd asked. There's no way you would've let me fuck you, or stay in your bed. You wouldn't have crawled into my arms or spoken to me the way you have tonight."

My throat tightens at the reminder of how much I've given him. "That's a lot of effort to get laid, buddy."

His eyes narrow to harsh slits. "I can get laid any time, any place. This isn't about sex. This is about you and me. It's about not being able to fucking walk away." He sucks in a breath and lets it out in a heave. "You can't deny feeling the same. I know you do."

"What I feel is anger," I snarl. "I feel disgusted and played. I feel like every word that comes out of your mouth is nothing but a lie." I square my shoulders and get in his face, almost nose to nose. "I feel like you've won this battle, but never again. I'm done. For good."

I glare at him for long seconds, then stride around him, making it to the door.

"We're not done," he growls. "We're not finished here."

"Yes, we are." I continue into the hall, hating the distance I'm putting between us, but needing it, too.

"Sarah," he calls after me. "You can't leave."

I briefly close my eyes, pained by the way he says my name. Loving and loathing in immeasurable quantities.

"*Sarah*," he yells, his footsteps following me.

I stride through the living room, toward Decker, who now stands between me and the porch door.

"I know how to find Jacob."

Hunter's statement stops me in my tracks. I meet Decker's gaze, and there's no longer any humor in his features. His face is emotionless. Solemn. A picture-perfect portrait of the truth.

This isn't a lie.

No. I can't be fooled again. I can't let myself believe that the man who torments me knows where to find the man who ruined me.

"Stop it," I whisper.

"Believe me." His footfalls move closer. "I know where he is."

It shouldn't matter. It *can't* matter. Staying here is a bad decision, no matter the reason. I will my feet to move and hold my head high as I continue to the door.

"We can help you take him down," Decker adds. "That's what you want, isn't it? To get him back for—"

"*Shut up*," I scream. "Just shut the hell up, and quit playing me. I can't take this anymore."

I focus on the freedom waiting for me on the other side of the wall of glass. There is a peaceful truth that comes with solitude. A clarity of vision unmarred by the opinions of others.

Yes, it's lonely. But there is harmony in that, too.

I lived in that existence for a long time, going through the motions of life yet not really living. Not really feeling in my self-imposed isolation. Then Hunter showed up, obliterating my truth. He destroyed the peace. He blurred the bigger picture.

And I can't deny I liked it.

He creeps into the reflection in the glass, approaching from over my right shoulder to meet my gaze. "He works for Torian. He's a small-time dealer in Newport who comes back to Portland every few weeks to check in."

He's tempting me with the one thing I want, manipulating me because I've let him know all the right buttons to push. I close my eyes and simply listen. Not to Hunter. Not to Decker. I tune in to my intuition, hoping against all hope that it steers me in the right direction.

After all his lies, I can't stomach the thought of trusting him. And then I think about him kissing me. I remember his notes. I hear his emotional admissions—*I had to see you... You've got me... I sold my soul for your safety*.

There has to be truth in those moments. At least the slightest glimmer.

"I know you think I've been fucking with you," he murmurs. "But trust me, you've done shit to me, too."

I open my eyes and glare at him through the reflection. "I haven't done *anything* to you. Not one damn thing."

"That's where you're wrong. You've fucked with me since the first time I saw you with Roberts. You messed with my head. You made me lose sight of everything." He gives a sad smile. "All I see is you, Sarah."

"Stop it." I shove my hand through my loose hair, pulling tight. I need the pressure to stop building in my skull. I need relief. I need... *Fuck*. I don't know what I need anymore.

"Let me help you with Jacob." He takes a step closer.

"Don't." I scoot away and turn to face him. "If you move

another step I'll..." What? Scratch his eyes out? Beat him? Cuss him to death? Maybe I could do all of the above.

"I followed you from the hotel room with Dan because I wanted to know who you were. I wanted to know why someone like you would be with a lowlife piece of shit."

"Bullshit," I spit. "You needed to find out what he told me."

"That was part of it, yes. But it didn't stop there. It never stops with you."

Oh, God. I'm succumbing. I want his lies. I crave the manipulation. Because even though his attention is fake, I keep convincing myself it's real. From the first night I met him, I saw things in this man that were never there—attraction, passion, protection.

None of it existed, yet the fiction weaves around me like tendrils of the finest silk, delicate and comforting in my denial.

"I needed to know more. Not just about Dan, about you." He remains a few feet away, somber with his deceptive conviction. "It got worse after we kissed. And then again when we fucked. Nothing made sense except my craving for more. It hasn't changed. Even when Torian was breathing down my neck. Even when you had a gun to my chest. And God knows it only got worse when Carlos ran you off the—"

"I need you to stop." My voice cracks and I give up the show of strength. "Please... Just stop."

"I can't. I've tried. When it comes to you, I don't have any control. I just want you, Sarah. That's all I know anymore."

I suck in a breath and glance to Decker, expecting a smirk or a grin at the very least. I get neither. His lips are tight, his brow furrowed. He's uncomfortable.

Well, goddamnit, so am I.

"I played you." Hunter moves toward me, stopping within reach. "And I get that you don't trust me. But I trust you."

He reaches out, and I stiffen as he grabs me by my jeans pocket and retrieves my knife. I watch in disbelief as he flicks it open and holds out the hilt for me to take.

"Do what you like," he offers. "Carve your name across my chest. Retaliate however you want."

"Jesus Christ," Decker mutters.

"I mean it." Hunter places the knife in my palm and wraps his hand around mine, raising the blade so the tip almost touches the skin across his ribs. "Do what you need to. Make this right."

My eyes are wide, my lips parted. He clutches my hand tight around the grip, and for the moment, I don't want to let go. I want to hurt him. I need to make him suffer.

I take a menacing step forward, and the tip of the blade pierces his skin.

I watch intently as his eyes flare, his jaw tenses, his chin lifts. I derive the slightest taste of justice from his pain, but the remorse hits me tenfold.

"Go on," he implores, his determination unwavering. "Do it."

I clench my fingers tighter, my throat closing. I increase the pressure, hoping for satisfaction to hit me by the bucket-load. But those hazel eyes... God, those eyes. They do things to me that the most malicious actions can't achieve. They strip my defenses. They strum my soul.

He sucks in a breath, and his grip loosens on my hand.

I glance down to find blood trailing over his stomach in a tiny rivulet to sink into the material of his black jeans.

"Get away from me." I scoot back out of his reach, and the knife falls from my fingers to clatter to the tiled floor.

"It's okay."

"No, it's not. Forgiveness doesn't come that easily. You have too much bullshit to make up for. No stab wound can amount to that."

"Then tell me how to fix this," he growls.

"How should I know?" I snap. "Haven't you heard the saying? You don't break a plate and expect an apology to make it better. You can glue it back together, but it's still not the same. The damage is already done."

"That's some philosophical genius, right there," Decker mumbles.

I ignore him, but Hunter's eyes flare with fury. "Fine. I'll give you space for now."

He turns to the kitchen and walks away, leaving me cold with the receding attention. Maybe I should've stabbed him after all.

Decker raises a brow as his gaze drops to Hunter's stomach. "You two are motherfucking crazy. I feel like I've just witnessed a satanic mating ritual."

"Nobody asked you to be here." Hunter rounds the island counter, grabs the scotch, and drinks from the bottle.

Blood seeps from the small cut against his ribs. He's never been more vicious with his harsh glare and flaring nostrils. He's never been more masculine. More fascinating. Alluring.

I march toward him, his eyes narrowing on me as I approach, and snatch the bottle from his hand. If I can't escape this torment, then I sure as hell won't let him do it via the reprieve of intoxication.

The asshole can suffer.

"Thanks." I turn away and storm to my new bedroom.

The last thing I hear as I close myself inside is Decker's laughter and his snickered, "You've got your hands full with that one."

21

HIM

I've been standing at the kitchen counter for hours, the sun now rising as I wait for Sarah to come out of her room.

She needs space, which I'm happy to give, since the window in her room can't be opened without a key. She can't run from me. At least not without me knowing.

"When do you plan on calling Torian?" Decker asks from his leaned position against the other side of the kitchen island.

"Not until she's ready."

"He's not going to be happy."

No shit. "I'll deal with it."

The soft click of an opening door sounds from down the hall, and Decker raises a brow. "How drunk do you think she is?"

Drunk enough to cause trouble would be my guess, especially since she isn't a drinker. Then again, she doesn't need to be drunk to cause problems.

Her padded footsteps approach, and I keep my focus

straight ahead, on Decker, determined not to let my gaze rush after her like an eager little puppy.

"Want me to leave you two alone?" he asks.

"Really?" I glare. "Now you ask that?"

The asshole could've left us alone earlier, but oh no, he had to bear witness to my idiocy. He'll never let me live it down.

He smirks. "Better late than never."

I sigh as her slim figure nudges the edge of my sight from the start of the hall. She isn't dressed in the jeans she had on before. It's something less than that. Something I can't quite determine from my peripheral vision. I clench the kitchen counter behind me and grind my molars, determined not to take a proper look.

"I'm ready to hear what you know about Jacob." She continues forward, increasing the temptation.

"When was the last time you ate?" I finally succumb to the need to visually consume her.

Fuck.

She's wearing the shirt I had on last night. The one I left on the floor in her bedroom. Now it's covered in cuts and slices as if she's spent the last hours performing a voodoo ritual on me through the large material that dwarfs her body.

She stops at the far corner of the U-shaped kitchen, her arms crossing over her chest. "Right before I stole a car," she mutters, "to save a friend you pretended to murder in an effort to get me back in your bed."

Decker clears his throat to disguise a laugh.

Great. I walked straight into that one.

"Well, I'm starving." And after another night without sleep, I need caffeine. I shove from the counter and finally meet her gaze. She's tired, the dark smudges beneath her eyes making this tough woman appear fragile. "Get changed. We're going out for breakfast."

"I'm not going anywhere," she says softly with the undertone of her iron-clad determination.

I drag my focus away and scowl at Decker, because if I scowl at her, we are only going to fight again. "You need to focus before we talk. I'm not going to waste my time if you're drunk."

"As much as I would've loved the escapism, I didn't drink your damn scotch," she growls. "I only took it because I wanted to make sure you didn't either."

"How about I go out and get food while you two have some time alone?" Decker walks to the sofa and grabs his jacket. "You can settle your unresolved satanic rituals and be ready to eat once I get back."

I'm not going to bite. I'm not even going to increase my glare. I've learned it only spurs him on. "Don't forget the coffee."

He jerks his head in acknowledgement and leaves via the porch.

The click of the latching door is deafening, closing me in with her anger-filled silence. I don't know what she wants me to say to make this right. There probably isn't anything in the English language capable of reaching the level of apology she needs.

"I'm going to take a shower." I stalk from the kitchen, toward the hall in the opposite direction to Sarah.

"You're angry at *me* now?" she accuses.

"No." I'm tired. I'm frustrated.

"Good, because you have no right to be angry."

I pause and bite my tongue like a motherfucker. "Go get dressed, Sarah. Decker doesn't need to keep seeing you like that." The exposed thighs. Those nipples beading behind the thin material.

"Decker can kiss my ass."

I give a caustic laugh. "Be careful what you wish for. He's more than likely to give you what you want if you keep strutting around the house wearing next to nothing."

I continue down the hall and enter my room, not waiting for her to snap. I need a shower to clear my head. To wake me up. To wash her scent from my skin.

I undo my jeans button and lower the zipper when the door creaks wider. She's there again, stalking in my peripheral vision like a temptress. "Do you plan on joining me?"

"No," she whispers.

I shove my jeans down my legs, giving her an uncensored view of my hardening dick. "Then I suggest you get out of my room."

Her hungry gaze takes me in, her interest straying over my crotch, then quickly diverting to my stomach. "Do you need stitches?"

"Don't worry, princess. You barely scratched the surface."

She raises a brow. "Then maybe you should give me another try."

I heave out a tired breath. "You want to cut me again?"

I'll let her, if that's what it takes. I'll let her take whatever revenge she needs, because I deserve it. But my willingness to admit my mistakes won't last forever. My stubborn pride will see to that.

"No." She continues staring, not meeting my eyes as long moments pass. "I want you to prove this isn't another one of your games. I need you to convince me."

"How?" I approach her and she holds up a hand, instructing me to stop. "Look, Sarah, I don't do this shit. I don't *want* to do this shit. But I fought to get you back, and I apologized for my less-than-stellar tactics—"

"Less than stellar?" She balks. "Whispering behind

someone's back is less than stellar. Conspiring against someone is less than stellar. But pretending to murder someone in an effort to get laid is a little beyond that, don't you think?"

I clamp my mouth shut, stifling a harsh response. I already told her this isn't about sex. If it was, I would've fucked her in every cheap-ass hotel in Portland. I wouldn't have merely watched her sleep. I would've woken her with my face between her thighs, my fingers in her cunt.

And I sure as hell wouldn't have let Decker see exactly how much of a vulnerability she is to me.

"Do you think I'd let you get away with stealing my car if this was only about sex?" I growl.

"Maybe this is retaliation for leaving the key fob in the console when I left the car unlocked in front of my building."

"You left the key?"

She beams an exaggerated smile.

Fuck this woman and my crazy infatuation that only seems to grow the longer she holds that expression. Even now, I want to laugh.

Laugh? She stole my goddamn car.

But none of that matters now. The only aim is convincing her this isn't all bullshit.

"How is exposing my home and my real name a retaliation? I've entrusted you with more information than I've ever entrusted with anyone. And you still don't get it. I don't know what else to tell you."

"Then don't tell me. Show me."

I frown. Is this some weird female fuckery? How the hell do I show her without words or the sex she claims this is about? Decker was right. I'm the dumbest asshole when it comes to women.

"If you care about me, you'll help me find Jacob—"

"I already promised I would," I growl.

She inclines her head. "*Then* you'll let me walk away."

I stiffen, my pulse spiking violently. "I can't do that."

I can't lose her. I don't know why; I just can't. Even the thought of it makes my chest tight. I already lost her once. I can't willingly do it again.

The determined gleam in her eyes transforms to a solemn stare of disappointment, and I hate it. I hate that she doesn't understand this shit is driving me to insanity. Isn't my inability to let her go enough? Doesn't that prove how much she means to me?

A woman has never come between me and my job before.

A woman has never stolen my focus and created havoc in my mind.

A woman has never controlled me. Not even a little bit. And certainly not with her level of effortless efficiency.

"Then this isn't about you caring for me. It's about you lusting after me." She pads from the room, her retreating steps fading down the hall as I stand in frustrated silence.

I wipe a rough hand over my face. Maybe she's right. Maybe it is lust. But even if it is, I still have no plan to let her go.

She wants revenge against a man who works for Torian. That won't come without consequences unless done strategically. Methodically. So, she needs me, no matter how much she refuses to admit it.

I mutter a string of curse words under my breath as I shove into my private bathroom, then lock myself inside and take a long shower. I take pleasure in the bite of pain as hot water breeches my cut. I take even more when I add soap to the mix. At least the distraction gives me a reprieve from thoughts of Sarah for a few short minutes.

I don't get out until the blood is washed from my skin and her scent no longer haunts me.

I should stay in my room until Decker returns. There needs to be a buffer between me and her. But as soon as I leave the bathroom, I pull on a clean pair of cargos and another black T-shirt, then stride right back down to the kitchen.

She's standing before the floor-to-ceiling windows, staring at my front yard. She's pulled her hair back into a high ponytail and is wearing tight leggings and the gray woolen sweater I fucked her in last night. The memory is a bitch—a haunting, conniving, sinister mistress that controls me like I'm a willing slave.

Problem is, she doesn't want me to be mastered. She doesn't want anything from me at all...apart from my dick.

I scowl, not appreciating the realization.

She doesn't hold the same fascination toward this thing between us that I do. For her, it's lust. Pure and simple.

I come up behind her, meeting her gaze in the reflection of the glass. She blinks back at me, no longer shooting spiteful daggers with her stare.

"Do you really want to walk after all this is said and done?"

She sucks in a deep breath and lowers her gaze.

She doesn't want to goddamn walk. She wants to continue this thing between us as much as I do—unwillingly and undeniably in equal measure.

"No," she whispers. "It's not what I want."

The admission makes a direct hit to my relief.

"It's what I need," she clarifies, stabbing the disappointment directly into my chest. "Because once I finish with Jacob, I'm going to need to find myself again. I'll have to start over and determine what I want from life."

"You want *me*."

She lets out a whisper of a laugh. "I do." She nods. "But that in itself isn't healthy. I doubt it ever can be. Not after everything that's happened."

An invisible weight rests heavily on my chest, growing more intense under her serene conviction. "Then I'll think about it."

"Really?" She turns, meeting my gaze with questioning eyes. "That means no following. No spying. No games. You need to let me move on with my life."

No checking in on her safety. No getting a fix from the distance between us by watching her sleep. No connection whatsoever.

I don't get it. I don't fucking understand why I want her so much. But even now, knowing she itches to run away from me, I can't stop wishing I had the words to make her stay.

"I said, I'll think about it." I step into her and wrap an arm around her waist. She doesn't flinch; she lets me hold her. "If that's what it takes to show you this isn't just about sex."

She licks her lower lip and then drags her teeth over the moistened temptation. There's no doubt she wants me. There's no doubt I could have her. Right here. Right now. On my living room floor.

"You don't get it. My concerns don't simply revolve around sex. They're more complicated than that."

"Then explain it to me."

Her shoulders slump as she releases a heavy breath. "The first boyfriend I ever had killed my entire family. He took everything from me, and I refused to let anyone into my life after that... Until you."

Until me, a replacement who was probably only a smidge better than her fucking psychotic ex.

"You've lied to me constantly," she continues. "You

hacked my video surveillance. You followed me to another city and stole secrets I never would've shared. Then you pretended my only friend—"

"I get it." I don't need the reminder of my rap sheet.

I've maimed. I've tortured. I've killed. But never before have I felt the remorse I do right now.

She needs to learn to trust me. *Me.* A man who barely trusts himself.

She rests her forehead against my chest. "You have to give me space, Luke."

Not only does it sound like she wants space, it's fucking clear she might never want to see me again. She has the determination to move on, regardless of this connection. This dependence. This addiction.

I hold her tighter, both arms around her back.

I don't think I'm that strong. Not yet, anyway. Maybe I will be after she pisses me off a few more times. Maybe... Then again, it's highly doubtful when it hurts to fucking breathe unless she's in my arms.

I press my lips to her hair and close my eyes. "I'm not making any promises, but like I said, I'll think about it."

22

HER

The sound of a car approaches in the front yard. I close my eyes, not wanting to leave the warmth of Hunter's arms.

"Decker is here," he whispers into my hair.

I nod.

Once I step back, I know I have to focus. There will be no time for fluttering hearts and craving attention. I have to take control. But I loathe to move from his arms when I know this could be one of the last times I'll be here.

"I think you'll change your mind about us once this is all over," he whispers.

He still doesn't get it. This isn't about our attraction. If it was, I'd never leave his bed.

"I'm not going to change my mind." I can't. Not if I have any hope for a mentally stable future.

I suck in a breath, fill my lungs, and retreat from his embrace. I don't look at him. I turn to the glass and watch Decker approach with food bags and a tray of takeout coffee.

Hunter opens the door, lets him inside, then leads the

way to the dining table.

"There are croissants, English muffins, and donuts, depending on your mood." Decker dumps the feast on the thick polished wood and pulls out a chair.

I take a seat across from him, while Hunter sits at the head of the table. Both of them focus on spreading the food and handing out coffee. Neither of them looks at me, as if fearing even a glance will bring up the topic we need to discuss.

Well, it's too late for avoidance.

"Tell me what you know about Jacob." I unwrap my croissant and take a large bite, the taste inspiring a hearty groan.

Hunter flicks me a casual glance, devoid of the feelings from our private moment. "He goes by the name Vaughn."

"Zack," Decker adds. "He's been working with Torian for years."

"Almost as long as I have." Hunter takes a sip of coffee, watching me over the rim of the cup.

"You know him?"

He nods. "We're not buddies, but yeah, I know him."

My appetite threatens to flee. "And you're still willing to help me take him down?"

"Yep." He takes another lazy sip of caffeine.

There's no concern. No building apprehension. Does he even understand my plans?

"You do realize I want him dead, right?" I glance at them both, expecting to see a glimmer of shock or foreboding. I find neither.

"I know." He places the coffee cup down and unwraps an English muffin. "It shouldn't be hard."

"Why is that?" I place my croissant on the paper wrapping, giving him my full attention.

"We're going to get someone else to do it."

"No." I scowl. "I don't want anyone else. I've waited ten yea—"

"Sending someone to meet their maker isn't all it's cracked up to be. You're not a murderer, princess."

I straighten my shoulders and want to snarl at how his gaze dips to my now thrusted breasts. "Let me worry about that."

"I can't. I won't." His attention returns to mine without remorse. "Do you really think you can look him in the eye and follow through with killing him?"

"Yes," I grate.

"And do you think you can spend the rest of your life seeing that face every time you close your eyes? Do you think you can live with his ghost haunting you? Always looking over your shoulder to see if the cops are following?"

"I handled you following me, didn't I?"

"That's nothing in comparison." His lip curls, but it isn't nice. It's cruel and derisive. "Have you forgotten what it felt like when you thought you killed Dan? Do you remember the nausea? Do you remember how you hid in your apartment for days?"

I remember.

But Dan was different. He didn't murder four people in cold blood. He didn't murder anyone. In comparison, Jacob turned my family to ash without remorse.

He didn't deserve this new life as Zack Vaughn. He didn't deserve a life at all.

"I. Can. Handle. It." I enunciate the words with vehemence.

I want the other Hunter back. The caring, pleasing one, not the harsh criminal who now sits in his place.

"And what if I don't want you to? What if I can't handle you handling it?"

The thick silence that follows his response is louder

than our argument. Static rushes in my ears. My pulse pounds in my throat. I don't want this to be hard on him, but neither can I let him distract me from what I've strived for.

"Sarah..." Decker places his croissant down. "Let Torian do it for you. That way you're still responsible, but not held accountable, and he will fuck Vaughn up better than you ever could."

I drag my attention to him and frown. "Torian? Why would he kill Jacob for me?"

"Because that's exactly what he does to anyone who crosses him."

"I don't understand." I glance between them, back and forth, trying to work out the puzzle.

"You're going to tell him that Dan gave you the name of the informant."

I gasp at the simplicity of their scheme. "I'm going to tell him it was Jacob?"

"Vaughn," Decker corrects. "You need to make sure you get the name right."

I nod, my lips curling in an excited leer. "That sounds..." I want to say easy, but this is a murderous plot. Surely it can't be that simple. "Are you certain it will work?"

"No, not at all." Hunter pins me with a stern scowl. "Convincing Torian will be a bitch now that I've already promised him you know nothing. He won't appreciate me going back on my word. He'll be skeptical from the get go."

"Which means it's best if the news comes from you," Decker adds. "We'll take you to see him or—"

"We'll fucking call him first," Hunter growls. "And pray to God that's enough. I don't want you there with him."

My throat dries at the unwavering concern in his eyes.

"But all this will put you in a dangerous position, too, right?" I ask. "It makes your original promise a lie."

"Don't worry about me. You're the one we're concerned about."

"Concentrate on getting your story straight." Decker balls his trash and throws it at the open paper bag in the middle of the table. "We need to go over the details again and again and again until it's memorized. It will take days to get this right."

"That doesn't work for me." The sooner this is all over, the sooner I can remove the shackles of Jacob's strangling hold. I won't wait a minute longer than necessary to be free from him. "I don't need to practice. Not when the truth is so close to what happened with Dan in the first place. The story will be simple and without complication. He can either take it or leave it."

"And if he leaves it?" Hunter asks.

"Then I deal with Jacob the old-fashioned way."

"You mean the way that gets you killed?" He scoffs, smug and superior. "I should just do this on my own."

"Don't you dare take this from me," I snap. "He's not yours to kill."

I can't believe we're bickering about murder. We're fighting over who gets to end someone's life. If my high school self could see me now, she would literally pee her pants.

"She's right." Decker raises his voice. "We already discussed this. If Torian found out you smoked one of his dealers, your life wouldn't be worth living."

"And besides," I add, "you act as though I'm new to this, but I'm not. Dan wasn't the first guy I fucked with. I've done this before. Many times." I grab the edge of the table in both hands to hold back my frustration. "Do you remember the priest whose child-molesting case was dropped? Do you also remember that same priest was admitted to hospital with self-inflicted cuts to his genitals?"

"Oh, boy," Decker mumbles.

"They weren't self-inflicted," I clarify. "And the investment banker who signed all of his assets over to the ex-wife he physically abused? Do you think he did that out of the goodness of his heart? Or the school teacher who secretly filmed high school girls in the shower? Did you ever wonder why he made the sudden decision to join a monastery?" I stab a finger at my chest. "I did all that. And much more."

Decker grins. "Is it weird that I'm a little turned on right now?"

Hunter glares at me, obviously not appreciating his friend's enthusiasm. "Congratulations." He leans back in his chair and gives a slow clap. "And how much time did you spend planning those jobs?"

Asshole.

Trust him to cut right to the only flaw in this plan. "I know what I'm doing, Hunter. And I already have a story straight in my head. A real one. *The truth.* I'll tell him exactly what happened. The only thing I have to add is the few seconds where Dan told me the name."

He continues to eye me, his focus bordering on a glower.

"Look," I plead. "This isn't new to me, and it sure as hell doesn't daunt me. I've wanted this for too damn long not to be enthusiastic to get it done."

"Then tell us your story." He spreads his arms wide. "Why were you with Dan that night?"

"To make him stop assaulting women. He'd been beating prostitutes on a regular basis and leaving them for dead."

"And why was that your concern?" Decker asks.

"It should be everyone's concern. Vulnerable women were hurt, and he had no intention of stopping. The police wouldn't do a damn thing and nobody held his father accountable—"

"So you beat him?" Decker interrupts.

"Yes."

They continue to bombard me with questions, one after another, but my responses are confident and given with conviction. I know my story. The timeline is infallible. The account is legitimate. All I have to do is leave out the parts about Jacob.

"And why would Dan just give you Vaughn's name without you having to ask?" Hunter raises a brow. "Especially when he demanded a large sum of money from Torian for the information."

"Because Rohypnol can be a bitch." I keep my expression blank. "In the minutes before he passed out, he was so confused he blurted a whole diatribe of what I thought was useless information. He said his father would kill him if another scandal got out. Then he pleaded once more for me to let him go, and told me Vaughn was the name I wanted. That Vaughn was Torian's informant."

Hunter's nostrils flare as he glares at me in an intimidation tactic. Or is it legitimate anger? I'm not sure. He pushes from his seat and silently begins snatching used food wrappers from the table.

"Is that it?" I follow him with my gaze. "Are you done grilling me?"

"Not even close." He shoves garbage into the empty takeout bags. "We need to keep going over this."

I sigh and glance to Decker for support. "I told you I won't do this a million times. I know my story. It won't change."

Hunter slams his palms against the wood. "And I told you that convincing Torian won't be a fucking walk in the park. You're not ready until I say you are."

I close my eyes briefly and find calm. He's upset that I nailed my account of what happened, because once this is all over, he knows I'll leave him. I get it. Really, I do. But I'm not going to wait around until he feels all warm and fuzzy about this. That shit could take weeks.

"You're angry." I look up at him, trying to reiterate how important the culmination of this moment with Torian will be for me. "I need this, Hunter. I'm ready."

His nostrils flare.

"She's right," Decker murmurs. "She's got this."

"How the fuck do you know that?" Hunter snarls. "I promised Torian she knew nothing. Going back on my word will make him suspicious. He'll come at her from every angle—"

"You don't know that, either." Decker stands. "He might not even want to talk to her in person. Having the conversation over the phone might be enough, seeing as he already knows there's an informant. But no matter what he does, we can't prepare for the unknown. We can only bank on her story being straight. And it is."

I give Hunter a sad smile. I can see the concern in his glare. He's worried. On edge. "I can do this. I promise."

"Go on." Decker jerks his chin toward the kitchen. "Get your phone. Call him. This could be as simple as a ten-minute conversation."

Hunter doesn't move. Not apart from clenching his fists in a white-knuckle grip against the wood.

"Please, Hunter." I clasp my hands in prayer and bat my lashes softly for dramatic effect.

He rolls his eyes and snatches the trash-filled bag from the table to stalk to the kitchen. My belly tumbles as he grabs his phone off the counter, then strides back in my direction, then past to the porch door, and outside.

I don't know if I should give him space or follow. Chase

after him, like he's always chased after me. Or remain in place, where it's safe and sterile from his affection.

"He's fucked up over you," Decker mutters. "Well and truly fucked."

I don't respond. I can't, not when I know what it feels like to be in Hunter's shoes. I feel exactly the same way. I experience it with every breath.

Hunter slumps onto the top step leading to the grass and stares off in the distance. He's picture perfect from this angle—the back view. The one where I can't see his massive scowl and harsh eyes. Looking at him front-on won't be as pretty—I know that. But I still want to be beside him.

I *always* want to be beside him.

"He won't call until you make him do it." Decker grabs the second bag of trash from the table and walks around me. "While you're here with him, he's going to try to protect you for as long as he can."

The beat of my heart quickens, in both sorrow and determination. There is always too much conflict when it comes to Hunter. We're opposing forces that continuously try to unite but consistently fail.

"I'll convince him." I drag my feet to the door and step onto the porch, the cool morning breeze sinking straight into me.

Hunter sits there cradling the phone in his hand with Torian's name displayed across the screen, the call waiting to be connected.

"Please call him," I beg.

His jaw ticks as he stares down at the device in his palm. "I need you to promise me you won't do anything stupid." His gaze flicks up at me, those gorgeous hazel eyes peering through dark lashes.

"Stupid is a really broad term. You might need to be

230

more specific." I smile, but he doesn't reciprocate the expression.

Instead, he sighs. "I'm just as likely to stop you from doing something stupid as I am of convincing you to stay with me, aren't I?"

I sit down beside him, our arms brushing. "I've wanted this for ten years. It's the only thing I've wanted. Well... I spent months wishing for the impossible—that I would wake up from my nightmare and my family would all be surrounding me. Eventually, I got sick of kidding myself and I focused on something tangible. Something I could actually achieve. And this is it. My family deserves to be at rest knowing the person who murdered them isn't capable of hurting anyone else. *I* deserve to know that, too."

He glances down at his phone, and the seconds tick by with the peaceful chirp of birds in the trees above.

"Don't say a word while I talk to him." He gives me one last glance, then presses the call button.

I hold my breath as he puts the loud speaker on, and the *ring, ring, rings* sail through me like arrows. The call connects, and the briefest pause of silence makes my stomach turn.

"You're up early," Torian greets.

All the air leaves my lungs in a sudden rush of anxiety. It's time to start the game. Out-master. Out-strategize. Out-play.

Hunter places his hand on my thigh and gives a comforting squeeze. "I've got news."

"What sort of news?"

Hunter closes his eyes, his face etched in pain. "It turns out Steph obtained information from Dan after all."

Neither of them speaks for seconds that tick by like tortured years. Torian is skeptical. Already. This doesn't bode well.

"Is that so?" Torian asks.

"Yeah, that's so. But I'll let you talk to her about it. She's here with me now."

"I don't want to talk to her, Hunt." The tone is lethal. "I want to talk to you."

My heart seizes. I'm frozen. Hunter stiffens, too, his apprehension clear.

"You already told me she knew nothing," Torian continues. "If memory serves, you vowed it to me."

Hunter releases his hold on my leg and wipes a hand down his face. "I was wrong. Apparently, she was too scared to talk."

"Hmm." There's a wealth of judgmental disappointment in that one sound. "You've been wrong a lot lately."

"Once *isn't* a lot." Hunter shoves to his feet and walks onto the grass, stalking back and forth like a caged predator.

"Give me the name. Who is it?"

Hunter pauses and meets my gaze, his eyes filled with bitter sorrow. "It's your dealer in Newport. Dan told her it was Vaughn."

I bite my lower lip, my fingers tangling in the warm wool of my sweater. Torian doesn't believe him. I can feel it in the sinking sensation taking over my stomach.

Please. Please. Please.

"Okay. Now, I'm willing to talk to her."

Hunter nods. "Good. I'll put her on the line."

"No. We do this face to face."

The strong man before me snaps taut. His eyes widen, his lips part, before he finally bows his head. Defeated.

I'm not going to panic. Nope. We're still on track.

"Tell me when and where, and I'll make it happen."

"I've got plans this morning. I'll call you when I have time."

Sweet relief rushes through me as Hunter disconnects

the call and places the device in his pants pocket. He remains on the grass, his brow furrowed in concern, his lips set in a tight line.

"This is good." I push to my feet. "We're moving forward."

I'd hoped Torian wouldn't want to see me. That all this could be fixed with a simple phone call. But after years of searching and scheming, that result wouldn't have given me closure.

I need to do this properly. To articulate my words with utter perfection to ensure my dance of victory is the sweetest imaginable. To see the hatred for Jacob in Torian's eyes and know he will punish my tormenter far greater than I could.

He approaches, climbing the step in front of me to wrap his arms around my waist. He tilts his chin, meeting my gaze. "Are you still confident?" His fingers rub up and down my back. Calming. Comforting.

"Yes. We've got this."

"*You've* got this," he corrects. "As much as I hate it, all the pressure is on your shoulders. I can only be by your side to help you through it."

"And I appreciate that." I drape my arms around his neck, wanting to stay like this for a while. Just the two of us. Just words. Not menacing actions.

"You know, you only have to ask, and I'll end this for you."

"No." I press my lips to his, breathing him in. "You're not killing anyone. Okay?" His risks are already too high without being held entirely responsible. "*Okay*, Hunter? Promise me."

He nods, his nose brushing mine. "I promise."

23

HER

I escaped to my room hours ago to catch up on sleep while we waited to hear from Torian. It took an hour before Hunter silently opened the door and crept in bed beside me.

I pretended to be asleep, not wanting to encourage the connection, but I had no intention of kicking him out. Not when the strength of his arms wrapped around me seems like a protecting force warding away the upcoming danger.

I even groaned a few times, feigning restlessness, so I could turn and snuggle farther into his chest.

Pathetic, I know.

I don't regret it.

Not even when Decker knocks on the door and walks inside the room, exposing my needy position.

"Torian is calling me." He flashes us his phone. "What should I do?"

"Answer it." Hunter sits up beside me, alert and ready for action while I struggle to shake my lethargy.

Decker nods and takes the call. "What's going on?"

There's a pause, and I lean on my elbow in an attempt to get a better view to read his expression.

"Yeah, I'm here with him." Decker keeps his focus on Hunter as he talks, a million and one silently relayed messages passing between them. "Yep. We'll be there."

He lowers the phone and disconnects the call. "We meet at Devoured."

"When?" Hunter asks.

"Now."

There's the slightest stiffening of Hunter's posture beside me. His anxiety is almost hidden.

"Right..." He slides from the mattress and turns to face me. "Are you still ready?"

"Yep." I move from the bed, hoping the nervous bubble of nausea threatening to burst from my throat isn't written all over my face. "But why did he call Decker and not you?"

"I guess he wants to know how deep this runs." Hunter starts for the door, and I quickly follow, pulling on my sneakers. "He's checking to see if I'm wasting his time with false information or if I've involved Decker because we mean business."

"So, it's a good thing?"

"I guess." Decker shrugs. "You can never tell with Torian."

The men lead the way out of the bedroom and down the hall. Decker grabs his jacket from the sofa while Hunter disappears into his room and comes back minutes later, shrugging into a leather jacket.

"We ready?" he asks.

"Yep." Decker starts for the hall leading to the garage. "Locked and loaded."

Shit. My lack of foresight is showing. "Do I need a weapon?"

"No. Torian will expect it from us, but might consider it

a threat from you." Hunter gives me a sad smile. "It's best to go without."

"Don't worry." Decker shoots me a wink. "The big guy will be your shield and your weapon if you need it."

That's what I'm worried about.

"Ignore him." Hunter jerks his chin toward the garage. "Let's do this."

I follow them down to the rental car and climb in, Decker in the back with me riding shotgun, trying not to burst an artery with my elevated pulse.

We drive into the heart of Portland, and the closer we get to the imposing buildings and busy streets, the more my stomach tumbles. I'm not concerned so much for my own safety. I've thought about this day for too long to not be at peace with whatever could happen to me—good, bad, or horrendously ugly.

What doesn't sit right is what Hunter and Decker are risking for my personal vendetta. This has nothing to do with them. Yet, they're here, driving me to a meeting they organized, to deliver a plan they came up with.

"If something goes wrong," I speak to the window, unable to face them, "you need to turn on me. If he finds out I'm not telling the truth, do whatever you have to do. Make him believe you aren't a part of this. Just get yourselves out of there safely. Okay?"

They don't answer. There's no response bar the soft hum of the radio.

"Hunter?" I turn to him. "Are you listening?"

"We won't go down like that." He flicks his gaze to the rear-view mirror, glancing at Decker. "Will we?"

"No, siree. We go down with this ship," Decker adds. "In a blaze of glory and bloodshed, if necessary."

Hunter sighs and focuses back on the road. "There won't be any blaze of glory or sinking ship. This is going to work. And if Torian decides not to believe you, then that's his problem. Just don't change your story, no matter how strongly he doubts you."

"But if—"

"We're not discussing this, Sarah," he growls. "Stick to the plan, and stop jinxing us."

Right. I'm jinxing us.

I turn back to the window and hold my apprehension in check.

"This is it." Hunter slows, pulling the car to the curb.

I glance around, trying to find our destination.

"Across the road." Decker releases his belt and scoots toward the front seats. "The restaurant with the ugly motherfucker standing out front."

I lean forward, taking in the quaint building and the overweight Italian-looking man standing at the front door.

"You wanted to know who ran you off the road." Hunter taps his window, pointing at the 'ugly motherfucker.' "That's him. My buddy, Carlos."

My palms sweat. That guy has information on my past. Information that could get us killed once we walk inside the restaurant. "Aren't you worried he's told Torian about my past?"

"I wouldn't have risked bringing you here if I did. I know him. I know what he's like. He's more scared of me than his boss and too spineless to do anything about it. After what I did to him the day he went to Seattle, I promise he won't dare to cross me again."

I want to ask what happened that day. What exactly did Hunter do? But the walking stick and full arm of plaster on the man at the door is a great indication. Especially after all the weeks that have passed.

"Should I be worried about approaching him?" I try to hide the concern from my voice.

"With me by your side?" Decker scoffs. "No way."

Hunter grabs my hand and gives it a squeeze. "You don't need to worry at all. Okay?"

I nod, trusting him.

Actually trusting him.

I unfasten my belt and meet them outside the car, Hunter yet again reaching for my hand as we cross the road.

The man at the door leers at me as we approach, his dark eyes spiteful.

"Carlos," Hunter greets. "How's the arm?"

"Fuck you, asshole."

Hunter chuckles, entirely unconcerned, and continues into the restaurant, me by his side and Decker close at our back. We pass a mass of filled tables and chairs with couples dining, and push by a staff entrance to enter a quiet hall.

"His office is the one at the end." Hunter stops and turns to face me. "Just remember what we said. Keep it simple. Then this will all be over."

I nod.

He's making me nervous. His palm is clammy, and he keeps scrutinizing me. He's panicked, and it's rubbing off on me.

This is like any other job. If something goes wrong, I bend and adapt. Bend and adapt. I don't stop until I'm safely on the other side.

I can do this. Easy.

I lean on the tips of my toes and place a kiss on his lips. Chaste. Quick. When I lower, he scowls and weaves an arm around my waist, yanking me back into him.

"Is that all I get?" he snarls and slams his lips against mine as if in punishment. Harsh and strong and deep. He kisses me and kisses me, making the world disappear and my heart sizzle.

Decker clears his throat. "I guess we all get a little horny when it comes to life-threatening situations. But can we save the celebrations until after we escape the drug lord's lair?"

Hunter inches back and rests his forehead against mine.

"It's just a thought," Decker adds. "If you two want to keep going at it, I'll wait. S'all good."

"Remember what I said," Hunter whispers.

I nod. "I remember it all. Don't worry. I've been doing this for years."

"Not with Torian, you haven't. He'll act as though he's your best friend seconds before he tries to gun you down."

"Stop worrying." I step back. "You're making me nervous."

I walk away from him, continuing down the hall to stop in front of the door. I don't pause. I don't contemplate. I knock and wait for a muttered 'come in' before I turn the handle.

The man from the funeral sits behind an elegant wooden desk, pages upon pages of scattered paperwork spread before him. He leans back in his chair and greets us with a welcoming grin. "It's great to see you all again."

He stands, moves around the desk, and stops in front of me. "You'll have to forgive me, but I've forgotten your name." His hand brushes my bicep in a soft slide. It's gentle and kind. Not exactly the reception I anticipated.

"Steph," Hunter grates.

"Ahh, yes. The infamous Steph." His touch falls from my arm. "A devilish vixen with a pussy capable of tempting even the most heartless of men. Isn't that right, Hunter?"

"Let's keep it professional," Decker mutters.

"Of course." Torian leans back against his desk and crosses his feet at the ankles. Calm, cool, controlled. "So, tell me, Steph. You were with Dan the night he died, is that right?"

I chance one last glance at Hunter who inclines his head in encouragement, then I face Torian head on. "Yes. For about an hour."

"And why were you with him?"

"He'd been assaulting women, and nobody did anything about it. I took it upon myself to make him stop."

His eyes glisten with a hint of pride. At least that's what I think it is until he opens his mouth. "You murdered him selflessly? I don't know if I should consider that admirably noble or entirely bloodthirsty."

The assessment isn't a shock. The remark that I murdered Dan, is.

I keep my focus straight ahead, fighting not to show my renewed horror. I can't let this get to me. Not even if I am Dan's murderer. Not even if Hunter has lied to me. *Again.* Not even if this is all a set-up.

"She didn't kill him." The words are snarled from beside me. "*I did.*"

"Really?" Torian cocks his head. "The investigator's timeline says otherwise."

I keep my chin high, my eyes focused.

Don't take the bait.

I pretend the news doesn't matter. That I'm so entirely heartless I don't even care. How can I when I'm about to cause another death?

"Don't believe him," Hunter mutters. "I swear to God he's messing with you."

I shouldn't look at him. I know I shouldn't. But my gaze goes rogue, taking in Hunter's tortured expression. My chest restricts. My throat tightens. I still believe him. I really do.

Torian chuckles. "Am I? I guess we'll never truly know."

"We know," Decker interrupts. "If Hunter says he did it, the only one who might have doubts is her, and you know it. Stop fucking around and ease up on her. You already know she was too scared to talk in the first place."

I remain quiet, reclaiming my focus while they bicker.

Torian walks around his desk and takes a seat, kicking his polished shoes onto the scattered papers. "So, you played vigilante with Dan," he muses. "When did Vaughn's name come up?"

"Once the Rohypnol kicked in, he lost his mind a little. He started blurting things that didn't make sense."

"What sort of things?"

I shrug. "He said something about not giving me information unless I paid him. But the more I hurt him, the more he talked. He laughed about what he did to those women. Then began to panic over what his father would do if another story broke. And he mentioned Vaughn taking everyone down. That he was the name everyone was after."

"And you're sure it was Vaughn?"

"Yes. I'm sure."

He nods, thoughts flickering in his eyes. "Are you aware that Vaughn has worked with me for a very long time?"

His tone changes. It has an edge now. A crisp bite of bitterness.

"What he is to you doesn't concern me," I answer honestly. "I'm only here to relay the information I was given. You can believe it or not. It doesn't matter to me."

He leans back in his chair, steepling his fingers in front of his chest. "Did he say anything else?"

"He said a lot of things. About how he would rape me raw—"

Hunter stiffens.

"He told me he would kill my family. He made numerous threats, and even tried to negotiate. But nothing else to do with Vaughn."

Torian stares at me, his gaze trekking my face with

enough scrutiny to make me shiver. I want to elaborate, to place more intricate details into the story to make it more believable, but that's where problems would arise. More details mean more lies, and more lies mean a bigger chance of getting caught in my dishonesty.

He turns his focus to Hunter. "You know vouching for her again will have significant consequences if she changes her story for a second time."

I stiffen. I can't help it. The stakes shouldn't be this high. Not for him. Not for anyone but me. "Hold me fully responsible. And you can double or triple your consequences. It won't matter. My account won't change."

He keeps narrowed eyes on Hunter. "He's already vouched for you once. I need to make sure he isn't making another mistake."

"Yes," the grated agreement comes from my left. From the lips of a man who shouldn't have to risk anything for me. "I believe her."

Torian nods and sits forward to open his top drawer. My heart rushes into painful arrhythmia waiting for him to pull out a gun. Decker must think the same thing because he steps closer, his chest brushing against my back.

Instead, Torian pulls out a cell and scrolls through it without a care in the world. "Do you know Zack, Steph?"

"I'd never heard the name until Dan mentioned it." That is the God's honest truth.

He presses buttons, ignoring me, disregarding the information. He's not buying it. He's not even listening anymore.

Shit.

I glance at Hunter, but he's staring at Torian intent, his jaw ticking. Watching. Waiting. Something has changed. Something I'm not aware of.

"Well..." Torian places the phone down and meets my gaze with a smile. "I appreciate the information."

That appreciation in his tone seems ominously fake.

"Good. Am I right in assuming you'll deal with the problem?" Hunter asks.

Torian sucks in a lazy breath and lets it out slowly. "Not yet. I want to make sure the information is authentic—"

"Authentic?" I glance at Hunter again, but his expression hasn't changed. He's still staring, chin high, shoulders straight. "How are you going to determine that?"

There's a knock at the door, and my throat constricts.

"Come in," Torian calls out.

The door opens, and Carlos limps inside, grinning. He's not the problem, though. It's the man who strolls in behind him and closes the door.

My heart stops.

I remember those blue eyes.

That sandy hair.

That confident gait.

I know.

I know.

Jacob turns from the door and follows Carlos, his steps faltering when his gaze reaches mine. He slows. Stops. Smirks. "Sarah?"

Everything burns. My limbs. Throat. Eyes. Heart. Oh, God, my heart. It threatens to take its final beat.

I stand tall, strong, and refuse to let the rage and rapidly building sorrow take over.

He's here. Right here. With his styled hair, expensive suit, and playboy looks that I itch to burn from his flesh.

"What the fuck is going on here?" Hunter moves to my right, unsuccessfully trying to block my view of the monster from my nightmares. But I can still see him, sense him, feel him. The hollow taint of what he's done wraps around me, tightening. Strangling.

"Pretend he's not here," Decker whispers in my ear. "Focus."

Focus. It's the one thing I can't do right now.

"Like I said, I need to authenticate the information, and what better way to do it than by asking the accused to come to Portland to stand trial?" Torian continues to steeple his fingers, his eyes sparkling with devious delight. "By the sound of it, we already have a flaw in your story, Steph... Or is it Sarah?"

"There's no flaw," Hunter snarls.

"What am I accused of?" Jacob asks.

"Breathe," Decker whispers in my ear. "Don't panic."

They all speak over one another, the voices garbled. I can't shake it off. I can't find the focus I need. Grief overwhelms me.

I'm failing. I'm failing. I'm failing.

"She claims Dan told her you are the informant who's been ratting to the police."

I swallow and find my voice. "It's not a claim."

"Like hell," Jacob snarls. "This bitch is setting me up because I killed her family."

"Is that true?" Torian's joker mask slips away under his deepening frown.

"You don't need to take my word for it." Jacob steps forward, pulling a cell from the inside pocket of his business suit jacket. "Look it up online. There are a million and one articles about what I did."

I'm fucked. No question.

Hunter grasps my hand, as if knowing I'm as good as dead. But I can't go down like this. I refuse to let Jacob walk out of here. No matter what it takes. No matter what the price. I have to turn this around.

I need to bend and adapt.

I drop Hunter's hand, gaining my independence, and

paste on a smirk. "It's true. He did kill my family. But I haven't seen this man in ten years. I didn't know he was still alive or that he changed his name. To me, this is fate."

Karma.

The room erupts in vocal conflict. Jacob curses. Hunter defends me. Decker keeps whispering unnecessary motivation in my ear while Carlos grins.

"*Quiet*," Torian shouts.

Hunter inches in front of me and widens his stance, parting his feet to act as a body shield. He knows what's going to happen. He senses it, and it isn't good.

Torian doesn't believe me. He knows I'm lying.

Jacob begins to chuckle, the sound of victory sinking under my skin like acid.

I rest my forehead on Hunter's shoulder blade and whisper a barely audible apology. I'm so sorry. So deeply, truly sorry as I place my hand on the low of his back, on the gun that always lies in wait.

He stiffens under my touch, fully aware of what's running through my mind. "It's okay," he murmurs.

He's certain he knows what I'm about to do. He knows the increased danger I will put us all in. He *knows*. And still, he doesn't try to stop me. He lets me know it's perfectly fine to risk his life. That he's here for me. Always willing to fight for me.

"I'm sorry, Torian," I say louder. "I don't expect you to understand." I reach under Hunter's jacket, remove the gun from his waistband and shove him forward, out of the way.

"*Stop*," Torian shouts.

But it's too late. I raise the barrel before anyone has time to reach for a weapon, Jacob's eyes widening in realization.

"For my family," I whisper, and pull the trigger.

Once.

Twice.

Three times.

And the last, for baby Thomas.

The bullets pepper his chest, jolting him with each impact. I breathe in his horror, delighting in his shock. I barely register Hunter stepping back into me, arms wide, returning to his role as human shield, while Decker smothers my back.

I'm sandwiched but all I can see is Jacob as he stumbles backward, collapsing to the floor, his hands clutching his chest in vain as blood soaks his clothes.

I hear shouts. Threats. My name. I hear instructions, but the words don't penetrate. The only thing seeping deep into my chest is victory. Relief. The bitter-sweet euphoria of vengeance.

Sarah, pay attention.

It's my father's voice, his guidance snapping me back to the present, to the room full of drawn guns.

Decker's is trained on Carlos. Carlos's on me. Torian's on Hunter. Mine on the wall, at the space where a murderer once stood.

"Her actions are justified," Hunter says in a rush. "He killed her family. You would've done the same."

Screams carry from down the hall. The rough scrape of chairs and scampering feet.

"Her justification means nothing when she brought this feud into my family's restaurant. She killed one of my men." Torian looms over his desk, the barrel of his gun aimed at Hunter's chest. "Step aside."

"Not going to happen."

"Do it." I push at Hunter's back. "Please."

He doesn't budge.

I could probably get another shot off and take Carlos down with me, but I wouldn't have a chance with Torian.

He would kill my determined protector before Carlos hit the ground.

"Move, Hunter," I plead.

If at all possible, he grows an inch taller with his dominant stance. He's not going to let me take the fall.

"*Move.*" I shove at him with my free hand, only to have Decker's arm grab my wrist, plastering it to my side as he holds me in place.

"The police will be here any minute, Hunt. What's your next move?" Torian blurts. "How are you going to play this?"

"I take responsibility. I owe you. I'll do whatever you want. *Be* whatever you want. I'll stop being a contractor and instead become one of your bitch boys, like you've always wanted. We can work out the details at a later date."

"No." I plead. "This was my fault."

"Let him sort this out," Decker whispers in my ear. "He's got it under control."

"No." I elbow him in the ribs, breaking free of his grasp. I stalk around Hunter, only to be engulfed in his arms and drawn into his body

"Don't move," Torian demands, his barrel trained on my chest.

"She's mine," Hunter snarls, taking the gun from my hand. "My responsibility. My debt. You shoot her, and you won't live to take another breath."

Torian's eyes narrow. "Do you really want to threaten me?"

"No. No. *No.*" I scramble to turn to face Hunter. "Don't do this."

A shot blasts the air, and his hands fall. His eyes widen. His lips part. I frantically search his face for answers, my mind screaming, until I hear a thud behind him.

Carlos is on the floor, blood seeping from a perfectly circular hole in his forehead.

"You should've done that weeks ago," Torian mutters, lobbing his gun at Hunter. "Put it in Vaughn's hand. As far as you're all concerned, they killed each other."

I stand rooted in place as Hunter wipes the gun of fingerprints, then places it in Jacob's hand. He does the same with his weapon, placing it with Carlos.

"What's going on?" I whisper.

"It's over." Decker puts his hands on my shoulders. "He's got it worked out."

"He's got what worked out?"

The wail of sirens increases. All I can hear is noise, the panic and chaos increasing.

"She needs to get out of here." Torian strides around the desk. "She'll come with me. You two can stay."

Hunter nods.

He nods.

"What are you doing?" I walk to him, searching those harsh eyes.

"You need to go. I'll meet up with you later."

"No. I'm not leaving you." And I'm sure as hell not going to run into the sunset with the man who seconds ago wanted to kill me.

"Sarah." He leans in, bare inches from my face. "You're covered in gun residue, and so is Torian. You can't stay."

"No." I shake my head and cling to him. "I'm not going without you."

I can't. I *won't*. I thought I could walk away, but it's an impossibility. I want him. I *need* him.

He winces and glances over my shoulder. "I'm sorry."

I snap my gaze to Decker, but I'm too late. I have a split second to brace for the butt of the gun before pain explodes in my head. Then the world fades to black.

24

HER

I wake up on a plush, unfamiliar sofa, dressed in nothing but my underwear. My head pounds as if I've been at a month-long rave and there's a sore spot that throbs even harder near my temple.

It takes seconds to blink away the groggy confusion. To remember what happened.

I don't move. I don't breathe.

I take in my surroundings—the sunlight streaming into the room, the expensive furniture, the scent of baked cookies or cake that makes my stomach growl.

Great. I killed a guy only to be abducted and stripped by Betty fucking Crocker.

"I think she's awake," a woman murmurs.

"About time."

The response chills my blood. It's Torian. I don't need to glance over the sofa to confirm, but I do. I sit up and find him in a million-dollar kitchen beside an equally stunning woman with sleek brown hair and mesmerizing blue eyes, just like him.

"Sleep well?" he taunts.

My head voices a protest, throbbing and pounding.

Decker knocked me out. At Hunter's instruction.

"Where is he?"

Torian raises a brow. "The surly one or his faithful sidekick?"

"Both," I snap, pushing to my feet, then wincing at the renewed burst of pain in my skull. "Where are they?"

"At the police station."

"Why?" Blood rushes from my head, the panic making me dizzy. "What's going on?"

"It's standard procedure for a witness of a double murder. At least it will be if they get released soon. Other-wise..." He shrugs. "Your friends might have to spend a generous amount of time in prison."

I reach for the sofa as my legs threaten to buckle.

"Don't be cruel," the woman chastises. "She's been through enough." She saunters toward me, her long, lean legs eating up the space between us. "It's only been a few hours. I'm sure they'll be back any minute now."

She continues by me to the pile of folded clothing on the coffee table. "Here." She picks up a pair of yoga pants and a baby blue sweater. "Put these on. They should fit. And your shoes are underneath the sofa."

I take the offering and pull them on with shaky arms. "Where are my clothes?"

"Incinerated," Torian mutters. "Just one of the many things I've done to cover your ass."

I wince, not appreciating the help, but thankful for it at the same time. I'm not naive to think his assistance is out of the kindness of his heart. I owe him now. Or worse, Hunter owes him.

That's a debt I need to clear.

"I'm sorry for involving you in this." I slide my feet into

my sneakers and approach the kitchen. "And I beg you not to hold my actions against anyone but me."

He reaches for a mug and takes a drink. "You're worthless to me, little girl. Hunter, on the other hand, has been an asset I've wanted to control for quite some time."

"What will you do to him?"

He takes another sip of tea, or coffee, or marijuana-infused water for all I know, and stares at me over the rim of his mug.

"Please," I beg. "I need to know."

Will he be tortured? Beaten? What will happen to Decker? Will they be treated the same? Punished equally?

Hunter vowed on his life that I was telling the truth. It should've been my goddamn life.

Torian cocks a judgmental brow, probably disgusted by my show of weakness. "I've worked with Hunter for years. But it has always been on a contractual basis. Under his terms. He had the freedom to pick and choose when and if we worked together."

"And?"

"And he will no longer get to pick and choose. He will no longer be a contractor. He will be a valued part of my team that will fulfil any job I see fit."

Anguish overwhelms me. "You can't make him hurt innocent people." I shake my head. "You can't. Eventually, he'll turn on you. You'll always have to watch your back."

"Nobody in my world is innocent. We all have a cross to bear. Even you." His lips kick in a devilish grin. "And it's not as difficult as you might think to break a warrior's back. You just need to know his weakness."

He raises his mug and inclines his head, as if toasting my existence. Toasting the vulnerability I bring to Hunter's life.

"*Cole*," the woman reprimands. "Stop it." She walks by me, squeezing my arm as she passes. "Ignore him. My brother likes to be dramatic. But deep down, he loves Hunter. We all do."

Torian gives a barely audible chuckle. "I love the debt he now owes me, that's for sure."

"Enough," she demands. "The poor thing is petrified. Leave her be."

I'm not petrified.

I'm angry.

Unstable.

She walks into the kitchen and opens a cupboard under the black marble bench. "Would you like a coffee? Or maybe something stronger?"

"No, thanks." I lean forward, looking down a hall to my right. There's a door with light streaming through the frosted-glass panels. The front door, I'm sure.

"Making an escape plan?" Torian taunts. "Don't bother. I don't want you here as much as you don't want to be here. You're free to go."

I snap my gaze to his in disbelief, my heart thundering beneath tightened ribs. Is this a trick?

"Go on." He jerks his head toward the hall.

"You're safe to leave," the woman reiterates softly.

I stare at the door, at freedom, as a shadow darkens the frosted glass from the other side. A knock sounds, and I hold my breath, hoping it's Hunter.

"Come in," Torian yells.

There's a click of the latch, the air in my lungs congealing as I wait, impatiently, to see Decker walk inside, closing the door behind him.

Where the hell is Hunter?

I stalk toward him, stopping him halfway down the hall to throw my arms around him.

He stiffens, long seconds passing before he drapes his

arms around me in an awkward reciprocation of the gesture. "Hey, tiger. How are you holding up?"

"I'm not sure yet. How about you?" I lean back to ask the question tightening my throat, but it lodges in my mouth as I acknowledge the extent of his drawn features. He looks exhausted, his skin pale.

"I'll be perfect once I catch some sleep." He winks at me.

I nod and wait for more, my gaze pleading for answers he doesn't seem to understand. "Please tell me where he is. What happened at the police station? Is he okay?" The onslaught bubbles from me in a garbled mess.

"You don't have to worry about a thing." He claps my shoulder and steps back. "Hunt took the fall, so you're all clear on murder one."

"What?" I stumble backward as he walks around me, continuing down the hall. Hunter took the fall? He confessed? "Why?"

Decker stops and turns back around to face me with a wince. "Sorry. Bad joke. He's outside paying the cab driver."

"He's here?" I swing around to the door as another shadow creeps over the glass, and seconds later Hunter walks inside.

"Oh, God." I rush for him, running the few feet of space separating us to engulf him in a body hug. He grunts with the impact, and I can't find the will to apologize. I wrap my arms around his neck, my legs around his waist, and bury my face in his neck.

"Hey, now, princess," he whispers. "It's okay."

I hold him tighter, squeezing until my muscles burn as his gentle arms wrap around my back.

"Come on now." His voice grows an authoritative edge and he pulls back, craning his neck to look at me. "It's over. He's gone."

"And you're not going to jail?"

"In your dreams, princess."

No. That's the last thing I want. I'm so unbelievably thankful for this man. Gratitude and respect flood me.

I cup his cheeks, his rough stubble teasing my palms as I take in every intricate detail of his harsh beauty. He's unbelievably gorgeous. Even more so now that I know him.

Trust him.

"Are you okay?" He rests his forehead against mine

"No."

He guides me to stand, keeping his hands on my hips as he scrutinizes me. "What is it?"

I glance down the hall, making sure we don't have an audience before I whisper, "What about Torian? What are you going to do about him?"

A half-hearted smile pulls at his lips. "Don't worry about him."

"But he practically said he's going to make you his bitch."

"He can't make me do anything." He leans in, placing his mouth deliciously close to my ear. "He knows he's nothing but another pull of the trigger if he gets on my bad side. As far as I'm concerned, he did us a solid today, and I'm thankful."

He retreats a step, his hands moving to my shoulders to give a gentle squeeze. The gesture is friendly, not affectionate. A goodbye, not a demand to stay by his side forever like I want.

He's pulling away from me, not just physically as he places farther space between us, but emotionally.

I frown. "What's going on?"

"I'm giving you what you need, Sarah." He sucks in a deep breath. "I'm letting you go."

My heart ceases to beat. My chest cracks open, exposing a hollow cavern.

"I won't follow," he continues. "I won't play any more games."

I should be relieved he's giving me what I asked for. He's giving me the space to get my life back on track, the solitude to regroup and reassess. But the celebratory emotions are non-existent.

I'm devastated.

Shattered.

"What about the police?" I ask. "What about the investigation?"

"You don't need to worry about either. As far as they're concerned, Jacob and Carlos killed each other, and you weren't even there."

"Go on." He jerks his head toward the door, his expression turning to stone. "I paid the cab driver to wait for you and drive you back to your apartment or wherever you want to go."

It's not my apartment. Not anymore. But that's the last thing on my mind.

"I'll organize a moving van and get your furniture back to you tomorrow."

I drag my gaze from him, unable to look him in the eye. "You might need to hold onto my things for a while longer. It's not my apartment anymore. Brent would've found someone else by now."

"I hope not," he murmurs. "Because I paid him to hold it for you weeks ago."

He did?

"I knew this would all work itself out sooner or later, and I didn't want you to lose your home," he answers my unspoken question. "You have nothing to worry about anymore, Sarah."

Nothing but loneliness and heartbreak.

I nod. "Right. I'll get going, then."

I don't move. I can't.

I want to stay. With him. With Decker. In this crazy life that not only tipped my world upside down but rocked my foundations. But maybe that's the adrenaline talking, or the pounding headache, or the lack of restful sleep.

He gives me a sad smile and swings out an arm to lead me to the door. He's calm. Stoic.

It tears me apart.

He pulls the door wide, giving me a view of the mansions and manicured gardens outside, along with the cab waiting in the drive.

How do I say goodbye to this man? The one who tricked me with his lies and won me over with his loyalty.

"Thank you for everything," I murmur.

"You're thanking me now?" He gives a subtle grin, that dimple stunning me with its exquisite allure.

"Yes. For what you did today, I'll be forever grateful."

He lowers his gaze, that grin turning somber. "Don't mention it."

I keep my head high, faking determination as I walk outside into the dimming late-afternoon sun, and approach the cab.

I don't want to leave, but it's the only thing I know. I'm always running, always seeking distance. I don't have any experience doing anything else. Staying and fighting for what my heart craves is a foreign concept I don't know how to battle.

"Wait," he calls.

I freeze, as if moving even an inch will stop him from trying to make me stay. My belly tumbles as his footsteps approach, then he grabs my hand and gently glides me around to face him.

My lungs seize as he leans in, placing the sweetest, softest, most flawless kiss on my tingling lips. I could die from the pleasure. From the affection and pure perfection.

Then he steps back, turns toward the house, and stalks away. "Goodbye, princess."

EPILOGUE

HER

One month later

I saunter into Atomic Buzz and approach Brent behind the bar.

"Your third visit this week," he drawls. "I don't know if I should be thankful for the company or concerned of impending alcoholism."

I roll my eyes and slide into my favorite seat. "I didn't realize I could become an alcoholic from two drinks a night."

"Everyone has to start somewhere." He grins at me and slides over a Long Island Iced Tea, my current drink of choice. "You're just a little slower at this than my regulars."

After I left Hunter a month ago, I came here. There had been nowhere else to go. I'd loathed the thought of spending another night in a hotel when I knew Hunter wouldn't come after me, and my apartment was nothing but empty space.

Brent had welcomed me back with open arms and a large amount of growled concern. He'd wanted to know what happened, and for the first time in ten years, I'd been willing to pour my heart out.

I told him everything.

Well, not *everything*.

I explained the situation with my family and went into detail about my search for the man who murdered them. He now knew that Hunter had helped me find Jacob, and thankfully he didn't pester me for more details when I gave vague references to why my time with both men had come to an end.

Brent looked after me for those first few days. He let me crash on his couch for a night, and helped the moving company place my furniture back in my apartment the next day when the truck arrived.

He became more than a friend in a short space of time, and quickly turned into someone I now consider family.

"How was the old duck today?" he asks, polishing the bar. "Did she make me any cookies?"

"The cookies are always mine, you know that." I smirk. "But she's good. We spent three hours in her kitchen while she unsuccessfully tried to teach me how to make a red velvet white trifle."

Brent snickers. "I guess you can't teach an old dog new tricks."

"I'm not old." I glare.

Betty had been another task on my newly made bucket list. It had taken me a week to work up the courage to return to Eagle Creek. When my cab pulled into her driveway, she had been standing on the porch, looking down on me as I stepped onto her lawn.

Turns out, she welcomed me back with just as much enthusiasm as Brent.

I crumpled in her arms. I actually had to fight not to sob like a little bitch. And as I explained my unworthy reasons for stealing her car, she filled my belly with coffee and homemade apple cake. She's been doing the same thing every Sunday for the last three weeks.

I've created a life and a home for myself in Portland, not just a place to hide.

The door to Atomic Buzz swooshes open, and Brent raises a brow at the newcomer. "I think this guy's lost. I bet you ten bucks he asks for directions."

"No way." I swirl my Long Island Iced Tea, not bothering to look over my shoulder. "I still owe you money from the last time we had this bet."

The time when Hunter had walked through that door.

The footfalls approach, and I cringe, not wanting my time with Brent to be interrupted with menial chitchat.

"What can I get you?" Brent lowers a hand to the fridge below the counter, waiting.

"A Corona." The voice is low and subtle, barely a whisper of a response.

My heart stops. It's him. The man I've dreamed about for nights on end.

From my peripheral vision, I see him slide onto a seat, leaving a vacant spot between us. Just like the first time we met.

"You lost?" Brent slides a coaster across the bar and places Hunter's beer bottle down on it.

"No."

"Looking for something in particular?" Brent taunts.

"Yeah."

I swallow over the tightening in my throat. "You're wasting your time with monosyllable answers," I whisper. "He'll keep pestering you until you divulge your deepest, darkest secrets."

"Is that so?" His voice washes over me, caressing all of

my erogenous zones, touching all my newly formed strength and making me even stronger.

"Yep," Brent admits. "So, spit it out. What are you doing here?"

I succumb to my visual thirst and turn to face Hunter.

He looks good. Really good.

A charcoal shirt is molded to the muscles of his chest. Rough stubble hugs his jaw, and those eyes are exactly how I remember them. Although, they're not harsh like when we first met, but they're equally intense. Then there are his lips —pure temptation in motion, the slight curve lifting at one side in a half-hearted smile.

"My sister got knocked up by a lowlife with a heavy hand. He left her as soon as my nephew was born. So, I quit my job, packed my things, and drove here."

"That's..." I want to keep up the recap of our first night together, but my palpitating heart won't allow it. "That's not funny."

"Sorry." He cringes, and it's kinda cute to see him uncomfortable. "I actually thought you would've come to find me by now. But seeing as you didn't, I came to offer my support in whatever way you'll take it."

"Support?" My brows pull tight as his gaze rakes me, from my face, to my stomach, then back up again.

My breath catches. "You think I'm pregnant?"

"The last time we were together we weren't..."

Safe. Protected. I was supposed to get the morning after pill and forgot in the mad scramble to regain control in my life. "I'm not pregnant."

"Not...pregnant."

I don't think he means to parrot me. It seems more like shock. Maybe it's even disappointment building in those clear hazel eyes.

"I just thought…" He sighs and grasps his beer, taking one large gulp after another.

Brent clears his throat then fakes a dramatic yawn, again, like the first night I met Hunter. "I think I might have to call last drinks."

This time I don't glare. I can barely hold in a grin. His eyes are gleaming at me, taunting in their memory.

Matchmaker, matchmaker, make me a match.

"It's barely dark out," I drawl.

He shrugs.

Hunter downs the last of his beer. "He's right. I should get out of here and leave you alone like I promised."

He slides from his seat and pulls his wallet from the back pocket of his cargos to slap some bills on the bar.

I let him walk away and remind myself of how much I've grown without him.

I've found myself in his absence. I've almost become whole again. But until now, I wasn't sure if I was ready for the final puzzle piece. The biggest, brightest part of being happy.

"Wait," I call out.

He plants his feet. His back straightens.

Brent grins at me, a pride-filled, happiness-rich grin.

"You're supposed to follow me out of here, remember?" I grab my purse from the bar and scoot off my seat to stride toward him. My legs tingle. My belly flutters.

I walk past him to the door, then pause to glance over my shoulder. This time, the tweak of his mouth isn't a threat or a taunt. It's pure elation. Undiluted relief.

There's still a hum.

An absolutely amazing zing.

It slides down my spine, tightens my nipples, and contracts my pussy in a repeat of the exquisite squeeze from when we first met.

I was right when I anticipated that Hunter would devastate me and leave me deliciously broken. I was wrong, too. Because he also made me whole again.

"You waiting for me, princess?"

My heart does a goddamn flip. It's enough to make my knees weak and my stomach tumble. "I've been waiting for a month."

The humor flees his features. "Are you serious?" He approaches to settle in beside me, peering down at me with beseeching eyes.

"Sorry, I broke character." I grin. "I'm supposed to point out that you're following me, then you ask if that's a problem."

His brows pull tight, then finally, he gives a succinct nod. "Is it a problem that I plan on following you?"

I want to laugh. Goddamn it. The vibration consumes my chest. This man, this murderer, is following instructions to do a cheesy re-run of the first night we met. And I goddamn love it.

I love *him*.

A breath shudders from my lips, and I blink back the burn in my eyes. "I guess that depends on what you want to achieve."

My vision blurs as I wait for his response. I remember what he said the first time. I remember the exact words—*I want everything.*

"Hey..." His rough palm glides over my cheek, his gentle touch inspiring the first tear to fall.

I haven't cried in ten years. Not in sorrow. Not in pain. And definitely not in the overwhelming happiness currently sinking through every inch of my being.

"I want you to move in with me," he whispers. "I want you to be mine. I want you to be as in love with me as I am with you."

He takes my mouth in a forceful kiss, curling my toes, stroking my tongue with his before pulling back to rest his forehead against mine. "I still want everything, Sarah."

I nod, the movement jerky and uncontrolled. "Then, no, Luke. I guess it's no problem at all."

The End

To read an exclusive BONUS scene, sign up to the Eden Summers' mailing list and receive—*an epilogue from Hunter's point-of-view*.

Visit here for details:

https://www.subscribepage.com/hunterepilogue

ACKNOWLEDGMENTS

This is always the hardest part of the book. I don't know why. I've learned the knack of writing stories, but when it comes to articulating my gratitude for those who helped along the way I never seem to have the profoundly monumental words necessary.

But here goes...just imaging me sitting here blubbering tears of appreciation.

- To my husband, kids and parents. I've never experienced a day without your support. It's always a case of you all jumping to help when I'm approaching a deadline or stressed to the eyeballs. Your understanding means absolutely everything. Always.
- To Doyle Davis, who fielded some of the most naive questions about weaponry and gave me an abundance of information. Your insight was brilliant. I couldn't have written Hunter without you.
- To Cathy Thiel, for your information on

Portland. You were my eyes on the other side of the world.

- To my editors - Lauren Clarke and Lori Whitwam. You both make my work profoundly better. Thank you for helping me grow.
- To my proofreaders - Lylian, Tamara, and Marci. Thank you for gifting me with your time and acting as though proofreading was an honor instead of the favor it is.
- And last, but definitely not least, to everyone who has supported me and my growing inability to adult properly since I started writing. I've forgotten birthdays. I've declined invitations. I've missed messages, ignored phone calls and been unresponsive to texts. I've been a neglectful friend, daughter, wife, mother. And yet, you've all still got my back.

Thank you. Thank you. Thank you.

Please consider leaving a review on your book retailer website or Goodreads

Titles in the Hunting Her Series

Hunter

Decker

Torian

Savior

Luca

Cole

Information on Eden's other books can be found at www.edensummers.com

Printed in Great Britain
by Amazon